Hoosier Dad

Elizabeth Seckman

This is a work of fiction. Names, characters, places, and incidents are products of the author's imagination or are used fictitiously and are not to be construed as real. Any resemblance to actual events, locations, organizations, or persons, living or dead, is entirely coincidental.

World Castle Publishing, LLC
Pensacola, Florida
Copyright © Elizabeth Seckman 2019
Paperback ISBN: 9781949812985
eBook ISBN: 9781949812992
First Edition World Castle Publishing, LLC, June 3, 2019
http://www.worldcastlepublishing.com
Cover: Karen Fuller
Editor: Maxine Bringenberg

Chapter 1

There are moments in a gal's life that she dress-rehearses repeatedly. Like saying "I do" with the temerity of a queen, while still blushing like a princess. And if there is no "I do" in her future, probably ever, then she rehearses that moment when she gets to look her worst heartbreak square in the eye and prove in a single, regal stare that she is so much more than good – she is better than ever. Unfortunately for Sarah, when that moment came, all she managed was an unflattering slack-jawed drop of her chin.

"Don't you need to write that down?" the handsome-as-ever Rich Cooper asked, nonplussed.

The man was, evidently, a moron. Sarah forced her mouth closed and picked up a pen. "So, what you're telling me is…you want to place a personal ad? For a fat, ugly, stupid wife?"

"Not fat," he said, as if explaining why he preferred white bread to wheat. "Plump. I want a woman who isn't obsessed with being skinny. But it's not like I'm wanting a sits-in-front-of-the-TV-all-day sort of behemoth."

Behemoth? Sarah's cheeks burned. She couldn't look up, couldn't make eye contact, or she might punch him. *Men.* They sickened her. Especially this one.

But he didn't seem to notice he was making her nauseous,

3

because he kept right on talking. "And I said I wanted decent looking, but not stunning. And I never said stupid...I said I didn't want a woman who was career oriented. I want a woman who is okay with working at home."

Sarah chewed the side of her cheek and scribbled the words on a notepad. The man was a Neanderthal, and should be skewered and roasted by any self-respecting woman. But the hell of it was...he was so damned easy on the eyes. She sighed as she glanced up at the casually tattered jeans, which revealed strong, muscular thighs, a small tear acting as a window to a light coating of blond, wiry hair. He was all man, smelling of freshly cut wood and...*bubble gum*?

Moving her eyes as quickly as she could from legs to eyes, she tried to pretend she didn't notice how his T-shirt stretched tight across his broad shoulders, but hung loose at his narrowed hips. She worked her ass off to keep her thirty-something body tight. The least Rich Cooper could have done to make up for being such an ass was to get fat and go bald.

It was only fair.

But no. The universe continued to crap on her. Even his face was still perfect. His easy smile and clear blue eyes hinted at mischief, and tricked a girl into thinking his misogynistic tendencies were simply a guise for something deeper.

But Sarah knew better. She knew that below the initial shallow surface was nothing but rock. *Total bed rock*. Sarah's blush deepened, and she squirmed in her seat at her own horrible analogy.

She never should have come back to Dodd, Indiana. This was a mistake. First day in town, and she runs into *him*. He evidently didn't remember her, but she'd never forget him. *Richland Conrad Cooper. King of the prom. Collector of hearts. Killer of virtue.*

She leaned back in her chair and crossed one leg over the other. Her foot tapped the air and her lips were drawn and

4

pinched. She took a deep breath. She dealt with murderers on a daily basis — she could handle him. "So, Dick. What you're telling me is you've lost your magic touch and need to advertise for a bimbo?"

He rested his body on the edge of the desk and leaned in toward her. He smelled delicious…definitely like bubble gum. She hadn't chewed gum in a very, very long time. It made her mouth water.

He gave her a wink. "It's Rich, and truthfully? Bimbos come a dime a dozen. I need a mom for my girls."

"And your idea of the perfect mom is a chunky gal without goals?"

Muscular shoulders rolled inside the faded T-shirt. "Sounds horrible, but yeah. I want an average woman. One who sees raising kids as something more important than a career."

"Why don't you give up your job? Raise your own kids?"

He stared at her as if she'd given him a crossword puzzle to solve. His blond hair needed cutting — it was beginning to curl, and lent him a boyish charm that was totally undeserved. "You think I can find a rich woman around here who will have me? Because I can't move either."

"Oh, my God. Seriously?" She pushed out of her chair and circled the desk. "Are you seriously stupid?"

He swiveled his body toward her, but didn't stand. "Serious as a heart attack. I'm in over my head, and I need help. Help I can trust. A woman who can be a role model for my daughters. I don't need any bar flies or bitches. I need a good woman who wants a home and a family."

Sarah shoved the notepad at him. "But doing this…it's…it's insulting."

He read the paper. "Okay, so maybe I could word it better — "

"Word it better?"

"Yeah. What if I say, 'Wanted: a woman who cooks, likes

5

kids, and would like to be a homemaker. And I will say I am a thirty-something construction worker who drives a fifteen-year-old pick up. That will weed out the gold diggers, the career women, and the hot babes."

There was no talking to him. He'd probably taken too many blows to the brain in his sporting years. And why did she care? Let him run his stupid ad.

"Fine." She scribbled the words on the paper. "How shall I sign it?"

"I thought of this on the way over — Hoosier Dad? I was going to go with Daddy. I thought that was catchier, but I'm trying to steer clear of that sort of element, if you know what I mean."

"Shocking," she mumbled. "Rich, avoiding skanks?" *Ha! But then he is evidently a dad. A dad who cares enough— Stop it! He is the enemy.*

"Not every girl I dated was a — skank? Really? You went with the word skank? All those years of college and you chose skank? But then I guess if you're back here working at the paper, maybe rumors of your rise to power weren't true."

Sarah took a deep breath through flared nostrils. Hands cold, cheeks burning, she wished she was out of there. What had made her think coming back to Dodd was a good idea?

He crossed tanned, muscle-lined arms over his chest and grinned at her.

The bell on the office door chimed.

"I'm back." Tonya Little, the editor of the small-town rag, *The Sunset Times*, swept into the office. She was short and plump with a radiant smile and a sporadic work ethic...the perfect woman for Dick. Too bad they were cousins. "Thanks for minding the shop." She set a brown bag from the hot dog booth on the desk. "Hey, Rich, what brings you by? Little birds in town tell you we had a new resident?"

"No, I was here on business."

"Oh? Well, if Harvey is hiring you to fix things in this place, you should start with the lock on the bathroom door. It's broken."

"No, he didn't call me, but I'll take a look at your lock."

"And my ice maker at the house froze up again. Come over and fix it and I'll make you dinner."

"Can't do dinner. Kari has a date tonight, and I need to be home to check him out. It's that Heath boy."

"Heath is a nice boy."

"I don't trust any boy. But I do need a favor. With Kari on a date, I have no one to watch Stacey. Can she stay with you tonight? My manager called off, and I'll have to be there until at least midnight. I should sell the damn bar and be done with it."

"Turn it into a restaurant," Tonya suggested.

"Booze makes the money. And I need the money right now. Do you realize prom cost me $1000 dollars?"

"It didn't have to cost more than a few hundred. You spoil them," Tonya said as she pulled foil wrapped hot dogs out of a bag.

"Well, she didn't have anything better than the other girls. Hell, I'm not going to tell my girls no because I don't want to work a little harder."

"Good lord, you work what? Twelve hours a day, six days a week? I'm sure no one would call you lazy."

"Whatever. I'll go check that lock." He turned his attention to Sarah as Tonya dug out fries. "How much do I owe for the ad?"

Sarah blushed. She didn't work for the paper—she'd only stopped by the office to tell Tonya she was back in town, and Tonya had insisted on running out and getting them lunch.

Tonya handed him a hot dog. "What ad?"

"I asked your new secretary to put me a personal ad in the paper."

Tonya laughed. "My secretary? Who? Oh my gawd, you thought— Rich, you idiot. Sarah is a lawyer. She wouldn't be working as my secretary."-

Sarah's throat was dry. She nodded and reached for her purse.

"I thought maybe all the super-Sarah stories were just stories. Maybe she built up some bad karma for dumping me." Rich grinned, his eyes crinkling in the corners.

Sarah's stomach did a barrel roll. Her *relationship* with Rich had been the beginning of the end. Okay, so *the end* was a bit melodramatic, but it had taken Sarah years to get over the pain this man caused her. Hell, she could still use a bit of therapy, or so she'd been repeatedly told by every guy she dated since Rich broke her. She didn't know what his game was, but she wasn't playing it. If he wanted to be the one who got dumped, so be it.

She fished her keys out of her purse. "Seems I was wise beyond my years."

"Ouch." Rich grabbed his heart like it hurt. "I don't recall doing anything to deserve that."

"Let's just say I was hedging my bets." She tossed the notebook toward him and said, "From the sounds of what you're looking for, we'd never have made it in the long haul."

Tonya reached out and picked up the notepad. She read it and laughed. "What the hell is this?"

"My personal ad," Rich explained.

"It's ridiculous," Tonya said.

"No, it's not." Rich sounded authentically shocked.

"Yes, it is." Tonya added, "And insulting. Makes you sound like an arrogant, juvenile pig."

"The words make the man," Sarah said as she slung her purse over her shoulder and headed for the door. "Tonya, I'll give you a call later. I have so many things to do to get the office open and the apartment livable, and I've already wasted precious time."

"Aw, come on," Tonya practically chased her with a silver package. "At least have a hotdog."

"No thanks. I've lost my appetite."

Tonya walked her to the door, gave her a hug, and whispered, "Sorry." She nodded her head in Rich's direction and added, "I had no clue he was coming by. I never meant—"

"It's all right. It was a refreshing reminder of what can be expected of men. But I do need to get things done. If I don't get my place fixed up soon, the city may condemn it."

"I'll stop by after work and help you," Tonya promised.

"You don't have to do that."

"I know. But I want to." Tonya squeezed Sarah's arms. "I'm so happy you're home! I've missed you so much. So glad you decided you weren't a big city girl after all."

Sarah nodded stiffly, took a last look over Tonya's shoulder at Rich, and then bolted for the door.

~*~

Rich watched as Sarah walked through the gravel parking lot to her shiny black Audi. He had to admit, he hadn't recognized her at first. And it wasn't that she'd lost weight or gone from brown hair to blonde. The change was deeper. There was a hard set to her jaw and a coldness in her stare that was never there before. The Sarah he remembered would have smiled...would have blushed when he made jokes.

That girl, that old Sarah, was the kind of gal he was looking for.

A punch to his ribs jolted him from his thoughts. "You dumbass! She's a perfect catch, and you come in here and act like some sort of backwoods, knuckle dragging buffoon? And for the record...I think you started dating that beast you married when Sarah left for college. So technically, if you two were dating—which is highly questionable, because surely I'd have been told about it—a break up would have been your fault."

"That's not at all how I remember it."

Chapter 2

Sarah's new office was nothing like the one she'd left behind. The glass and steel tower was replaced by a squat, brick rectangle. No more polished revolving door — the warped wooden one with the cracked glass was her new gateway. She was no longer part of Stollings and Reed. It was just Sarah Andrews, Attorney at Law. Or at least it would be once she had someone paint her name on the front window. As she dipped out of the bright sunlight into the dim interior of the building, she wrinkled her nose against the musty smell of the place. It was cool and dank, in desperate need of windows and light.

The unpacked boxes lining the cracked plaster walls left her tired. She didn't even know which box held her pillow. The whole place was in shambles, like someone had picked up her life and tossed it across the county line. A light flickered above her head. The place probably had shoddy wiring too. Maybe she'd get lucky and the place would burn to the ground, and she could cash in the insurance for a beach shanty. She had considered that option when she received her severance package, but she chose to come home instead.

Looking at the gloom that would one day be her office, she assured herself she'd made the smart choice. Now she just needed to get her ass moving and get it all together. *I am woman...hear me roar.*

She locked the office door and headed for the stairs to the one-bedroom apartment above her new work space. The tiny hovel was also a far cry from her norm. Her modern furniture looked awkward and out of place with the aged hardwood floors and carved, antique wood work. The building had been erected in the 1920s. In its former lives, it had been a drug store, a dance studio, and before she bought it, a thrift shop. Multi-purposed, old, and almost used up.

It was a tired place in need of rehab, but she'd paid cash for it, with a little left to spare. Last year she wouldn't have hesitated to take out a loan on a nicer place, but experiencing the reality of a life crash had taught her to be more careful.

She poured a glass of wine and settled herself on the white leather wrap-around couch. Her run-in with Rich was a depressing reminder of what happened when a smart girl repeatedly made the wrong choices, especially where men were concerned. Rich was her first love. He'd stolen her heart—by ripping it right out of her chest. She still had the scars to prove it. The hell of it was, he had no clue. To him, she was just one of many. For years she'd tried to hate him, but the truth was he had never made her any promises. Never told her he loved her or promised her a future. She was the fool. What was it her mother always said? *The only way to make a man respect you is to demand it.*

She swallowed the glass of wine in a gulp and pressed her head against the back of the couch. She had to let it go. The memories. The pain. The obsessive what ifs….

"Forget about Dick!" Her words echoed off the empty walls.

Taking a deep breath, she reminded herself that she had better things to worry about, like getting her office up and running. First and foremost, she needed to hire a secretary. Needed to get the front glass repaired. Needed to get the place painted so it looked less like a haunted house and more like a business. She should have stayed at the paper and gotten some advice on renovating from Tonya. But she couldn't stand being in the same room with *him* another second.

God, when did I become such a chicken shit?

She went to the fridge and poured another glass of wine. Chugging it, she poured another. She was about to polish off a third when a call from the sidewalk caught her attention.

"Sarah. Sarah Andrews. You up there?"

She rubbed the dust off the window, reminding herself that a good cleaning was also in order. As she cleared away the grime, her heart skipped a beat, infuriating her.

Dick was paying her a visit. She tried to pry the window open, but it was painted shut and wouldn't budge. She went to another window and shoved until she was breaking out in a cold sweat from exertion…or nerves and alcohol. She managed to crack it about six inches wide, then leaned down and yelled, "What do you want?"

"Let me in. I want to talk to you."

"Go away."

"Come on, Sarah. Come down from your tower and talk to me."

My tower? My tower! Her cheeks flamed. She stormed downstairs and flung the door open. It hammered off the stoop wall, making the aged wood quiver. From that point, it all seemed to happen in slow motion — the bang of the door off wood; the creak of the shifting window casing; and the slow slide of the pane of glass as it fell and then shattered in a spray of shards as it hit the sidewalk. Screaming like a high-strung twit, she jumped back from the explosion and covered her mouth with her hand.

Rich was on the stoop in a flash. "You all right? Any of it hit you?"

She looked herself over. "I don't think so. It just scared me."

"Scared me too. That should have been taped until it got

fixed. If a kid had been walking by—"

"That would have been a serious liability."

"Spoken like a true lawyer."

"I didn't mean it like that. I just meant…."

He stepped past her, moving about her space like he owned it. "You got a broom? Dust pan?"

"I think."

She looked around the box-filled room, not at all sure if she had one or not. She'd been here less than twenty-four hours, and in that time, she had closed on the place, stuffed too many belongings into too few square feet, and filled the fridge with wine and cottage cheese. Today she'd been determined to make a plan. But Dick kept getting in her way.

Rich stepped past her and opened a closet. There was an old broom. He took it outside and started sweeping. Sarah regained her train of thought and dug through the closet for a dust pan. Finding none, she ripped apart a box, fashioned a dust pan, and carried it outside and held it as Rich swept the shards onto it.

"When did you get such a temper? They teach you that at Stanford? Replace your sense of humor with rage?"

Still holding her piece of cardboard filled with glass, she faced him. "Uh? Excuse me?"

"I asked—"

"I heard the question."

"Then why ask why?" He kept sweeping glass into a tidy pile.

"Because it's a stupid question. I do have a sense of humor, and I am very much in control of my temper."

He laughed, a loud, genuine belly chuckle.

Sarah threw the piece of cardboard in the trash. She didn't need this. Who was he to taunt her? To laugh like nothing in this world mattered? It was men like him, who saw life as one casual connection after another, that had damn near ruined her.

13

It was the rage she felt that drove her, not some logical plan. It was like her foot had a mind of its own, kicking through his tidy pile of glass. He looked instantly shocked—eyes round, mouth hanging open. No doubt he thought she'd lost her mind. Instantly embarrassed, she stormed past him, heading for her apartment steps.

"Seriously?" He dropped the broom and followed behind her, catching her by the arm. "Did you kick glass at me?"

"Hardly at you," she said, jerking her arm away.

"You did. Like a spoiled brat, you kicked glass at me."

"Quit acting like a baby. It barely hit you."

"I'm acting like a baby?"

"Yeah, you're acting like a baby."

"What the hell is wrong with you?"

"With me?" Her voice was a few octaves higher than she'd planned. Her cheeks blazed and her hands shook. "There's nothing wrong with me. You're a pig. An insulting pig! I didn't ask you to come here, so go away." She turned and made it up two stairs before turning and asking, "What the hell are you doing here?"

"I came to apologize. I'm sorry if my ad in the paper insulted you."

"It didn't insult me. I don't care if you want to make an ass of yourself."

"I was desperate. It seemed like a good idea at the time."

"You? Desperate? Ha!"

He leaned his back against the banister, crossing his arms over his chest. "Have I done something to you? Pissed you off somehow?"

He probably didn't even remember...had just turned her life upside down and smashed her heart to pieces for fun. It only mattered to her. Her eyes stung with the revelation.

Sarah bit her lip hard and spun away, moving as quickly as

she could toward her steps. In her haste, her toe caught on the step and she fell forward, barely getting an arm in front of herself fast enough to break her fall. Her forehead smacked against a step and her arm lit up with a lightning bolt of pain. Before she could even consider her bad luck, she was scooped up and being carried through the office.

"Put me down," she demanded.

"No. I'm taking you to Fast Care."

"I'm fine."

"You're bleeding."

"I am?" She touched her fingers to her burning hairline and came away with a hand covered in blood. "I am."

Her imagination went wild. Pictures of a mangled face made her stomach tighten and her head spin. She might throw up. No, she couldn't throw up. Dick deserved it, but she still had some self-respect left.

Or so she hoped.

Chapter 3

Self-respect told her to insist he put her down, but being tucked tightly against solid, warm flesh felt good. Sarah rested her head against his shoulder and closed her eyes. Her cheek rubbed against the cotton of his T-shirt with each footfall. It was almost enjoyable, if only her head didn't burn and ache. She probably looked like Frankenstein, or at least his bride.

His breath was warm against her cheek. "It'll be all right. Doc will fix you up."

His comforting words brought the tears to her eyes. She didn't quite understand why, but they made her sadder and lonelier than she had ever felt—and she was the queen of getting dumped and left behind.

Her tears brought more assurances and a tighter grip of his arms. Kicking open the clinic door with his foot, he carried her through the waiting room. A nurse in hot pink scrubs must have decided he had no intention of waiting in a seat for the doctor, so she held the door to the exam room open and waved them on in. He set her on the exam table and knelt before her, holding her hand.

"You'll be all right." Her smile was shaky. He frowned and stood. Gathering her in his arms, he pulled her close. "I'm sorry. I had no right give you hell."

She shook her head against his chest.

"I'm a pig," he said.

She nodded. A small laugh escaped her lips.

Taking a step back, he tipped her chin so she was looking at him. "You didn't have to agree so damn fast."

She grinned and wiped at the tears. She came away with a blood-soaked hand. Her hands shook. Logic told her not to worry, head wounds bled a lot, but still….

Touching a finger to her wound, she felt the raw, swollen flesh. "Oh God." Fresh tears sprung to her eyes. "Is it ugly?"

It wasn't until then that she realized she'd bled all over his shirt, and hers. She was never one to be called vain, but suddenly having a scarred face mattered way more than it should to a sensible female. There was a mirror on the wall. She had to see for herself just how hideous her face was. One foot on the floor, her body felt hollow, as if only a part of her was present in the room. Two feet on the floor, and she felt her world go dark.

When she woke, she was lying on the table, her head on a pillow. A man stood over her, checking her pupils, while hot pink scrubs lady waved an ammonia pack under her nose.

"Welcome back." The man dropped his light into his pocket and frowned down on Sarah. "I'm Dr. Mitchell. Seems you've had an accident?"

"She fell up some steps, Doc," Rich offered.

So, this was Doc? Sarah had assumed a plump, gray-haired man with breath like garlic would be Doc, not a young, dark-haired guy with way too many muscles and far too good of a tan. *Doc is hot.* The only thing that stopped him from being a picture-perfect specimen of maleness was his height. He was a little on the short side, and Sarah was a little on the tall side, and towering above her dates always made her feel like some sort of Amazonian woman. Which was totally ridiculous, and she was too smart to think that way.

17

"So, this happened at home?" Dr. Mitchell asked as he checked her injuries.

"Um, yes, well, at my office. I moved in to the empty office on Main Street, used to be Donaldson's Thrift Store?"

"Office?" Doc asked.

"I'm opening my law office."

He paused his medical perusal. An eyebrow arched slightly and he seemed to nod in approval. "An attorney, hmm? Interesting." He grabbed her wrist and checked her pulse as he asked, "What have you eaten today?"

"Toast…and a glass or so of wine."

"Or so?"

"Two or three glasses…tops. No, it was two. Dick interrupted the third…I think."

Doc put his stethoscope in his ears and listened to her chest. "Dick?"

Rich laughed from his corner. "Just a pet name, Doc. She means me."

"Oh. Okay. Sorry. Long day. Started at five at the ER, and I'll probably be here until midnight."

"That is a long day," Sarah offered. "Every day like that?"

"Oh, I get the occasional day off. Get to spend some time on the lake. You ever go to the lake?" He asked her, then turned to his nurse. "Get a stitch tray ready. The head laceration is pretty deep. I doubt derma glue will hold it."

"Yes, sir." Pink Scrubs moved about the room opening doors and drawers.

"I haven't been there in ages," Sarah admitted. "I've been living in Indianapolis."

"Really?" Doc sounded impressed. Sarah started to think maybe she didn't look too hideous…she seemed to be getting hit on—by a doctor.

She couldn't help but sneak a glance at Rich, though why it

18

mattered if he noticed made zero sense. Okay, so it made a little sense. Rich had broken her heart. She hoped he was taking notes that she was a catch. Prime, grade A, and getting bandaged up by a hot doc with a roving eye—meat! Suck on that, Dick.

Rich was too busy reading a pamphlet on cholesterol to notice. She sighed and concentrated on Doc. He had stubble on his chin, the makings of a five o'clock shadow. His hands were soft—*too soft*, but she shunned the thought. He asked her to lie still, then he and hot pink scrubs worked together to clean away the blood from her forehead. Next came the numbing needle. Sarah gripped the edges of the table as all thoughts left her head besides, *damn, that hurts*!

Rich abandoned his study of lipids and stood beside her, taking her hand in his and giving it a gentle squeeze. His hand was warm and rough. She gripped it tighter as the needle popped into her skin. She couldn't feel it, but she could feel the tug pulling through her flesh, and it made her stomach knot.

Doc worked quickly—the stitching was done in a matter of seconds. He snipped the thread with surgical scissors, "I have a boat I like to take out on the lake. Great way to relax. Not that being a doctor is hard work—nothing like lugging drywall like Rich—but it can be draining. You probably deal with that in law, right? The emotional drain of the job?"

Sarah nodded. She could have sworn Rich rolled his eyes at Doc's statement. She supposed it might have been a little tacky and braggadocios, but still, Rich was the enemy. Why did she care if he was offended?

"There you go. Three little stitches fixed you right up...one for each glass of wine," Doc said with a wink.

"Will it scar?" she asked.

Doc leaned close, looking over his handiwork. "Not too badly. It is very close to your hair line, so your hair should cover it." Doc covered the new stitches with a bandage. "Besides, a pretty face like yours, it'd take a lot more than a little scar to mess it up."

Rich sighed as he helped Sarah sit up. He kept a hand at her back.

Doc gave her knee a pat and declared, "All done. Told you it'd be nothing."

"Thanks." Sarah touched her forehead gently.

"Don't touch," Pink Scrubs scolded as she handed Sarah a mirror. "See? It's not so bad."

The white bandage on her forehead made her look like a cartoon soldier. Her upper lip was swollen to double its usual size, and black and blue marks were beginning to show on her cheek.

"Oh my," was all she said.

"It'll be fine," Doc said, pulling off his surgical gloves. "Keep it dry and clean and you'll be good in no time."

"When do I come back to get the stitches out?"

"Well, either you can come back, or you can go boating with me Saturday and I could take care of them then."

"Oh," Sarah said, a little stunned. She never had been a good flirt. Born too serious, her grandmother used to say. But she caught Rich's frown of disapproval, so without any further thought, she said, "Of course I will. That sounds wonderful, and probably cheaper than an office call."

"Certainly," Doc said. "Especially if you agree to go to dinner with me. I mean, where can you get free health care and food?"

Sarah laughed. "No place that I know of."

Doc scribbled on a pad then ripped it off and handed it to her. "Here's a script for a few Vicodin. Don't mix with the wine. And here." He ripped off another piece. "Here's my phone number. Give me a call and we'll set something up."

"Sounds good," Sarah said as her attempts at a smile made her reach for her lip again.

"Ah! No touching until you see me again." Doc winked at

her.

"Thank you," Sarah said as she scooted off the table with Doc holding onto one arm, Rich helping with the other.

She said goodbye and stopped at the desk to sign papers. Rich stuck with her, saying nothing until they were outside, walking down the sidewalk.

"Isn't it against medical ethics to pick up patients?"

Sarah laughed. "Like I'm going to turn him in."

Rich frowned and gave her a look.

Sarah shrugged as glee bubbled through her. It might be immature to get so much pleasure out of his displeasure, but so what?

"Oh well. You're more Doc's type, anyhow."

Yes, she thought, they were both professionals. "What type am I?" she asked, feeling rather smug.

"Bitchy."

She came to an instant stop. "Me? Bitchy?"

Rich slowed, but didn't stop. "Uptight. Difficult. Most certainly high-maintenance."

Sarah moved forward as quickly as she could to keep up, and said, "Do you get some sort of sick pleasure out of insulting me?"

Rich shook his head slowly, without even bothering to look down at her. "No, you're just easily offended. I came to apologize to you earlier, but you threw your little temper tantrum and busted your glass. I, again, tried to be a nice guy and clean it up, and you acted like a brat and kicked it at me."

"I...." She barreled toward him, arms swinging, feet stomping on concrete. "You insult me at every turn. You intentionally push my buttons. You know how to make me angry, and make me do stupid things."

He laughed, a big, wide-smiled chuckle that made her want to punch him in the face.

"Oooh!" was all Sarah could muster. She took off again. She

was going home—she didn't care if he called her every name in the book, she wasn't talking to him a minute longer!

Five steps away, she hit a buckle in the sidewalk and down she went. Fully expecting her face to bite cement, she was pleasantly surprised to be swooped into the air before her body made contact.

"Looks like we're back to this. You know, you really should eat—you're way too thin."

"Says the guy looking for a fat chick."

He set her on her feet, but kept an arm around her shoulders. "Come with me—I'll feed you. No strings. No insults. You need to take the pain pills, and you don't want to do that on an empty stomach."

"I think not."

"I think so. Don't be a girl about all this. Just come and eat."

"What's that supposed to mean?"

"It means stop holding grudges. Just like a woman to be pissed about something that wasn't even intended for her. Hell, you're probably still mad at me for something I did in high school."

"I can't believe I ever liked you. Your mouth opens, and the most absolutely stupid drivel rolls out of it."

"Well then, let's get food and we can both shut our mouths."

"I think I'd rather go scrub the grout from my shower than spend—" Her rant was cut short.

Tonya pulled up in her mini-van. "Rich. Dammit. Do you ever answer your phone?"

"What?" He pulled the phone from his pocket. There were sixteen missed calls. "Oh, hell." He looked panicked. "The girls all right?"

"They're fine. Jess stopped by. She brought this." Tonya handed him a paper through her van window.

Rich stepped off the curb and took it.

Sarah watched as his face went from stressed to worse...like a guy who'd lost everything in a tornado.

"Damn her. I knew it. I knew she had something up her sleeve." He looked over the papers, his head shaking as he read.

"You two haven't been cage fighting, have you?" Tonya nodded toward Sarah's head.

Sarah looked to Rich, who was still reading, then back at Tonya. "I tripped going up the steps."

Her injuries were forgotten when Rich wadded up the papers and said, "It says I have five days to respond. I can respond right now—this is bullshit."

"I don't think that's what they mean by responding. You need to get a good lawyer, Rich. Give those to Sarah," Tonya said, her eyes glancing to Sarah and back to Rich. Neither Sarah nor Rich moved for several seconds.

Sarah was the first to soften. She knew how it felt to lose something precious; she wouldn't wish that feeling on anyone— not even Rich. Sarah held out her hand, "May I?"

He handed the papers to Sarah and she looked them over. "She's challenging your custody?"

Rich nodded.

Are those tears in his eyes? Sarah softened. "Do you have the money for a lawyer?"

"I have a little. And I can mortgage the house, and maybe get a second one on the bar."

The guy was a jerk, but the kind of jerk who obviously loved his kids. Sarah was spiteful, but not heartless. And it wasn't like she had an abundance of cases to keep her busy. "If you can come up with enough for the court costs, I'll waive my legal fees. If you trust me to take the case."

"You can trust her, Rich. She's the best. Aren't you, Sarah?"

"I've won a few cases, but I've never done family law. You may be better off with—"

23

"Shush, Sarah. You're being humble. She's the best you'll get, Richie. If there's a way to win, Sarah will find it."

Rich ran a hand through his hair. "If you can help me, I swear to God, I will be eternally indebted."

Hmmm…Dick as a man slave? What an excellent position to have him in.

Chapter 4

The little town of Dodd suddenly felt quaint and comforting from Sarah's lofty perspective. Richland Conrad Cooper needed her. Doc Mitchell wanted her, and that seemed to bug the hell out of Rich. Her life still sucked, but she had learned long ago to appreciate even the smallest wins.

Sarah looked over Rich's court papers. "Your first hearing is scheduled for next week. First thing we'll do is get that moved. No sense letting her set the agenda. I'll make that call as soon as I get back to the office."

Rich looked stunned, and scared.

Sarah touched his arm and promised, "We'll beat this. I'll do whatever it takes."

A horn blew behind Tonya's car. "It'll be all right, cuz, I swear." The horn blew again. "Oh, holy hell. Hang on to your pants!" Tonya yelled out her window to the driver behind her. "Take care of him, Sarah. He may be a dipshit, but he's a good guy way down deep." One more horn blow prompted her to put the car in gear and drive off.

Dinner forgotten, they walked on to her office. The front door was wide open and the glass still needed cleaned up. Sarah pointed to the building. "You got a few minutes? I'll need some information."

"Yeah. The girls are in school." He checked his watch. "I have about an hour before I have to pick them up."

"Then let's get started." Sarah closed the door behind them. "Guess I better call and get this repaired."

"I'll do it. It's an easy fix. It's the least I can do."

They stepped into her "office," a small room off the main entrance. It had a desk, a chair, and cardboard boxes stacked on more cardboard boxes. The desk and chair were cheap faux wood from the local department store…nothing like the mahogany she'd left behind.

"Looks like you're still moving in."

"Yep. You will be my very first client in my very own practice. Hell, I don't even have a secretary yet."

Rich sat on the edge of the desk. "Rumor has it you were quite the hotshot attorney in Indianapolis."

She rummaged through a few boxes until she found a notepad and a pen. "Is that what they say?"

"Yep. Got to work under Evan Stollings, the boy wonder… Mr. Future President."

Sarah dropped her pen on the floor, her hands shaking as she picked it up. "I'm sure Mr. Stollings has a long career ahead of him."

Rich settled himself on top of her desk, crossing his arms over his chest. "Just curious, but why do you think he gets a pass on all the sexual harassment charges? Think it's his good looks, or is he misunderstood?"

"I can't say I know what you're talking about." Sarah took a deep breath.

"Really? Seems every month there's a new bimbo scandal. I hear this last one, he got caught with his pants down, right in the middle of the act, by his wife. I hear he's paying out the nose to keep it quiet."

"Well, he's obviously not paying enough. You heard about

it."

"Only through the grapevine. You never see any stories on the news about his scandals. Maybe they're just rumor—"

"Seriously? Did you come to gossip, or discuss your case?" Sarah snapped at him.

Rich shrugged and sighed. "Sorry, you guys are probably friends."

"Hmmph. Hardly." Sarah sat and turned the tablet to a fresh sheet of paper. "I simply think we'd better worry about your case, not Evan Stollings." Sarah brushed a loose piece of hair behind her ear. "If I can't get the date moved, it won't give us much time to prepare."

"You're right. What do you need to know?" Rich asked as he pulled his long legs under him and made himself more comfortable on top of her desk.

Assemble more office furniture, she thought as his knee bumped her hand. She'd insist he get off the top of her desk and sit on a chair, but she had none to offer. They were hopefully in one those boxes stacked up the walls.

Scooting the legal pad farther away, she cleared her throat. "For starters, is this the same court that granted you custody of the girls in the first place?"

"No. We've never been to court. When the girls were little, Jess up and left me. She divorced me from Nevada. Those papers were the last word I had from her."

"How many years went by with no word?" Her pen scratched quickly across the yellow paper.

"Four. She left right after Stacey's first birthday."

"So, she abandoned the kids for four years without a word? Did she ever send money, any gifts? Cards on holidays? Anything?"

"Nothing."

"Well, this might be easier than we think. It's clearly

abandonment," she said, looking up at him. An instant flush moved up her neck. *Grown men shouldn't sit on desks. It's childish and—damn it, why does he always feel so close?*

"That's my hope, and I don't think Stacey will be a problem. It's Kari I worry about."

"Why's that?"

"Well, Jess had Kari before we got married. Kari was three and had never met her father, so I just sort of filled in."

Her pen came to a stop. Her heart did that weird skip-beat that made her lungs freeze. "You're not Kari's dad?"

"Not technically." Rich rubbed his thumb over the stubble on his chin. "But I'm the only dad she's ever known."

"Oh." She chewed the side of her cheek. Why would he lie to her? Jess had told her she and Rich were having a child. One that would have had to have been conceived when he was supposedly with Sarah. She cleared her throat and forced past the lump that settled there. "Did you adopt her?"

"Jess always said it was unnecessary. She said Kari's dad died before she was born. I couldn't exactly adopt the girl against her mom's will."

"After Jess left, why didn't you do something then? Take custody of her?"

Rich took a deep breath and shrugged. "I guess I was afraid to go to social services and make a deal out of it. I mean, what if they dug up her real dad and he wanted her back? For all I knew, she could have been lying about the dead dad. After being married to her a few years, I knew you couldn't trust a damn thing she said. The guy might never have been told, and who's to say if he suddenly knew he had a daughter, he wouldn't want her? I couldn't take that chance. I may be a shit for thinking that, but I love that kid. As far as I'm concerned, she's my daughter."

Sarah frowned and made a few notes on the paper. "As your attorney, don't mention that again."

"Which part?"

As she flipped to a new page she said, "That you intentionally avoided legal action to keep the child's paternity a secret."

"Say it like that and it sounds pretty bad."

"Mmm, hmm," she said, chewing on the end of her pen as she thought for a minute. "Has Jess ever said why she was absent so long?"

"She says she became addicted to prescription pills while we were married, and that she left to save the girls from being hurt by her addiction."

"Noble of her," Sarah's voice was flat.

"Bullshit, noble. After Stacey turned a year old, Jess complained about being home all day and night, so she convinced me to buy the bar. I worked during the day and she ran it at night. It wasn't long before she was screwing half the clientele. She was never addicted to anything but men, and it was a man she ran away with. Not drugs."

"Impossible to prove, and we'd look like we had no compassion for her if we tried to prove her wrong."

"You telling me I don't have a chance?"

Sarah dropped her pen and looked up at him. "Not at all. I am counseling you NOT to mention your reasons for avoiding social services. You will take Jess at her word. She said the dad was dead, the dad is dead. She says she was hooked on drugs, she was hooked on drugs. We can't pick and choose believability."

Rich let out a long sigh. "I suppose that makes sense."

"Of course, it does." She picked up her pen. "I need all the information you have on Jess. Names. Dates. Birthdate. Social security number—if you know it. Hell, if she has a dog—what did she name it? Everything you can think of, write it down here. I'll get started."

Rich took the tablet from her.

Sarah tried not to let his hand touch hers when she handed

29

him the pen, but it was unavoidable. To make it worse, he gave her a wink — like he knew his touch made her heart race. While he filled the page with almost illegible scribbles, Sarah took a few deep breaths.

He handed it back to her. She looked it over and nodded. "Good. Looks good. I'm going to hire a detective. If she so much as cheats on her taxes, I want to find out. That all right with you?"

"Anything it takes. Let me know what this will cost. I'll pay you back. About how much did you charge in Indianapolis?"

"Six hundred an hour plus expenses."

"Holy shit."

"Fix my door, and we'll call it even."

"You'd do that for me?" He looked beautifully grateful, like a puppy being offered a treat.

Sarah frowned. "Jess and I didn't exactly part company as friends. Call it just desserts."

As soon as Sarah was out of the country, Jess had moved in on Rich, even after he broke Sarah's heart — a real friend would have shut him out, not dated him.

"I don't care what you call it. I'm just glad you're home, Sarah Andrews." He smiled down at her. "I honestly didn't realize just how much I've missed you."

Chapter 5

Sarah pushed herself away from her desk and Rich. She didn't need this, this blurring of the lines between professional and personal. Not to mention he'd burned her once already, why let him do it again? Dear lord, she was almost thirty-three, old enough to know better.

Saying nothing as she rounded the desk, she didn't speak until she opened the office door. "I think I have enough to get started. If I need anything else, I'll give you a call."

He slid off her desk, but didn't make any effort to leave. Crossing the room until he was within inches of her, he said, "What have I done? Why are you so mad at me?"

She opened her mouth to lie that she just had a lot to do, but he cut her off.

"Yes, I acted like an ass at the paper…but I think you'd realize I saw this fight coming. I heard Jess was moving back to Dodd, and knew I'd be hearing from her in one way or another. She's cleaned up…fresh from rehab, and newly married to a guy with money. Me, on the other hand? I'm single. I run a bar, and have a sad little construction company on the side. But I love my girls. There's nothing I wouldn't do to protect them, including getting married to look like I have a better family environment than Jess. I know her, Sarah. I know Jess will look real good to the outside world. Cookie-freaking-baking perfect. But you've got to know…I lived with her. She's a lying, conniving tramp. I know she has an agenda, and she'll do anything to get her way. That's why I thought if I had a wife by the time this hit, I'd look better in court."

Sarah's heart broke at his confession. It wasn't his fault he'd never loved her. They'd been friends — good friends. She was the one who'd blurred those lines by falling in love with him. Not him. She couldn't keep blaming him for her mistakes.

She took his hand in hers and gave it a squeeze. "You can't just marry someone for show. That's not fair to you, the imaginary wife, or your daughters. But I do understand how you feel. I promise you, I'll do everything I can to beat her."

His hand tightened around hers and he stepped a little closer, his head dipping lower. She jerked her hand from his and grabbed the office door, motioning for him to leave.

"Can I buy you dinner?" he asked.

"No." She pointed toward the door with her head.

"Why not?"

Closing her eyes for a moment, she explained, her voice maybe a bit too crisp, "This isn't personal. I don't want you to confuse professional concern with any sort of other relationship."

The brute laughed — head tipped back, beautifully shaped throat muscles working under tanned skin. Once his delight subsided, he asked, "No relationship? Why not?"

"Well," her eyebrow arched. "For starters, I'm not fat, and I have a career."

"Some things are negotiable; some things are fixable."

"Oh my gosh, I can't believe you just said that. You never learn. You truly are a pig."

"No, no." He put his hands over his ears. "Not going back to that. I'm leaving and not listening. I'll be back later. Hopefully sweet Sarah will be here." He leaned closer and whispered in her ear, "Please tell bitchy Sarah to relax a little. I offered dinner, not a ring."

"Well, I...." Her words came out in a shrill hiss.

He turned and left.

"Sweet Sarah," she grumbled after he left. "He can kiss bitchy Sarah's ass. He's such an ass. I can't believe I ever—good God, what did I see in that man?"

"You talking about Rich?" Tonya grinned at her from the doorway. "I didn't bother to knock. You have a big hole in your door, so I just stepped through."

"That's Rich's fault."

"He broke your door?"

"No, I broke my door, but he's the one who made me mad, so ultimately, it's his fault."

"I see." Tonya's grin grew wider.

"Stop it!"

"Stop what?"

"Grinning like you think him pissing me off so easily means there's something between us. It's ludicrous."

"Obviously there is some history here that I was never trusted with, which hurts because I am your very best friend."

"Nothing. We went to prom together. You knew that." Sarah kept unloading stuff from the box and setting items neatly on her desk.

"Oh, come on, you look at him like you'd like to rip his heart out. Something happened between you two."

"Nothing of any relevance."

Tonya stared at her, eyes boring into her with so much intensity Sarah finally broke. "Fine. I had a crush on him. A stupid, school-girl crush. I thought...well, we had fun at prom. I thought he might like me, but he didn't."

"He says you left town to live with your mom without even saying goodbye."

"Whatever. Ancient history. Rich Cooper means nothing to me. Never did. Never will."

Tonya laughed. "Whatever. I know you're too stubborn to admit it, even to yourself."

"I —

Tonya put up her hand to hush her. "No arguing. I'm just teasing you, and I swear, I didn't come here to bust your chops. I wanted to invite you to lady's night. Once a month, the girls and I ditch our men, mix up some drinks, and hang out."

"I don't have a man to ditch, and I think I have already replaced my blood with wine. So, it looks like every night is lady's night for me. But you ladies enjoy. It sounds quaint."

"Sarah Mae Andrews! You're coming to my house, and before you do, you're going to pull the broomstick out of your ass so you can have fun. Tell me no, and I swear by all that is holy that I will tell Rich you like him. That you confided in me that you've had a crush on him since you could wear a training bra."

Sarah dropped the stapler she was unpacking, and it made a chip in the faux wood of the desk. "That is a complete and total lie."

"Is it?" Tonya cocked an eyebrow at her.

"Yes."

Tonya shrugged and grinned. Sarah could see the family resemblance — smug, arrogant pains in her ass.

Sarah let out an exhausted breath. "You know, I was going to come to your lady's night, but now that you're —"

"Yay! Last Friday of every month. Put it on your calendar. I'll pick you up at eight. My house is hard to find. Love you, girl!" With that, she left.

Sarah set her desk to rights and then went to her apartment. Though eager for a glass of wine, she resisted, opting instead for coffee. She didn't want to be found dead because she mixed pain pills and alcohol. It'd be her luck that it'd take days to find her, and she'd be bloated and fly specked. People would come to her funeral and say how natural and beautiful her puffy body looked, and she'd have to haunt their crazy asses for their stupidity. She'd never have a moment's peace in eternity.

Wrapping the mug in both hands, she settled herself on the couch. She quickly outlined a plan of attack, making mental notes on case histories that might be used as precedent; what their defense could be against Rich's many short comings; and what exactly about Jess's life could she attack? Settling her head against the back of the couch, she closed her eyes and thought. Everything the woman did wrong prior to rehab would mean nothing. Even if she left the kids while sober and sound-minded, no one would care. She got help. Once a victim, now a victor... she'd get brownie points for that.

She groaned and leaned forward. Her head was beginning to hurt. Rubbing her temple, she realized she could use help. Sarah dug her phone out of her purse and called her mother.

She answered on the first ring. "Sarah. I was just talking about you. I was telling Ed what a stupid choice you made returning to Dodd."

"Not again, Mother."

"Aren't you touchy. Going worse than you thought?"

"It's going fine. That's why I called. I have my first case, and I wanted to know if I could borrow your PI."

"Of course, though if you'd forced Stollings to find you a job at another firm—"

"I wanted a simpler life, not a transfer to more of the same."

"So, is it simpler? You sound as tense as a hooker at Sunday services."

"Gee thanks, nice analogy."

"You know I didn't mean it toward you—how were you supposed to know Evan was married? I mean, he's only the fastest rising star in the Midwest."

35

"I suppose I don't get out much."

"Or read many newspapers."

"This has been fun, but I better go."

"Oh Sarah, stop. I'm sorry. I have skin like rhino hide and forget you're still sensitive. Tell me about your case. Will it be brutal? Something good and nasty you can sink your teeth into?"

"It's for Rich against Jess."

"Weekend cabin boy and your friend, Jess? Good God, Sarah, maybe you'll make a fine good soulless attorney after all."

"It's not that. It's just…you can tell he really loves his kids."

Claire's laugh was more of a snort. "He didn't show much concern or affection when it was you in the predicament. But then maybe it's like my mother always said about your father— he couldn't stand you because he couldn't stand me. Personally, I think that's bullshit. Why always blame the woman? Isn't a man a deplorable human being if he doesn't take care of his kids? Even if he loathes her mother?"

Sarah took a deep breath. She knew her mother meant well, but talking to her for more than a few minutes at a time always made her feel like she should get a therapist.

Before Sarah could end the call, her mother pushed ahead with more theories and insights. "Or are you just trying to torture yourself? Some sort of self-flagellation? Helping the man who broke your heart, does that offer some sort of penance for ultimate forgiveness? Would you rather I just buy you a whip and you can do the job right?"

"Mother, please. Will you help me or not?"

"Of course. Email Naomi the details. I've already told her she'll be hearing from you."

Sarah rubbed her hand across her now-aching forehead. Ever since she'd seen his reaction to the mere possibility of losing his kids, she'd known he cherished them. Probably would have loved hers—in time. It prodded her to voice the question that kept her up at night. "Why couldn't I have kept it? I could have been a single mom. You did it."

"I already had my law degree and a job. You were a mistake I could deal with."

"I could have—"

"Stop being ridiculous, Sarah Mae Andrews. You had a scholarship to Stanford. Those don't come a dime a dozen. You were in a position to do amazing things. I couldn't let you throw that away for a crush on a guy whose most amazing life skill was hammering things."

"I should have talked to him."

"Well, you didn't. And there's no way to get a re-do, so get over it and move on with your damned life. I swear, I honestly think you try to self-destruct. You could be having the most amazing career—"

"I know. I know. I'm a disappointment."

"The self-pity won't work on me, little lady. You're over thirty. It's time to get yourself together. Forget the Cooper boy. Your instincts on men are horrendous. You haven't ever chosen wisely. From Stollings to the prom night screw to the guy who used you as a drug mule—"

"That wasn't my fault. How was I supposed to know what was in the bag?"

"That's my point—your taste in men sucks. Ignore your loins and your heart, and please, for once in your life, use your head. If you're not going to pursue a real career and want a kid, you better get your shit together. The clock is ticking."

"Thanks."

"You're welcome."

"I was being sarcastic."

"I know you're under a lot of stress, so I'm ignoring it. I'm honestly worried about you. I could take some time off and come there and help you—"

"No, no. I'm fine." Sarah imagined her mother's help, AKA constant bitching, and quickly tried to offer her assurances. Sarah took a deep breath and, "I met a cute doctor."

"Now, that's promising. Does he have a specialty?"

"He works in the ER."

"Oh. Well, still beats the ex-jock with no goals."

Sarah bit her lip. She didn't understand why she felt compelled to defend Rich, but the urge was strong. "Doc seems like a nice guy."

"Doc? His name is Doc? Is he a dwarf?"

Sarah laughed. A real laugh. The first in weeks. "He is pretty short."

"I suppose good things come in small packages. Take care, Sarah. I know I've never been the perfect mother, but you're my daughter and I only want the best for you."

"I know you do. Don't worry. I think I'm going to be fine. Head over heart. Gotcha. I'll get that tattooed on my wrist."

Chapter 6

A sudden crash made Sarah jump in her seat. Closing the laptop screen, she hurried to the window facing the street. She saw nothing but the same quiet Main Street that had been there since she was a little girl. If she were still in the city, her first thought would've been intruder…call 911. But here? Crashing and hammering could only mean one thing: *Rich.*

She headed downstairs. As soon as she opened her apartment door, she could hear voices. One of them sounded like a little girl. Rich was busily working on her door as his little girl helped and the older one leaned against the wall.

The younger child was dressed in green sweat pants and an orange hoodie. Purple shoes rounded out her outfit. Her hair was cut short, so the ringlets of springy red curls clung to her head. The older girl, Kari, was dressed in jeans and a T-shirt, her straight blonde hair pulled back in a ponytail. The little girl turned and smiled at Sarah as she approached. The older one shot her a look that would have frozen moving water.

"I'm Stacey," the little girl offered. "I'm helping my dad. Why'd you break your door?"

"It…. Well, I—"

"Mind your own business," the older girl ordered.

Stacey stuck out her tongue and shook her head at her.

"Brat," Kari said.

"Dad, Kari called me a brat."

"I heard. Kari, don't call your sister a brat. Stacey, quit telling Sarah things I say. She has no sense of humor and won't understand."

"Really?" she asked her dad, then turned to Sarah. "Why don't you have a sense of humor?"

"I do. It's just that some people aren't as funny as they think they are," Sarah said with a smile.

"My daddy's funny. Isn't he, Kari?"

"You're so ignorant," Kari said.

"Dad!"

Rich drove the last nail in with a little more oomph than necessary. "Both of you stop. Sarah, your door is done. I couldn't get glass, but the plywood will hold until I can order a pane. You two, get on out to the truck."

The girls followed their dad's orders slowly, looking over their shoulders at Sarah and bumping into each other in the door frame, which resulted in some pushing and name calling.

"You see why I can't lose them?" Rich laughed as he gathered his tools.

"They are beautiful. You're a lucky man." She amazed herself with her self-control. She was able to spit out compassion without choking on it or blurting out the awkward — *why, why did you forsake us?* Her mother was right. It was history and couldn't be undone. No sense picking at wounds that needed to heal.

He stood to full height. "That I am. Even their most trying days are better than the best days without them."

She nodded.

His voice was quiet. "I'm scared, Sarah. Especially with Kari. That attitude she's copping? That's all new. Her mother makes a few phone calls to her, and my once happy kid morphs into a moody teen."

"What about Stacey? She taking it all right?"

Rich nodded. "She was one when Jess left. She has no memory of her whatsoever. Kari was eleven, and I think she has enough memories of her mother to last her a lifetime."

"Was Jess abusive?"

"She was unpredictable. The night she left she was supposed to be at a mother-daughter sleepover with Kari. She told me she was going, told Kari she'd be late, and then she never showed up at all."

"So, Kari's what? Fifteen?"

"She'll be sixteen in December."

"So, Jess was pregnant with Kari before I left for school? And she's not yours?"

"It was some guy she met at college. At least that's what she told me."

"And you're sure she's not yours?" Sarah leaned against the door jam.

"Why do you keep asking that? Hell, if Kari was mine, I wouldn't be sweating all this so much."

"True. It's just that, well, I thought you guys were dating then."

"No. I believe I was trying to date you, but you blew me off. I guess a college dropout isn't nearly as exciting to you as the Harvard types."

"It was Stanford, and for your information, Jess told me you two were dating. You seemed to be with her enough."

"Hell, we were the only two dumb enough to stay in this town. I guess hanging out together just happened. If you would've ever talked to me again, you would've known we didn't date till Kari was three."

Sarah crossed her arms over her chest. "You don't have to explain yourself. We weren't exactly a love match. I didn't expect anything from you."

"I thought we were friends. Sometimes I look back on that weekend and I wish I hadn't—we hadn't—because I lost a friend. But at least I can say I took a chance. Damn, but I liked you."

"Seriously?"

"Hell yeah. What wasn't to like?"

Sarah started to grin, but only briefly. She truly wasn't stupid enough to fall—again—for mendacities. There was a reason that men were at the root of the word. As a species, they had zero qualms about spewing whatever sweet-smelling bull they had to get them what they wanted. She'd already agreed to help him—why play the games?

"You know, Rich, you're a handsome guy, and you could get ladies to drop their drawers with a smile. I don't play games, so don't try it."

"Why does everything I say have to be a fight with you?"

"It doesn't have to be. Stop trying to convince me I ever meant anything to you and we'll be fine."

"Fine, Miss I-Know-Everything." He turned to leave, but then spun to face her. "But for the record, I did like you. I don't know what your problem is now. Maybe you're short-tempered from too many years on the Angelina Jolie diet plan."

"There you go again, looking for fat chicks. I'm sorry I grew up and left the fat, wimpy girl behind."

"Leave her alone. She wasn't fat; she was perfect—she had an awesome rack and a nice ass." Rich shoved the door open and took a step outside, but then turned back around and added, "And you know what else? That Sarah was fun. She used to smile and laugh. Maybe you should stop starving her and lighten up a little!"

Sarah's jaw fell open, but not a single word came out. He was in his truck and gone before she could utter, "I never!"

Kicking the door closed, she locked it—she didn't need him sneaking back in here. To think he wanted her help. He could burn in hell before she would help him. *Used to have a nice rack. Used to have a nice ass.* She still had them, they were just smaller than when she was a chubby seventeen-year-old. She worked her ass off to stay trim! She ran six miles a day, and hadn't eaten a spoonful of sugar in ten years. *Who the hell is he?*

Chapter 7

"It's okay. I love you, Daddy." Stacey patted Rich's arm as he put the truck in gear.

"Buckle up, princess. And thank you; I love you too."

"Oh my God. I can't believe Aunt Tonya thinks you guys would make a good couple," Kari said with a disgusted shake to her head.

"Your Aunt Tonya said that?"

"Seriously, Dad, don't sound so hopeful! I mean, she obviously can't stand you."

"Because she misjudges me," Rich said as he looked over his shoulder to pull onto Main Street.

"Really? You think that's all? I mean, let's just pretend you never said such stupid things like she was too skinny…which for the record, you might have gotten away with. But you added that she had no boobs."

"You heard that?"

"You two were *yelling* at each other, practically in the street."

"Oh, I didn't realize." Rich was quiet a minute, then he asked, "Okay, so let's say I can smooth all that over…then what are my chances?"

"You don't need chances, Daddy! You have me." Stacey grinned up at him.

He winked at her. "Yes, I do, pumpkin." He shifted uncomfortably in his seat as they rolled up to a stop sign. "But let's just say...I might be interested in her. What are my chances?"

Kari thought a minute. "Ask me later. I need to consider this longer."

"Gee thanks, eight ball; you're a big help."

Kari broke into a laugh. "Look, I am the number one matchmaker at my school. Everyone I set out to fix up, hooks up. But I don't have my awesome stats by luck. I only play Cupid with people I know will like each other. And sadly...right off the bat, I wouldn't see you two ending up together. It's like that fantasy of the brainy girl falling for the jock. That happens in movies. In reality, the jock dates the cheerleader, and the brainy girl goes out with the brainy boy."

"I see. So, I'm the jock?"

"Sort of. Though you are old and not really an athlete anymore, but you get my point."

"Unfortunately, yes I do," Rich said with a sigh.

Kari flashed him a pleased smile.

The kid is right. Sarah would call Doc, they'd go out, and Rich would be the loser getting drunk at their wedding. Then he'd probably head home to an empty house after Jess took his girls. Life truly was a bitch when you married one.

"Take her flowers, Daddy. It works in movies," Stacey offered.

"I *was* rude. I mean, I should apologize for that at least."

He pulled the truck to a stop alongside a vacant lot with overgrown grass and yellow-headed dandelions. Jumping out, he grabbed a handful of the flowers, then jumped back in. He made a U-turn and headed back.

He pounded on the door, but Sarah didn't answer. He yelled up at her window, making a note to himself to add an entrance to her apartment from the outside. Screaming from the street was a nuisance. He yelled again, in case she was upstairs.

The door swung open and there she was, looking as annoyed and pretty as ever. He suddenly felt as nervous as he had the first time he realized she wasn't just his cousin's little friend. Sarah and Tonya had been underfoot most of his life. Sarah was Tonya's tag-a-long friend, showing up to every family gathering and holiday. When he got the call from Tonya to do her a super-big favor, he did his best to dodge her, but dodging Tonya wasn't ever easy. He finally caved and agreed to come home the weekend before finals and take Sarah to prom. He'd been so busy at school, he hadn't realized awkward little Sarah had become a stunning beauty in a shimmering emerald gown that clung to her curves and—

"What?" Sarah asked.

He suddenly felt hot. He shook off the memory and managed to spit out, "I lost my temper. You make me…I mean, I'm under stress, and I'm not being very nice."

"Well, I do understand being under stress. You simply need to realize you don't have to play games with me to get my help."

"I swear, I wasn't doing that. And I promise, somehow, I'll pay you. And, I want you to know, I'm not asking you to do this because you're cutting me a deal. I'm asking you to do this because I trust you. You're the smartest person I've ever known, and if anyone can help me keep my babies, it's you." He pushed the flowers toward her.

"You're offering me weeds?"

"Keep them long enough, they turn into wishes."

She gasped. He felt a surge of hope as she stepped toward him and plucked the flowers from his hand. "Of course, I'll help you. And the weeds are, uh—sweet."

"Not weeds. Wishes."

She sighed, looking up at him with a look he could only call defeated. "I'm not exactly the wishing type, but thank you."

He smiled as he reached for the door handle. "Okay, well, if there's anything I can do, anything you need, let me know." He thought of asking her to dinner again, but decided he'd crashed and burned plenty for one day. Tipping his head to her, he left and joined the pair of ladies who were always eager to spend time with him.

Rich jumped into the truck, and asked, "Who wants to grab dinner at the diner?"

Stacey lifted an arm in the air like she was in school. "I do. I do!"

"Then dinner it is."

Rich headed on down Main Street, parking beside a meter. As he fed a few quarters in the machine, he thought of how Doc would probably have gotten Sarah roses. Doc also had a boat and a house on the lake.

A tiny hand grabbed his and pulled. "Come on, Daddy! We're hungry."

They headed to their booth. Stacey read over the menu, though Rich knew she would order the same thing: chicken nuggets and fries drowned in ketchup. He didn't even pick up a menu. He'd have a bacon cheeseburger and onion rings. But Kari would surprise them. The older girl thumbed through the plastic-coated menu. She even asked Nick, the owner/waiter, if there were any specials. Nick smiled at her as he stroked his mustache. Nick never had a special unless Kari asked for one.

"Seems," Nick said slowly, "we have a pineapple chicken salad with a light cranberry dressing."

Kari nodded as she handed him her menu with a smile. "I'll have that."

"I'll inform the chef."

Rich grinned. Nick performed the job of "chef" also. The only time the diner had extra help was during lunch hour, when Nick's wife came in to wait tables and run the register. At any other hour, the little diner rarely had more than two tables filled at a time. It wasn't a fancy place. The fake red leather seats were cracked, the splits repaired with red duct tape. Pictures of the town at various times in the last century covered the walls.

Christmas bells hanging on the door chimed, announcing a new arrival. Nick yelled from the kitchen, "Be with ya in a minute. Have a seat."

Rich and the kids turned to the sound. Rich instantly lost his appetite.

Kari turned white, her words quiet, unsteady. "Mom?"

Chapter 8

Sarah carried her flowers up to her apartment and stuck them in a water-filled wine glass. If she was ever to make a wish, what would it be?

Her thoughts were interrupted by her ringing phone. She didn't recognize the number, but she answered. It was Doc. Disappointment made her frown, but she said brightly, "Why, hello. What a surprise."

"I got your number off your file. I hope you don't mind."

"No, not at all," she said, grabbing her glass of dandelions and setting them in a sunny window.

"I could pretend I'm calling to see if the stitches are holding up okay, but I put them in, so I know they're good." He laughed.

Sarah tried to laugh with him as her fingers traced the velvety tops of the flowers. "No, I'm fine. Stitches are fine."

"See? I do good work."

"Yes, you do." Sarah settled herself on the window sill.

"Seems I'm free tonight, so I wondered...would you want to grab a bite, maybe a drink...unless you're taking the Vicodin."

Sarah laughed. "Just the first dose, then I weaned myself off."

"Great. There's nothing fancy in Dodd, but The Recline has good food, and we could have that drink."

Reasons to say no flashed through her head. When those

49

reasons hit on the pain in the ass with the blond hair and warm brown eyes, she instantly said, "Sounds great. What time?"

"Eight all right?"

"Eight is perfect."

Hanging up, she couldn't help but feel a twist of regret in her gut.

~*~

Dressed in jeans and a pink cashmere sweater, she pulled most of her hair up, carefully placing her bangs over the stitches on her forehead. She had iced her lip for most of the evening, so it didn't look any worse than a Hollywood starlet with a bad collagen implant.

Doc called from the street—seems his knocks on her front door had gone unheard. She would have to get an entrance to the apartment and a bell for the front door. Grabbing her purse, she headed downstairs to meet him.

He looked different without his stethoscope and five o'clock shadow. Still cute, but freshly shaven and dressed in khakis, he looked a bit like the saboteur she'd left behind in Indianapolis.

"Hey," he said as she stepped out the front door. "These are for you." Three pink roses.

"Thank you," she said politely. "I'll just put these in water." Not offering to let him in, she hurried to her office and tossed the flowers on her desk. Evan had brought her roses on their first date. Was this some sort of omen?

"Mind if I leave my car here? The Recline is right down the street, I figured we could walk."

"Of course, perfect night for it." And it was. The stars were bright and the fall air was still warm enough to be sweater-only weather. "So, how did you escape the ER?" she asked.

"The doctor on call was able to make it in. She'd called me earlier; her son was feeling sick and she wasn't sure if she wanted to leave him with a sitter. I told her I'd cover if she needed me.

Seems she didn't need me."

"That was thoughtful of you."

He shrugged. "It's easy for me. No kids, no wife...hell, I don't even have parents to occupy me."

Stealing a glance at him, she noticed that he looked as content as he had at the clinic. There didn't seem to be any self-pity in his statement, just a guy telling the facts. "So, if it's not too personal, why no parents?"

He flashed her a smile. "Not too personal at all." They stopped to check for traffic as they crossed to the next street. A lone car was traveling down the road. After it passed, they crossed. "I grew up in foster care. I vaguely remember my mother, know nothing about my dad. Honestly, I don't think my mother ever knew who he was. But anyhow, by the time I was eight, I was in foster care." She was about to tell him how sorry she was for him, but before she could, he asked her, "How about you? Big family?"

She laughed. "No. Not at all. I'm an only child. My parents never married. I met my dad once, when I was thirteen. I think he's working in Israel; I'm honestly not sure. My mom lives in London. She's with the State Department. She joined the diplomatic corps when I was four."

"I take it you've traveled a lot?"

"Oh no. My grandparents raised me. My mom's parents. They insisted I was better off with a stable home than moving all over the world with my mother."

"And that was okay with her?" Doc asked.

"Of course. Mother loves her career. I was a speed bump."

"Seems we have that in common." Doc grinned at her.

Sarah could see the sign for The Recline up ahead. It was a sport's bar, the only bar she'd seen during their stroll across downtown. Suddenly, she hoped beyond all hopes that this wasn't Rich's place. The blinking neon sign and the huge front glass window painted with a frog with an umbrella drink chilling in a recliner matched. There was a time when she was nuts about frogs. After her mother vetoed the puppy, she'd tried talking her grandpa into getting one. He countered with a fish, and she came home from the pet store with a frog. Rich was her and Tonya's escort to the pet store. They were only eleven, and weren't allowed to ride their bikes across Main Street yet. Rich had been violating the rule for years, and traversed Main Street with ease. Looking back, that day may have been the day Rich became her childhood crush. He was a wise old thirteen-years, almost a man to a child of eleven who still had to be in bed by 9:00 p.m. He led them across town, weaving them through traffic. When Sarah started looking at the fish, it was Rich who suggested the frog — it had more personality. Sarah agreed, though honestly, had he suggested she get a box of mill worms as a pet, she might have been just as eager to buy them.

"We're here," Doc announced, pulling the door open and ushering her inside with a light hand on her back.

Instantly surrounded by the sounds of conversation and clashing pool balls, she could tell this was a popular place. The hostess, a very cute, very young-looking blonde, greeted them. "Hi, Doc! Welcome to The Recline. You here for a bite to eat, or just here to play some games and have a drink?"

"Mandy? I didn't know you worked here," Doc said.

The hostess nodded. "A girl's got to take care of herself."

"I suppose," Doc said with a smirk. "If all else fails, right?"

Mandy didn't seem offended. She laughed and gave Doc a big smile, but Sarah couldn't help but wonder why Doc would say something so rude. Did he have that general opinion of women, or just the blue-collar variety?

Doc cleared his throat and glanced nervously at Sarah before answering Mandy. "A bite to eat." He placed a hand at the small of Sarah's back. Sarah squirmed away, pretending to look at a framed poster on the wall. She wasn't avoiding touching Doc, but there was no point in allowing this date to get any more intimate if Doc had latent, sexist issues with women. Though she did give him points for not checking out the hostess's most impressive set of breasts. Even Sarah couldn't help but notice and envy them. Just a little.

They followed Mandy to a booth in a dimly lit corner of the room. As they sat, Doc requested a beer; Sarah ordered a glass of wine—red or white…didn't matter. She wasn't picky. Once Mandy left, Doc offered Sarah a sheepish smile and explained, "I don't care much for Mandy. Or her type. It's a long story, but let's just say that Mandy has caused a friend of mine considerable grief. The woman is always looking for someone to pay her way, and she usually manages. I suppose Rich is next in the cross hairs."

Sarah tried to look nonchalant, like she didn't care one way or another if Rich and the busty waitress were an item. Didn't his ad rule out shallow bimbos? But, no matter—Rich was not her business. She turned her attention to the menu. Nothing but grill items—hot dogs, hamburgers, fried jalapeño bites. Sarah looked front and back for a salad. Closest thing to one was the loaded nachos with onion and tomato.

"Hey, Doc. Sarah."

Washed with instant, unreasonable guilt, Sarah looked up from her menu to face Rich. Dressed in loose jeans and a green Recline tee, he looked relaxed, like he owned the place.

"Glad to see someone talked you into getting some food… though you should have taken me up on my offer to go to Nick's. His food is way better than mine."

Sarah felt the red creep up her neck. Before she could say a word, Doc was answering, "It's not the food, Rich—it's the superior company."

Rich laughed and nodded. "Hard for a guy like me to compete

with a guy of your stature, that's for sure."

Sarah couldn't help but notice Doc's grip on his menu tightened.

"Sarah, would you mind if I dragged you away for just a minute?" Turning to Doc, he said, "Business, I swear. Sarah is my attorney."

Doc didn't look at all pleased, but nodded politely.

Sarah followed Rich back to his office. She expected a disaster area, but the place was surprisingly neat and very professional... all but the alcohol memes scrolling across his computer as a screen saver. He offered her a chair as he went to his desk and sat.

"I think you insulted Doc," she said.

"Yeah, I know. He can't stand short jokes," Rich said, with a wink and a grin.

"I didn't realize he was that shallow."

Rich laughed. "Now who's making short jokes?"

Sarah felt flustered. Shaking her head, she said, "I didn't mean that, I meant —"

Rich was suddenly serious. "I know what you meant." He leaned back in his seat and stretched his long body out. "Look, Doc is a good guy. You're smart to go out with him. If I was a chick, I'd pick him. Especially over...well, the stock in Dodd is thin."

"It's just a date," Sarah said.

Rich held his hand up to shush her. "I swear, I didn't lure you back here to ruin your date. I seriously need some advice."

"Okay."

"Jess caught up with us at dinner. She said if I allowed her to have visitation with the girls, she wouldn't challenge my custody. Says she wants to start with visits with Kari, and then later do visits with Stacey...to ease her in."

"Do you trust her?"

Rich took a deep breath and made a grimace. "Not at all. I

mean, her dropping in on us at the diner was the first time I've talked to her in four years. I don't know anything about her, or her new husband. The offer sounds like the answer to my prayers and is very tempting. But then I think anything that seems too good to be true usually is. That's why I wanted to talk to you. What should I do? Go ahead and fight her, or take her deal?"

Sarah thought for a minute. "I've barely done the research, but my guess would be that if we go to court, and you refused a common-sense solution, it could be held against you. Perhaps that's her angle. Maybe she's hoping you come across as difficult to deal with, possibly accuse you of trying to alienate her from her children."

"So, I should take her up on her offer?"

Sarah nodded slowly. "I would come up with a legal agreement. I wouldn't just do it with a hand shake. This could even be the paper trail you need to prove custody later if she decides to challenge you."

"Could you do that? Make it legal, that is?"

"I'm sure I could figure it out."

Rich was up and in her comfort zone in a stride. Taking her in his arms, he squeezed her so tightly she could barely breathe. She closed her eyes and took a deep breath. He smelled delicious. Seriously, bubble gum sweet.

"Thank you, Sarah. I have been sweating this all evening. You don't know what it means to me to have your input. I feel like a huge weight's been lifted."

"Glad to help. I'll call you when I get the paperwork written up." Sarah pulled herself away. Looking up at him, she had to admit, he really was a handsome man, in a carefree, I-don't-mind-holes-in-my jeans sort of way.

He opened the door to the office and the bar sounds surrounded her. "Now, let me get you back to your date."

Chapter 9

On his way home from the bar, Rich debated going to Tonya's and picking up Stacey. They could watch *Frozen* for the millionth time. Normally, Rich swore he'd end up letting go if he had to watch that movie one more time, but even that was preferable to going home to an empty house.

The dash clock blinked 1:08 a.m., and logic told him there was no way he was waking his little girl up. He could promote Mandy to night manager and hire another waitress, but that would flip Tonya out. She was still mad that he'd hired the woman at all. Seems Mandy screwing Tonya's best friend's husband was supposed to be countered with ostracism, but Tonya failed to send Rich the memo. When the girl showed up asking for a job, any job, he hired her. And he still hadn't heard the end of it from his cousin.

Pulling into the driveway, he noticed the living room light was on. He hoped one of the girls wasn't sick. The TV was on, so he followed the sound. There was Kari, curled up on the sofa with a bowl of popcorn.

"What are you doing home? I thought you were spending the night with Leanna."

"Meh. I got into a fight with Heath and didn't feel like going to Leanna's. She'd spend her whole night telling me how she has the perfect boyfriend. How he buys her flowers…blah, blah, blah. I'm in a pretty evil mood, so I might've throat punched her."

Rich chuckled as he sat down beside her, stealing her bowl of popcorn. "Screw Heath. Asshole doesn't deserve you."

Kari laughed. "I didn't tell you what happened."

Rich shrugged. "Call it father's intuition."

"Well, it was his fault. You know David Hilbrandt?"

"Chess club king?"

"Yeah, him. Heath and I were at the movie and David comes up and says hi to me, and Heath shoves him. I was like, *what the hell*? And Heath said, 'I don't want him talking to my girlfriend.' And I was like, 'I'm not your girlfriend.' And he was like, 'Then get the fu…fudge out.' And I was like, 'Screw you a…butthole—' and got a ride home with David."

"How old is Heath?"

"Sixteen."

"Damn. If I beat the hell out of him, do you think I'd get jail time?"

"Most certainly. Best let me deal with him."

Rich stuffed a handful of popcorn in his mouth. "Why don't you just date David?" Rich asked, talking as he chewed.

"Uh…. Duh, David is a dork."

"I like dorks."

"Of course, you do, you're a dad."

"Seriously. You should give him a chance. He's a nice kid. Honest, dependable, trustworthy."

"All perfect dad-chosen-boyfriend traits."

"What the hell are you looking for?"

"I don't know. Someone who makes my heart race."

"Oh Jesus. My heart just stopped," Rich said. "I think I need a beer." Rich handed her the bowl of popcorn and headed to the kitchen.

"And is a good kisser," Kari yelled over her shoulder with a giggle.

"You're grounded until you're twenty and your brain is rational," Rich yelled back.

Opening the fridge, he took out a beer and grabbed his daughter a soda. There was a pile of dishes in the sink from dinner. That was Kari's job, but after the night she'd had, Rich was willing to let it slide. Besides, no one ever died of day-old dishes.

Kari was still giggling when he came back to the living room. Jumping the back of the wrap-around couch rather than walking around it, Rich made himself comfortable.

"Did you have any luck with the lawyer lady?" Kari asked, taking the soda from him and popping it open.

His brow shot up. "I thought you weren't a fan of the idea."

"If you like her, I suppose I can try to help."

"I'm not promising to return that favor. I may not like any guy but dorky David…ever." Rich grinned, then asked, "How did you know I saw her tonight?"

"I had David drop me off at Leanna's. At the time, I was thinking I'd still spend the night, but then changed my mind and walked home. I passed Sarah and Doc walking down the street near The Recline. I assumed that was where they were headed."

"And they were." Rich took a long swallow of beer. "Which sucked more than I imagined. Maybe this is what a mid-life crisis feels like—irrational jealousy."

"So, you only plan to live to be seventy?" Rich shrugged. Kari rolled her eyes. "And why is the feeling irrational? You like her, don't you?"

"I feel like I do, but I can't. I barely know her anymore."

"Aunt Tonya said you guys were good friends…went to prom together."

Rich took another drink. "Aunt Tonya talks a lot. What else did she say?"

"She said Sarah always had a crush on you when they were kids, but that she could never get Sarah to admit it."

"We were good friends, but then she went to college and I never saw her again until yesterday."

"I suppose you should ask her out."

Rich rested his head on a blanket he rolled into a pillow. "She seems content with Doc."

"Nah. She doesn't really like him. She flinches when he touches her."

"How so?"

"Like, walking down the street, you know how a guy will put his hand on your back, or your arm?"

"No. Guys should keep their damn hands to themselves."

"Oh quit." Kari poked him. "When you're out with a girl, if she likes you, she won't really notice the touch, or she'll relax into it. If she doesn't like the guy, she's overly conscious someone is touching her, and she will flinch. And I watched. Sarah flinched."

Rich thought of how fidgety she was when he talked to her. She was constantly moving away from him. Maybe she just didn't like to be touched? "She always acts like I'm invading her personal space, too."

"But she openly loathes you." Kari said the words like they were good news.

Rich's laugh was quick and loud. "So, you think I should ask her out? The guy she openly loathes?"

"But you have to ask yourself why she hates you. If you meant nothing to her then, you'd mean nothing now. But she's out for your blood."

"It's sounding more and more hopeful by the minute."

"Remember, Dad, the opposite of love isn't hate…it's indifference. There is a fine line between love and hate."

"Interesting theory." Rich tucked his hands behind his head and stared at the ceiling as he wondered whether or not Sarah could be holding a grudge, much less be harboring feelings for him. Or was he grasping at straws? Either way, he had to admit, his daughter was one smart cookie.

He nudged her with his foot. "So, Miss Kari Renee, how did you get to be so damned smart?"

"I have a dad who needs me to raise him."

Rich laughed. Thank God for his girls. Where would he be without them?

~*~

The next day, Rich decided he'd meet with Sarah and lay out some of the plans he thought would make her home and office space more livable. He bribed Kari with relief from dinner dishes for a week if she'd go with him for moral support, and to judge just how deeply Sarah's hatred of him went. He got her number from Tonya, so he didn't have to yell at her from the street, and arranged a meeting time.

She was waiting for him when he arrived. Dressed in jeans and a worn-out hoodie, he thought she looked more gorgeous than ever. Her hair was pulled back in a ponytail that hung to her shoulders. Opening her door before he and Kari were even out of the truck, she waved at them from the stoop. Rich grabbed his yellow legal pad and pencil.

"You know," Sarah said, "you don't owe me. I haven't done anything."

"Of course you have. Hell, you know how rumors fly in this town. I wouldn't be surprised if Jess heard you were on the case, and that's what made her so reasonable."

"I doubt that," she said. "But I do need some help, so I will take it. The first thing I'd like to have is a way to get in and out of my apartment without having to come through the office."

"I thought you might think that, so I drew a few sketches." Rich flipped through his yellow pad to the pictures. He noticed Sarah's shoulder brushed against his as she leaned in to see what he'd done. Her clean, flowery smell forced him to pause and gather his thoughts before explaining, "This one is just a basic set of steps leading to a door at the back of the building." He turned the page. "Now, on this one, there is a little porch. Maybe do some built-in seating? It wouldn't be a big space, but it would give you outdoor space."

"I don't go outside much. I think simple steps would be fine."

"Okay. How about window boxes? Plant some flowers in them, give the building a more feminine touch? Maybe do a few eight-foot windows with Juliet balconies?" He showed her the pictures of the flower boxes overflowing with pink blooms and trailing ivy. Wrought iron gratings would cover the double-opening windows.

Sarah aahed over the design, leaning even closer. "Did you draw these?"

"Yeah. It helps people visualize the changes."

She took the notepad from him and smiled. "I never realized you were so talented."

Rich couldn't stifle a burst of ornery pleasure. "Oh, I've got all kinds of skills."

Sarah's brow lifted, and she shook her head as she handed the notebook back to him. "If that's not too much work, I would like that."

"Now, for your office space...I was thinking you need a reception area here at the door. Leave your office where it is, but put in a fancier door. It should be impressive. Maybe we could even find a salvage door with some old-style grandeur."

"I'd like that," Sarah said with a nod.

"In this area of the work space, we can keep the kitchenette, but add a small eating area. I assume one day you might have employees who need a lunch room."

"One can only hope," Sarah agreed.

"And in the back, I'm thinking a boardroom style area for

meetings. And there is enough room for either storage or a few small offices."

"You've thought of everything. What would it cost?"

"I told you I'd do it."

"You can't think I would hold you to that? I didn't do anything."

Rich shrugged. "It's Jess I'm dealing with—I doubt very seriously it's over."

Sarah nodded, and placing a hand on his arm, she gave it a squeeze. "Well, send me all the bills for the supplies. And I'll give you a key, in case I'm not home and you need to get in. I'll just run upstairs and get it. I'll be right back."

Once Sarah was gone, Rich turned to Kari. "Well? Does she hate me?"

"She seems very comfortable with you, until you say stupid things."

"What did I say that was stupid?"

"You have lots of skills? What the hell, Dad? You'd expect me to throat punch a guy for that."

"Shit. You're right. And you should. I'm going to have to class myself up. The problem is, I've never been the classy guy. I am the guy we don't want you to go out with."

Chapter 10

First thing Monday morning, Sarah filed the legal papers necessary to request an official custody arrangement between Rich and Jess. Confident that this would be a simple issue, Sarah wasn't at all prepared for the backlash. When she returned to her office, Jess was there, sitting on the stoop. Jess stood as Sarah approached.

Jess was prettier than Sarah remembered. As a youth, Jess had a horrible over bite and dishwater blonde hair that always looked greasy and stringy. Now she was a knock out. Her platinum blonde hair was cut so short it looked thick and full of volume, and her make-up looked professionally applied.

Tonya had never liked Jess—had always complained when Sarah invited the girl to hang out with them. Sarah wasn't sure, in hindsight, if she'd actually liked Jess or simply felt sorry for her. Jess's dad was the town drunk, and not the happy sort of friendly drunk, but the scary, most likely to one day snap and kill someone kind. When he was loaded, he'd yell at people on the street—*what are you looking at?* Rumor was that Ben Mudd would take that anger he spewed at strangers on the street and unleash it physically on his son, Jess's older brother. The boy went out hunting one weekend and died in a gun accident. He *accidentally* put the barrel in his mouth and fired. Sarah's grandpa always wondered why the boy hadn't used the gun on Ben instead, and saved the whole family a lot of grief. How could Sarah refuse to be friends with a girl like that? The only thing that seemed to keep Jess from becoming a teen statistic was her dreams of a fantastic future—one where Jess was so rich she could tell everyone in Dodd to go to hell.

Jess had started her climb to stardom by taking Rich. Sarah always wondered if Jess put Rich on her radar after Sarah confided in her that she loved him, or if it was just coincidence. Either way, it ruined their friendship. As Tonya would have said, Sarah called dibs on him, and Jess should have respected that.

"Jess," Sarah said. "What brings you here?"

"We need to have a little chat."

"Okay." Sarah unlocked the door and led her to her office. The place was still stacked in boxes, but all the furniture was assembled. Sarah sat; Jess remained standing.

"I want you to back off with Rich. Him and I can work this out without your meddling."

"I told him to take your offer. How is that meddling?"

"It doesn't need to go through the courts."

Sarah shook her head. "Rich needs to protect himself. He's cared for those kids for too long on a handshake."

Jess grabbed a chair, pulled it up next to Sarah's, and sat. "These are my kids, Sarah. I don't want you involved."

"Well, I'm sorry, but Rich does."

Jess poked Sarah in the shoulder. "Try to play house with my family and I swear, you will regret it."

"Are you threatening me?"

"Damn, you are smart."

"Okay, I'll bite. What do you think you can do to me?"

Sarah immediately thought of her affair with Evan Stollings. It was humiliating, but not horrid enough to make her quit helping Rich. And she lived with the knowledge that their liaison could be revealed any day, maybe even on the news. That was a reality she had already came to terms with, and decided if the story leaked, it leaked.

"Rich doesn't know what you did."

Sarah smiled at Jess. "I'm afraid you'll have to be more specific."

"He doesn't know you were pregnant."

Sarah's mouth went dry. She tried to remain calm. Taking a deep breath, she said, "You said —"

Jess laughed. "You're seriously stupid for a girl everyone says is so smart. I lied, you dumbass."

Sarah's mind froze. It couldn't process what Jess was alluding to. Snippets, fragments of memory sped through her head. Asking Jess to help her get a message to Rich. Giving her the phone number in London where he could reach her. Jess telling her Rich said he couldn't be bothered with this right now. He was only nineteen; his parents were going to kill him.

"He had you mail that money…to take care of things."

"Yeah. Not Rich. I sent the money. You see, I was in a very similar situation to yours — with Kari — and her dad did say he was only nineteen and his parents would kill him and he gave me more than enough to take care of things. Unlike you, I couldn't do it, so I sent the money to you, just hoping you'd do the right thing."

Sarah's chest hurt. She couldn't pull in a full breath.

"Poor Rich. He missed you so much. Dumbass thought you guys had something…what did he call it? Something real… something special. Pretty soon, he was convinced you had just used him to pop your cherry and went off to conquer the world. And your dear mother was a very willing accomplice. She trusted me, you know, especially after I was a concerned enough friend to tell her you were trying to hide your pregnancy from her."

"Why? I was your friend."

"You had something I wanted. The Coopers are an awesome family. My family, as you know, sucks. I thought maybe I could be happy with Rich, give my baby a decent family. I'd tried to find a rich man at college, but that was a total fail. Funny thing about people with money...greedy bastards assume everyone is coming after it. I couldn't get past the grand matriarch of any clan with two pennies to rub together. I swear to God, they clone those nasty bitches and put one in every family—sensible shoes, brown pantsuit, and of course, the obligatory rope of pearls."

Sarah could hear her words, but she wasn't comprehending them. It was as if her soul had lifted out of her body, leaving only a shell sitting there stiff-backed and white-faced.

"Now...." Jess scooted closer and snapped her fingers in Sarah's face. "Listen up, Sarah. You need to pay real close attention. Back off Rich. If you have some insane notion of a rekindled romance where you get to play momma to my kids, I will destroy you."

Sarah's body started to shake. She tried to control it, not wanting to give Jess the satisfaction of watching her break down. But she couldn't, and Jess's grin indicated that she knew she was winning.

Jess stood. "I'll leave you to absorb all this new info. And just to make it clear...if you think the answer is to call and cry to Rich, just imagine how he's going to react once he knows what you did."

"I was only seventeen. I was scared; I was—"

"You think that will matter to him? To any Cooper? They are all about family. You chose convenience over responsibility. They'll love that."

Sarah could understand how reasonable people were goaded into murder. She hated Jess at that moment. She'd been her friend. How could she have done this to her?

"I see the cat got your tongue...finally. Sarah Mae Andrews, struck speechless. That's a day to mark on the calendar."

"Why? Just so you could have Rich?"

Jess shrugged. "I've thought of that a lot myself. Did I ever love Rich? I'm landing on no. I realize now that I had very little interest in Rich. I think I wanted him to not want you, but as a keeper for myself? No. Not for the long haul. Your mother was right; the guy has no ambition. He isn't ever going to leave this town. He is content to have a few kids and live paycheck to paycheck." Jess looked around the office, as if evaluating the value of the place. "I didn't truly set my sights on Rich until I had Kari, and her loser father turned out to be flat broke. I could have sworn the guy had money. Boy, was I wrong. So, I had a kid and no money. I was stuck. No way in hell I was going to live with my parents, and I wasn't doing the public housing thing, so I moved in with Rich."

"So, when you told me all those lies, it was just to hurt me?"

Jess shrugged. "Because I hate you. You were given everything, yet you acted like you were abused. Oh, poor Sarah. Her mommy is rich and makes her live with grandpa, who gives her anything she wants. I'll bet you've never had your ass beat with a hairbrush or whipped with a willow switch until you couldn't sit."

Fifteen years ago, Sarah might have felt sorry for Jess, but right now, she could only imagine choking her to death. Sarah stiffened her spine and drew on every ounce of strength she could muster to look Jess in the eye and say, "Poor, poor pitiful Jess. You think just because your life and your family sucks that you have the right to ruin other people's lives? Well, you can just take your threats and go straight to hell. I'll do everything I can to make sure Rich never loses his kids."

"That's your choice. You think you'll ever have a relationship with Rich once I tell him what you did? Where is his baby, Sarah? You ready to answer that question?"

"Like I give a damn. If you haven't noticed, Rich and I are hardly a match anymore. Go ahead and tell him. We're barely even friends, much less a couple. And then when you do, I'll be sure to inform the court that you tried to blackmail me."

"Who would believe you?"

Sarah set her phone on the desk. "I hit record as soon as you sat down. You want me to send you the recording of our conversation to share with Rich, or do you want me to?"

"I know you love him. You don't want him to know. You're bluffing."

"You don't know me. You're making decisions based on the girl you knew sixteen years ago. I have zero interest in Rich Cooper. I *was* helping him because he was Tonya's cousin. Now, I think I'll help him just to make your life miserable."

"Don't push me, Sarah. You have no idea what I'm capable of."

"You're right there, Jess. Here I always thought you were a decent person. My mother was right, I am *not* a good judge of character."

Sarah showed Jess to the door, locking it securely behind her. Sarah covered her face with her hands, forcing herself not to cry until she heard Jess's car pull away. Then she slid to the floor and cried. Her whole life ruined by a few lies. The memories that had haunted her for so long—caused by spite.

Rich. He never knew. Never turned his back on her. He'd have loved their child if he'd had the chance. She had the urge to call him and tell him everything. Make a full confession. She clicked on his contact on her phone and stared at his number. How would she start the conversation? How would she justify what she did to a man who put nothing ahead of his kids?

~*~

Sarah lost track of days as she unpacked, sorted, and got her abode into a livable space. Jess never made good on her threat to

68

tell Rich about the pregnancy. That should have brought relief to Sarah, but it didn't. She had a gut feeling that Jess wasn't at all intimidated by Sarah's counter-threat, but was holding her information for a time when it would do Sarah the most damage. Logic told Sarah to simply tell Rich the truth, but she knew that would never happen. She couldn't think about the past, much less talk about it. It was safe to assume he'd hate her if he knew.

And her not being able to hate him became a gigantic elephant that sauntered into the room every time she was with Rich. She could not relax around him. Without her angry wall to protect her, she was wide open to a flood of emotion. And guilt. What she wouldn't give to have just one chance to change the choice she'd made.

But a do-over was irrational, and Sarah was extremely rational by nature. Becoming romantically entangled with Rich would be a mistake. It was better to be friends. People didn't break up with friends. The standards for behavior were lower and the solidarity was stronger in friendships. And if Jess believed there was nothing romantic between them, her biggest motivation to tell on her was eliminated. If they were in a relationship that went awry, she'd be cut from his life. Cut from his kids' lives. She couldn't risk that. In the short time she'd known the girls, she'd grown to love them.

To keep it all clean and separate, she focused on Doc. At some point, she was certain she could make herself, maybe not love him, but be comfortable enough to build a solid relationship with him. Doc was a good guy. He even found time in his busy schedule to help her lug boxes and move furniture. Each time he brought her dinner and flowers. Each night ended with an awkward kiss. But it was becoming comfortable.

Unlike the time she spent with Rich. Rich made her heart pound and her palms sweat. Knowing he was a good guy only made the suffering worse. When the custody agreement between

69

him and Jess was signed and sealed by the judge, Sarah held her breath a moment to see if she was about to be outed. Instead, Jess signed with a smile and suggested that Rich and Sarah made a cute couple.

As a friend, Rich showed up every day, as promised, and worked. She was also blessed with after-school visits by Stacey. The child was all levels of wonderful — sweet, funny, thoughtful. The little girl helped her decorate, and thanks to her expertise, Sarah now had a Hello Kitty nightstand clock and sunny yellow bedroom walls.

Kari came the first few days, but as her mother began exercising her visitation rights, Kari's time was absorbed. And according to Stacey, there was a new boy in Kari's life. She shared this information with Sarah on the very strictest confidence. A pinky-swear had to be shared to get the dirt. Sarah thought it was sweet that Stacey was so awestruck by her sister having a *boyfriend*. Sarah missed the days when talk of holding hands and stolen kisses on the playground were a big deal.

What she wouldn't give to feel innocent again.

Today, she expected the little girl to make good on her promise to help her set up the newly renovated kitchen. Rich had to take a break in the work he was doing down in the office area while he waited for the drywall crew. He got all the walls up, but they were like skeletons with the wiring exposed like veins and arteries. The new windows were also on hold, since they needed to be specially ordered. The door was done, and she had a bell that chimed in her office and her residence when someone either rang or entered the front door.

Sarah assumed Rich would take a break during the down time, but he did a kitchen overhaul, instead. It even had a mini-dishwasher. Amazed with the speed at which Rich finished jobs, Sarah had to give him credit for being one hell of a hard worker.

Grabbing a box that said *kitchen*, she hauled it in and set it on the floor. A knock on the new door grabbed her attention. She yelled, "Come in."

The door swung open and Stacey's little voice yelled back, "You'll never guess who's here to help you!"

Sarah couldn't help but chuckle. "Oh, I don't know…could it be the tooth fairy?"

"The tooth fairy? That's a silly guess. I'll give you a hint; she has a bag filled with presents."

"Santa Claus?" Sarah guessed.

"I said I was a girl."

"Oh. I know who it is. Geesh, I'm so silly. Come on in, Mrs. Claus."

Stacey appeared in the doorway, a plastic shopping bag hanging from her hand. Oddly, the child and Mrs. Claus seemed to be sharing the same closet. Sarah was no longer surprised by the fantastic fashion combos, though today's green skirt, purple pin-striped socks, and black puppy sweatshirt was a step above average.

"My, don't you look fancy." Sarah whistled. The child did a spin to show off how well the skirt flared.

"My dad bought this for me. It's a fancy skirt. I'm like a princess or a ballerina."

"Yes, you are." Sarah smiled. Rich followed in behind her and cleared his throat. Sarah looked up at him. He really was the best dad. Thoughtful and sweet. The pain of regret cut through her chest and almost took her breath away. "I, uh, was just thinking…." She coughed and cleared her throat. "What a nice job you did on the kitchen. It's such an amazing change. I think the granite counters are my favorite."

"I like the purple walls, though I think they should be brighter," Stacey said.

Sarah looked over the deep plum walls, trying to imagine them the shade of purple that Stacey would have chosen. "But we needed to match the granite."

"I'd have gotten the orange one—remember the orange?"

Sarah took a breath. The child would grow to be a great artist or a tacky eye sore. Or possibly both. "I have to be honest with you, Stacey. I don't have your vision. I'm stuck in my boring brain and like my boring colors."

Stacey nodded and patted her arm. "It's all right. My daddy says all the time that you're stuck in your ways, so I understand."

Rich turned several shades of red and rubbed the back of his neck.

Sarah shook her head at him, but said nothing. Instead, she turned her attention back to the child. "So, what's in the bag?"

"Oh, just you wait!" Stacey dropped to the floor, legs crossed, bag in her lap. Pulling out a white bear with a big pink bow, she held it up to Sarah. "Here, I got you this. I noticed you didn't have any toys."

Sarah took the fluffy white bear and instinctively hugged it. Her eyes burned, but she blinked back the tears. "Why, I think this is the sweetest gift ever."

"What will you name him?" Stacey asked.

"I don't know. Why don't you name her for me?"

"Okay. RC. That's a good name. That's for my daddy's name, and since he gave me the money, we'll name him after him."

Sarah looked over the white bear. "Wouldn't a girl name be better?"

"He's a boy, silly. Bears are boys."

"But he has a pink bow...."

"Boys can wear pink, duh." Stacey stood, shaking her head.

"And you call me sexist," Rich said, leaning against her doorway. Muscles flexed against his body weight—a stance that should be outlawed.

"So, well, thanks for my bear...is your dad just dropping you off?" Sarah asked. *Please say yes and get the original RC out of my atmosphere. I can't manage this today.*

"I need to add a coat of varnish to the floors in your office," Rich said.

"You really don't have to do that. You've done too much already."

"I told him I had to help you with your kitchen," Stacey chimed in.

"Seriously Rich, you've—"

Rich held a hand up to stop her. He eased himself off of the wall and started backing toward the door that led to her office below. "I'll finish what I started. You ladies have fun."

Stacey wasted no time. Grabbing Sarah's hand, she pulled her into the kitchen and attacked the box on the floor. It was amazing how her small hands moved so quickly and deftly. Sarah could only assume that was a trait she shared with her dad. The thought brought an instant flush and heat to her cheeks. Rich was downstairs working his magic, making the huge space into a proper office.

"Ta-da!" Stacey said as she finally made her way deeper into the box where the wrapped-up glassware was located. The little girl pulled one out and unwrapped it, handing the tall glass to Sarah and diving in for another. "You will have a for-real house in no time. I'm a good worker, huh?"

Sarah took the glass and wiped it free of dust and set it in the cupboard. "You're an amazing worker. I'd be lost without you."

"I know. Cause I'm big, huh?"

"Well, you're the most mature five-year-old I know."

Stacey pulled out another glass and unwrapped it. "That's what I told Kari, but she won't believe me."

"She won't?" Sarah shook her head. "Why not?"

"I don't know," the child said with a shrug as she sat cross-legged by the box and looked up at Sarah. "Her and Mom have big girl secrets that I'm not allowed to know about. Cause I'm a *baby.*"

Sarah felt a chill run up her spine. She sat on the floor by Stacey, "What kind of secrets?"

Stacey whispered, "I don't know. That's why they're secrets."

Sarah's gut screamed. Jess was capable of anything, but what could she be doing to Kari? She thought of the new boyfriend. "Have you ever gotten to meet Kari's new boyfriend?"

Stacey shook her head. "No, but I saw him."

"You did?"

"Yeah. He picks Kari up at school for Mom. He's old. I like David, but Kari thinks he's a dork. I think he's nice. David says hi to me. The new guy tells me to mind my own business. And he said I suck my thumb. I don't suck my thumb. He's telling lies."

Sarah almost cringed. "Of course, you don't suck your thumb. And he's also wrong about your sister not being your business. You have every right to get to know him."

"That's what I said."

"Why is he only picking up Kari? I thought you were going to start visiting your mom too?"

The little girl shook her head. "No, I went once and didn't like it. Phil is mean. I don't like him. Mom says I don't have to come visit if I don't want to. So, I don't."

"Who's Phil?"

"Mom's husband. First day I went there, he made me eat peas. I hate peas. And he yelled at me for petting a dog. You're supposed to pet dogs, right?"

Sarah nodded. "Is he nice to Kari?"

"At first he wasn't. Then Mom said, 'If you want to make this work, she has to be happy here.' I guess it doesn't matter if I'm happy there."

Sarah smoothed some wayward hairs behind the little girl's ear. "Well, I'm glad they aren't trying very hard. I'd be lonely without you. I'd still be up to my nose in boxes without you."

Stacey grinned. "Yes, you would. I don't really care so much anyhow. As long as I don't have to go there." The look on the little girl's face said she cared quite a bit. Sarah added hurt look on the little girl's face to her growing reasons to despise Jess. Sarah turned to Stacey with her hands on her hips and asked, "How 'bout we take a break and go for ice cream? I'm suddenly not in the mood to work."

"Sure." The little girl clumsily got to her feet. "Can we ask Dad?"

Sarah's heart did the stutter-flutter that annoyed the hell out of her. "Sure."

Off the child went, running through the apartment and down the steps. Sarah followed on her heels. Rich must have heard her coming and dropped the paint roller to be able to catch her as she barreled toward him. Her momentum almost knocked him off balance, but he didn't get mad. He swooped the girl up and held her.

"What the hell, princess? The place on fire?"

Stacey chuckled, head tossed back, eyes crinkled closed. "No, Daddy! Sarah and I are getting ice cream. You want to go?"

Rich shook his head. "Daddy has work to get done, so Miss Sarah can get this place open. But you go and have fun." With a kiss, he set her on the floor. "Where's your sweater?"

"I don't need it."

"Oh yes, you do. Scoot. Go get it."

She grabbed Sarah's hand, pulling her back toward the steps. Rich shook his head and said, "No princess, you let Sarah stay here. I want to tell her what kind of ice cream I want."

The little girl rolled her eyes as she stomped toward the steps. "Chocolate on a sugar cone. I coulda' told her that."

Once Stacey was out of range, Rich leaned close to Sarah. "I appreciate this more than you know. Jess is completely uninterested in her. She only has time for Kari. So far, Stacey doesn't seem to notice because she has you. I owe you for that."

Sarah nodded as her mind wrestled with what to say. Something was off with the whole thing, or was she making mountains out of mole hills? She looked over her shoulder to be sure they were still alone before she said, "We may need to talk, in private."

Rich nodded. "Stacey is going to a sleep over tonight, and Kari will be at Jess's. Would Doc give you the night off?"

Sarah bit her lip. Rich wasn't making it easy for her to think of him as a friend, especially when he acted like a jealous boyfriend. "I'm supposed to go to Tonya's tonight. It's lady's night."

"After that works for me."

"Pick me up around 11:00?"

"Good then. It's a date," Rich said.

Chapter 11

Sarah practically pulled Tonya through the door. Sarah was eager for her to see her home. And it was a home. The first Sarah had in years. She'd even donated the white leather furniture to the Salvation Army and replaced it with a couch and loveseat with elegant lines and soft, comfortable fabric.

"I'm almost ready. You can have a seat, or check out the kitchen…or the balconies. You can pretend you're Rapunzel — Stacey does." Sarah went to her bedroom to finish dressing.

Tonya talked to her through the open door. "The place is looking good. I keep telling John I want to hire Rich to knock out the wall between our kitchen and living room, but nooo. John says he'll do it himself…one day. Story of my freaking life."

Sarah emerged from the bedroom carrying a pair of slick leather boots. Tonya whistled from the kitchen, leaning across the counter and shaking her head. "Look at you. Bringing the sexy to lady's night!"

Sarah looked down at her curve hugging jeans, black sweater, and silver jewelry…then to Tonya's Colts sweatshirt and ponytail. Sarah blushed. "I should change."

"Why? You look hot. Doc coming over later?"

Sarah shook her head. "I sort of had the idea we'd be going out. Just give me a sec, I want to change."

Sarah could hear Tonya's giggle from the bedroom as she stripped off the jewelry and sweater and pulled on a T-shirt and a cardigan. Twisting her shimmering blonde hair into a sloppy bun on top of her head, she looked herself over in the bathroom mirror. Her make-up was still a little heavy for a night in, but she was excruciatingly mindful that she would be seeing Rich later.

I like Doc, she reminded herself. *He's stable and predictable.* The kind of guy she could maybe have a family with…if…well, she wasn't thinking about that. She quickly washed off the better part of the make-up. Keeping the boots, she slid them on then met Tonya in the living room.

"Ready?" Tonya asked.

Sarah grabbed her purse and followed. Climbing into Tonya's mini-van, there was a pink pig on the front seat. Sarah picked him up and sat him on her lap as she buckled up.

"You can throw him in the back. That's little John's oink-oink. John says he's getting too old for the damned thing, I suppose he is nine and getting a little old —"

"Oh, don't take him!" Sarah petted the stuffed pig like he was a real pet. "Remember my Sally Sue?"

"Oh my gosh! The Raggedy Anne looking doll? I remember you carried that thing everywhere."

Sarah nodded. "I know. I loved her."

"You still have her?"

Sarah shook her head. "No, Mom threw her in the trash. She also said I was too old, and I was embarrassing myself. I used to have nightmares about her ending up in a landfill with worms and crows."

Tonya nodded slowly, but said nothing. Sarah knew Tonya was probably thinking what a horrible mother Claire Andrews was, but being such a good friend, she knew she'd never say it. Instead, Tonya asked, "How is your mom?"

"Living in London."

"Impressive. Have you gone over?"

"Not recently. Weekly phone chats are enough. I can't imagine spending any amount of extended time with her. Do you realize my mother just divorced husband number four? Yet, I'm the loser."

"Four husbands, huh? Lordy, I married John when I was twenty. First guy I'd ever been with. I often wonder…is he really as good in bed as he says he is? I mean, how would I know? He could be doing it all wrong."

Sarah laughed. "There's not too many ways to do it. I think you were lucky to find the right one on the first go-around."

"Now, I'm not saying I'm thinking of shopping around. I'm just saying these women with like four husbands, I wonder if they think, hubs number one was better at oral, but failed in the deep stroke."

"Tonya!" Sarah squealed, holding a cool hand to her now burning cheeks. "I can't believe you just said that."

"Holy shit. You're over thirty and still uptight, aren't you?"

"No."

"Say blowjob."

"No!" Sarah gripped the pig closer.

"You can't say it!"

"I can. I just choose not to."

"You're still a little frigid around the edges, aren't you?"

"Of course not!"

"Remember the time Brandon Seymour tried to feel your boob and you punched him?"

"I don't see where me refusing to be felt up like a common tramp makes me uptight."

"It was just boob. He just wanted to cop a feel. I mean, tell the guy no, don't punch him."

Fiddling with the pig's tail, Sarah thought of that dance all those years ago. Poor Brandon never saw her right hook coming at him. When it landed, it was instant blood and screams. He called her so many horrible names—ice queen was the one that stuck and followed her through school—but he had much juicier choices as he backed down the gym hall and out the doors. She had to call her grandpa, who congratulated her for her dexterity, for a ride home. She never got asked on another date. Tonya had to beg Rich to come home from college and take her loser friend to their senior prom.

Sarah said quietly, "Maybe I over-reacted a little."

Tonya got a good laugh at Sarah's confession before admitting, "You know I'm just messing with you, right?"

"Go ahead, laugh at my misery."

"You don't need to be miserable."

"I'm not—

"You are! I'm your best friend. Dear lord, I can feel your unhappiness. It's like your life is at a crossroad. The choices you make now will—"

Sarah's fragile laugh interrupted Tonya's lecture. She knew she had to switch the conversation before her friend got on a roll. "Oh quit. You're being such a clairvoyant drama queen. I'm adjusting to a new situation. It's hardly a crisis."

Tonya sighed. Her pursed lips and knitted brows made Sarah want to leap from the moving vehicle before her friend started her a pity party. Fortunately, geography was on Sarah's side.

Tonya pointed to a hidden drive. "Here's the turn. My road is difficult to see with the trees and shrubs and all. I keep telling John we need to clear them out and put up a sign or something, but he doesn't see the problem."

Turning off the black top, they traveled about a half-mile down a smooth dirt road. After a few seconds on the road, Sarah recognized the place. Tonya's family once had a cabin on this land. There was a pond with a rope swing where they used to swim in the summer time.

"I knew how to get here. All you had to do was tell me you were living in the old cabin."

"Oh, my God, Rich brought you here? There WAS more between you guys — and neither of you ever told me. I'm so hurt."

"It wasn't like that. And I've been here with you a thousand times."

"Huh uh. We always used the entrance on Milo Road. To get to the cabin this way ten years ago, you had to have a four-wheel drive. Only Rich came this way. He'd sneak in the back way so Aunt Debbie and Uncle Ron couldn't tell his mom and dad he was here. Ooohhh, I can't believe you never told me. I'd have been so happy. You know, I seriously thought after seeing you two at prom that you guys would become a thing — like a more than friends sort of thing. I wanted you two to be together. Oh, my God, why didn't you tell me you guys were a thing?"

"We weren't a *thing*. Yes, maybe he brought me out here once or twice, but it was never — I quickly realized I was — We were headed down different paths, and it was better to just be friends."

"Friends, huh? Is that why you get all red and flustered around him?"

"Truthfully? I think I'm inept and ridiculous around all men."

"I think you two would be perfect together."

Sarah gave her a head shake and a frown.

"I was so disappointed when he started dating Jess. Until then, I harbored hope you'd be back to live happily ever after," Tonya admitted.

Sarah nodded, but said nothing. She'd been quite disappointed when Jess told her they were dating too. So disappointed that she'd stopped talking to Jess completely. The last thing she wanted to hear were updates on the happy couple, when even thinking of Rich was enough to make her feel like she was bleeding out.

81

"Home sweet home," Tonya said as they pulled into her driveway.

The cabin of debauchery had been replaced by a brick ranch. The porch was littered with bikes and plastic cars. Dump trucks were parked in what should have been flower beds next to the house. Jess was right. The Coopers were all about family.

Sitting on the steps, waiting on them, was Angie Grant. She stood and waved as they approached. As Sarah got out, Angie gave a high-pitched squeal and a bone-bruising hug. "Look at you! Still so pretty and…oh mah goodness…so skinny! You can tell you don't have kids!"

"Nope, no kids," Sarah agreed.

Angie wasn't exactly chubby, but she was a bit rounder than her former cheerleader self. She was still pretty, but looked seriously tired, with dark circles under her eyes and sallow skin. Sarah wanted to ask her if she was feeling all right, but she didn't. She just hugged her old friend tighter. Seemed only Tonya had found the for-real happily ever after. Or maybe Sarah was just imagining things.

Tonya ushered them inside. The house was comfortable and clean, decorated in country crafts and photos of Tonya's three kids.

"Have a seat, ladies. I made up some snacks and frozen daiquiris. I invited Mary Shepherd and Michelle Harvey, but I'm not sure if they'll come."

"Do I know them?" Sarah asked, totally feeling like an ass that she didn't even remember, with any degree of confidence, the names of the people she'd graduated with.

"Not likely. Mary moved here a few years ago, and Michelle was three years below us in school. But they both work with Angie at the hospital. You'll like them."

"Michelle Harvey? Isn't that Jess's cousin?" Sarah asked.

"Yeah, but trust me—they don't get along. Michelle is cool.

You can trust her."

"I thought I could trust Jess," Sarah mumbled.

"You never were a good judge of character," Tonya laughed.

"Tell me about it," Sarah added with an eye roll.

"Speaking of the she-devil, Ang and I ran into her at the mall." Tonya turned to Angie. "Tell Sarah about running into Jess—that evil bitch—at the mall while I get the food."

Angie rolled her eyes and let out a most exhausted sigh. "She has these new, huge knockers."

Sarah knew something had been different about her other than her hair. She was about to admit that, but then closed her mouth. They'd want to know all about it. Better to say nothing than try to lie to this group.

Tonya poked her head around the kitchen doorway. "Seriously freakish ta-tas. But I didn't mean for you to tell her about the boobs—tell her what she said."

"I was getting to that," Angie said. "Anyhow, she has these huge boobs, and her face is so full of plastic, it barely moves. And her new husband? He's a freaking child. I swear, I think he was just potty-trained."

"Tell her what she said," Tonya ordered from the kitchen.

"You want to tell this story?" Angie yelled back, lifting her chin toward the ceiling as if the sound would travel better thrown into the air.

"Maybe, if you don't get to the good part."

"Fine. She told us that she was coming into big money soon. That she was only staying in this two-bit town long enough to get things settled, and then she's out of here."

"Good riddance, I say," Tonya yelled over the clatter of dishes and closing cabinet doors. Then she popped her head around the doorway again, "But that wasn't what I was talking about, either. Tell her what she said about us."

Tonya came in carrying a tray of drinks. Setting it down, she went back to the kitchen, then returned quickly with a tray of loaded nachos.

"Oh yeah. She called Tonya and I fat," Angie said with a shrug as she grabbed herself a drink off the table.

"She called us brood cows!" Tonya said. "What a bitch." Tonya grabbed a drink and stuffed a straw in the top.

"So, brood cows…is she saying we're moody and fat?" Angie asked with a giggle.

"Not brooding cows. Brood cows, genius." Tonya rolled her eyes, then added, "She could only wish she had half — no, a quarter of our maternal instincts. She's no more a mother than a freaking cat."

"My cat was a good mother," Angie offered.

Tonya took a big sip. "You know what I mean, Ang. Geesh."

Angie took a long drink, giggling the whole time. "I just wanted you to know cats everywhere don't deserve to be compared to Jess."

"How the hell did Rich fall for her?" Sarah asked, grabbing herself a drink off the tray.

"Oh, she can sell it when she wants. When she had her sights set on Rich, she was my best buddy. Sugar wouldn't have melted in her mouth. And she had Kari, who was simply an adorable little heart-stealer." Tonya grabbed a nacho and popped it in her mouth. "Kari was so shy, but she took to Rich, and I think that won him over. Hell, even I thought it was going to be a good match. I hate to admit that, but it's true."

The doorbell rang and Tonya jumped up to answer. Voices from the hall told Sarah the other two ladies had arrived. Sarah cradled her drink and scooted to the corner of the couch. Kicking off her boots, she curled her legs under her and got comfortable.

After Tonya introduced her, Mary offered Sarah a high five. "So, you snagged Doc, eh? Well played."

Angie choked on her drink. "Doc? My…I mean, our Doc?"

"Yeah," Mary said as she shrugged off her coat and took a seat. "It's the talk of the hospital."

Michelle picked a spot on the floor in front of the plate of nachos, which she dived right into. The woman was as thin as Sarah, but ate like a horse. Her voice muffled by chips, she added, "Yeah, you're despised by all the single ladies, and some of the married ones, for pulling Doc off the market like that."

"He's not off the market," Sarah said with a bit too much vigor. "We've had a few dates, that's all."

"I should make more drinks," Angie said, grabbing the tray and heading out of the room.

When the blender started in the kitchen, Mary leaned forward and whispered to Tonya, "I keep forgetting about Angie and Doc. If she is going to get all jealous and neurotic when he dates people, she should just dump Donnie. It's not like Donnie is staying faithful. I know I saw his car at Mandy's the other night. I swear to God, I think we should tell Angie."

"John told me to stay out of it. Which I will, because she never believes us, and it always starts a war. I'm more worried about Rich. I'd like to smack that stupid SOB upside the head for hiring the bimbo. What the hell was he thinking?" Tonya said with a frown.

Sarah sipped her drink and listened. Images of Rich and the bimbo tortured her. They would make a handsome couple. And Rich did seem to go for self-absorbed, low-life kind of women.

"I'm sorry, Sarah!" Mary blurted. "I forgot, you and Doc—"

"A couple of dates, I swear. It's not a relationship. You're fine."

"Oh, I thought you looked a little green around the edges."

"What really pisses me off," Michelle interjected, "is how Donnie uses Angie's guilt to get away with his seriously stupid excuses. Every time she calls him out on his crazy stories, like, *'I'm late because I had a flat tire...for the fourth time this week.'* He reminds her of what she did, and she shuts up. So pathetic!"

"What does Angie have to feel guilty about?" Sarah asked.

Tonya looked over her shoulder—Angie was adding more ice to the blender. Once it started spinning again, Tonya said, "Angie kissed Doc. We all told her to lie about it, but—"

"She didn't even have to lie, just NOT confess!" Michelle said, licking her fingers.

"Anyhow, she told Donnie all about it. He tried to make her quit her job, but they needed the money, so she couldn't. Now, every time he wants to be an ass, he throws that kiss in her face and suggests the two of them still have a thing going," Tonya explained.

"Remember the New Year's party?" Mary asked.

"I swear to all that is holy, I'd have divorced him for that. Angie announced to everyone she was pregnant with their first baby, and Donnie told everyone—a whole party full of people— that he'd celebrate after he got DNA. He told Doc if the kid came out short and dark, he was the one paying for college."

"What did Angie do when he said that? Did she punch him?" Sarah asked.

"She laughed it off. What the hell could she do?" Mary said with a frown. "I thought Doc would punch him, though. Kinda wished he had."

"Yeah, especially knowing Donnie has been keeping his little cream puff on the side for years." Michelle said.

"What?" Maybe Sarah was glad she wasn't married. They all seemed to be miserable.

"Rich's hostess—the big-chested bimbo, Mandy? That's Donnie's woman. Donnie and her have been going at it since she moved here a few years ago. Him and Ang were barely back from their honeymoon when he started sneaking around with her." Michelle took a sip of her drink. "She was a secretary at the garage where Donnie worked, and they were caught—by a customer—making out in the break room, and they both got fired. Angie's mom and dad bought a garage and hired Donnie to work for them. I think to keep an eye on him, and to get rid of Mandy. I mean, he couldn't exactly ask his in-laws to hire his twit. I was hoping she'd go back to where she came from, but then Rich hired her. Now, Donnie has to spend every minute he can spare making sure Rich doesn't end up with his side dish."

"I'd kill him," Tonya said.

"You really think that will matter?" Mary asked. "Eventually, Rich and Mandy will hook up. I'll put money on it."

"Why would Rich do that?" Sarah's question came out a little louder than she expected. "I mean, she hardly seems like a good influence on his kids, and he's crazy about his kids."

"I didn't say he'd marry her, but I will guarantee he'll be banging her in no time. Mandy would ditch Donnie in a heartbeat for a guy like Rich," Mary said.

Sarah frowned and turned her attention to her drink. Images of The Recline's curvy blonde hostess filled her head. The woman was hot, in a cheap, bottle-blonde sort of way. Was Rich dumb enough to fall into a slut trap? Most certainly.

Men sucked.

Chapter 12

When Angie reappeared with fresh drinks, the conversation turned to kids and busy schedules. Sarah curled up with her drink and listened. She had nothing to add, because she'd lost her chance to be a mom. Being over thirty, with all her relationship issues and bad karma, she'd wisely tossed being a mom from the bucket list.

It wasn't like she didn't want to nurture a creature. She'd often thought about getting a cat. As she sat there downing her drink, the thought crossed her mind again. It would be nice to have something to come home to, even if it was just a furry feline.

On second thought, maybe she ought to get a dog. A cat would simply be too stereotypical.

Before she realized, her straw was gurgling. Tonya reached over and filled her glass from the blender pitcher. The fancy pitcher had long ago been abandoned. They were sucking the daiquiris down so fast, they were no longer bothering with the trappings of good manners. Sarah polished that one off, and had started on her third when Angie turned her attention to Sarah.

"Spill it, Sarah. Have you slept with Doc yet?"

Momentarily shocked, Sarah wondered how the conversation had gone from kids to sex. Her mind was feeling a little fuzzy, and her cheeks might have gone a little numb.

"Come on, Sarah. Dish," Mary goaded.

Poor Angie looked so miserable and unhappy, it was impossible not to realize that she was still emotionally invested in Doc. By sharing info with her, Sarah felt like she was creating some sort of odd threesome. But she had nothing to hide—yet—so she supposed it was safe to answer. "I swear, there is nothing to tell. We've had a few dates. All platonic."

"Boring," Angie said, like she was talking through a megaphone. "So, you think you will soon?"

"Dear Lord! How should I know?" Sarah laughed off the question, but she was suddenly wishing she was at home. With her imaginary cat. No, her dog. Damn. How much alcohol was in those drinks?

"Leave her alone, Angie. Sarah has intimacy issues," Tonya said, patting Sarah on the leg.

"I do not!" Sarah leaned forward, shaking her head. "I'm perfectly normal…ish…in that department."

Mary burst out laughing, "What the hell is normal…ish?"

Sarah tried not to slur, but her tongue felt slightly heavy. "Normal…ish means I get all the urges I'm supposed to have—just like anyone else—but I can always count on my judgment to muff it up. Every single damn time. You want the truth, Angie? I'd have to force myself to have sex with Doc. He does nothing for me. I may as well kiss my grandpa when I kiss him. No matter how badly I want to be attracted to a guy who won't send me straight to hell, I just can't manage it. That's normal…ish, right?"

A silence fell over them. Mary scratched her head. Michelle stopped eating and stared at Sarah.

Angie chewed her lower lip. "Maybe Doc just isn't the one. Maybe you should look around more—find someone who makes you happy."

"Oh, hell no. I am not following my heart again. I'm keeping Doc, and I am going to freaking live happily ever after if it kills

89

me. I'm done. Doc is a good man. A stable man. He's single and breathing, and he is exactly what I need."

Tonya's eyes were wide, like she'd witnessed a horrible crime. She grabbed Sarah's hand and gave it a squeeze. "Sarah, what the hell happened in Indianapolis?"

Sarah wrapped her arm around her once dearest friend and pulled her close, laying her head on Tonya's shoulder. "It's not Indianapolis, sweetie. It's me. I'm naturally attracted to poison."

"So that makes Doc poison?" Angie asked.

Sarah straightened up. "No! You're not listening. That's what I'm saying—he can't be poison, because I'm not attracted to him."

"So, you don't like him, but you're still going to date him?" Angie sounded offended.

"Yup," Sarah said. "Head over heart…and loins. It's the way God intended. For the head to be on top. I should call him and tell him," Sarah said, digging through her purse for her phone.

Tonya grabbed it from her and shoved it under her leg. "Oh no, you don't. No drunk calls or texts."

"I'm not drunk. I only had three drinks."

"Five, but who's counting," Mary said with a laugh.

"You can tell him tomorrow, when you're sober. Okay, hun?" Tonya said, rubbing her back.

Sarah wanted to argue more, but the front door opened and Rich walked in. Sarah looked at her watch. It was already eleven? Maybe she did have more than three drinks.

Bending over, she did feel slightly lightheaded as she tried to work the zipper on her boots. Finally getting it together, she caught the tail end of Tonya's conversation with Rich.

"…drunk. Don't mind what she says…."

Sarah wrapped her arm around Rich's as she winked at Tonya. "Don't worry Tonya, I'd never tell my good buddy Rich anything. Come on, Rich, take me home, 'cause we done screwed the pooch forever."

Chapter 13

The row of steps leading to her second-floor apartment looked long and endless. Gripping the handrail, she let her body slide until she was seated, her head resting on a spindle. "I'm gonna sleep here."

"Shit, Sarah, how much did you drink? Or are you still on the pain meds?"

Sarah closed her eyes and enjoyed the feel of cool night air blowing across her excessively hot face. Well, she enjoyed it until Rich cradled her face in his hands and ordered, "Answer me, dammit. Did you take any pain pills today?"

Dear lord, he is taking this too seriously, Sarah thought. *What did it matter? Alcohol, pills...pills and alcohol....*

Before she could answer, he scooped her off her comfy seat and was carrying her back to his truck. The sudden motion left her as dizzy as a rollercoaster ride. Slapping him on the chest, she warned, "I'm gonna be...."

Sick. She was going to say she was going to be sick. Rich had her on her feet and pointed toward a trash can at the back of the building before she could finish the sentence. Clutching the sides of the metal can, she emptied herself of too many daiquiris and too few bites of food. When she finished, she felt shaky and weak. Wiping her mouth with the back of her hand, she felt like crying, but only because her life sucked. Everything she'd ever wanted was a step away, but she'd have to admit things to him that she couldn't even admit to herself.

Pressing cool hands to hot cheeks, she assured him, "It was just one too many drinks."

Rich's grip on her shoulder tightened a little. Taking a step back, she tried to break away, but he wouldn't let her go.

"I'm fine. I swear, no pills for days. I'm just tired and haven't drunk this much in ages...hell, maybe not ever."

"Well, I'll walk you up and get you cleaned up."

Sarah looked down at herself. Was that vomit? Dear lord, if she wasn't so damned drunk, she'd be humiliated. Instead, she was hit with a bad case of giggles. She laughed until her sides hurt and her eyes watered. Committed to salvaging her self-respect, she started toward the steps as she dug a tissue out of her purse. Not watching where she was going, she caught her heel in a sidewalk crack and stumbled a little. It was enough to bring Rich in to scoop her up again. Before she could complain, they were at the top of the steps. Rich opened the door and carried her all the way to the bathroom, where he sat her down on the closed commode and started removing her boots.

"I can do that myself, ya know," Sarah said, but made no move to help.

"I'm sure you can."

"So you can go."

"No," Rich said as he pulled her socks off.

"No?"

"No." Boots and socks removed, he stood up and looked down at her. "We are supposed to talk about Kari. That's why I picked you up, remember?"

She closed her eyes for a long moment and then nodded slowly. "I forgot."

"I didn't." He leaned against the sink.

"I've made forgetting things a specialty. God, I feel so old. And tired," Sarah said as she stood, waving him out of her way so she could brush her teeth. On the first attempt at hitting her mouth she swiped peppermint across her cheek.

Rich shook his head and took it from her and set it on the sink. "One night won't kill you." He poured a cup with mouthwash and handed it to her. "Rinse and spit, you'll be fine."

"Damn right, I'll be fine," she said, head swaying back and forth. Without saying another word, she walked past him to her bedroom. Stripping off her jeans and sweater, she grabbed a T-shirt from the floor and pulled it on. Climbing on all fours from the bottom of the bed to her pillow, she tugged at the duvet. Not realizing her body weight was holding it down, she muttered, "Stupid, uncooperative bastard of a thing." Then she dropped, face first, into her pillow.

Chapter 14

Waking to bright sunlight, Sarah threw an arm over her eyes and groaned. Like a baby vamp, the harsh rays burned, making her head ache.

"Aspirin?"

Her head jerked against her pillow and she peeked out from under her arm. Rich was crouched by the edge of her bed.

"You're here?" She groaned as she imagined how puffy and horrible she had to look. She covered her face with her hands.

"You were so stinking drunk, I couldn't just leave you. You might've puked and drowned in it or something."

"Thanks, you're such a gentleman. I'm alive; you can leave."

"Not a chance. You said you had something to tell me about Kari."

"Oh God, I forgot." Sarah moved her arm and lifted her head from her pillow. It felt like a hundred-pound melon, fragile and heavy.

Rich stood, hands in his pockets, staring at her. "What's going on, Sarah?"

"I think I'm hung over."

"No joking. There's something going on. This isn't the Sarah I know."

"That could be because you don't know me. I'm not the

person you remember, or invented in some weird need to create yourself a woman."

"Oh, so this is all my problem?"

Sarah bit her lip and shrugged. She shouldn't be having this conversation right now, not when she was possibly on the verge of a mental breakdown. She'd come to Dodd to get herself sorted out, and all she'd accomplished was the creation of more problems. "I didn't mean you have a problem. I just…I'm just… dear lord, my head feels like an over-ripe melon."

"You know, Sarah, you can talk to me about anything."

Sarah sat up and swung her legs off the side of the bed. *Oh, the things I could tell him,* she thought. *He'd never want to look at me in the eyes again.* "I need coffee," she said. "And some aspirin."

"Why don't you take a shower and I'll make the coffee? Then we can talk about Kari."

Sarah rubbed the back of her neck. "Give me ten minutes and I'll be more — well, less of a bitch."

"Promises, promises," Rich said with a wink and a grin.

Sarah made a face at him, one that was reminiscent of elementary school. After he left, she stripped and headed for the shower. As the hot water streamed over her shoulders, she leaned her head against the shower wall and tried her best not to cry. He was such a decent man. He could never understand the choices she'd made.

She stood there until the water ran cold and Rich pounded on the door. "Sarah? Are you okay?"

"I'm fine." She shut off the water, dried quickly, and dressed in sweatpants and a tee. When she opened the bathroom door, Rich was waiting on her. He had that look of concern that made her want to crawl in bed and cry.

"The coffee's ready."

She followed him to the kitchen. There were two mugs of coffee on the table, along with toasted bagels. Her stomach turned at the thought of food, but her heart swelled at his thoughtfulness. Sitting at the dining table, she grabbed the mug. It smelled delicious. She took a drink. Rich was an excellent coffee brewer. The man was full of magic.

She blushed at the thought and tried to focus on what was important. "Kari."

He gripped the mug with both hands and nodded.

"I have zero proof. It's just something that Stacey said that has me worried."

"I trust your instincts; what is it?"

"Stacey was telling me the new stepdad only has an interest in Kari. That it's Kari that Jess and Phil are trying to keep visiting. Stacey said it doesn't matter if she goes or not."

"I figured Jess was closer, more comfortable with Kari because she's older."

"But they're both her daughters. She should at least be trying to get to know Stacey. It's not like she's a hard child to love."

"That's true. She warmed up to you in days, and you're hardly easy to get along with."

"Ha ha, aren't you a comedian?" Sarah took a deep breath. "And then there's the boyfriend. At first, I thought it was just a regular boyfriend/girlfriend sort of thing, but then Stacey said she wasn't allowed to tell anyone about the new boyfriend. That he picks Kari up at school, but never at home. And Stacey says the guy looks old. Now, I know—"

Rich was up out of his chair, pacing. "She knows she's not allowed to date anyone without approval. And the guy's old? How old?"

"I don't know. I mean, Stacey is five, so old could be fifteen. But…well…what if old is old? There has to be some reason she's sneaking around. Well, unless you are insane about your rules—then I could understand sneaking around."

"I'm not insane about the rules. I just have to meet the boy first. I let her go out with Heath and I thought he was a little shit — I was right about him, by the way. She hasn't said anything about any other guys. She doesn't usually hide things from me."

"Stacey saw him. Now, maybe this boy is just a friend and Stacey is a little girl who is misunderstanding."

"True, and Kari would never defy me."

Sarah toyed with the handle of her cup. "My mother forbade me seeing you...I still did it. I lied to my grandpa to get away that weekend."

Rich rubbed his hands through his hair. "The weekend at the cabin." He looked up and grinned, his loathsome dimples puckering in as he remembered. "That was a good weekend."

"I got caught, and oh my God, I got in so much trouble, and… well, it doesn't matter. My point is, she may not be listening to you."

"She always listens to me." Rich sat back down.

"Come on, Rich. You can't be this naïve. Do you know a girl who listened better than me? But when I thought…well, when you invited me to the cabin. And dear God, I feared my mother."

"But that's the thing, Kari doesn't fear me. We've always been honest with each other. She listens because she trusts me."

Sarah shook her head. "Stacey said she is sneaking around. Maybe it's a relationship she knows you won't approve of?"

Rich looked like he'd been punched in the gut. No dimples. All frown lines. "Should I call her on it?"

Sarah rubbed her temple. "I don't know. Stacey will know I told you, and I know she's just a little girl…."

"But you still want to keep her confidence?" Rich finished for her.

Sarah nodded. "It might seem silly, but it feels good that she trusts me."

"I'd want proof anyhow. Not just something her little sister said. I mean, you're right — old to Stacey could be fifteen. Sneaking could be telling her she had to ride the bus."

"All valid points."

There was a quiet pause. Only the refrigerator hummed in the kitchen.

Rich broke the silence. "Kari is supposed to be at the lake with friends today. Jess and Philip are taking them boating."

"If Jess is helping her sneak around, a boat is a smart place to hide."

"No doubt. She knows I won't bump into her on the water."

"You could with Doc. He asked me to go boating this afternoon."

"I appreciate the offer, but going out on a date with you and Doc isn't exactly my idea of fun."

"I wasn't suggesting I go. I could ask Doc to take you instead. I figured I could watch Stacey. You don't want her to know you're spying on her mother and sister, do you?"

He shook his head. "You're pretty damned good at being clever, Ms. Andrews."

"I have my moments." She looked around the kitchen. "Did you see where I put my purse?"

"It's on the couch."

Sarah got up and went to the living room. As she texted Doc, she said, "I was thinking of getting a puppy today anyhow. I bet Stacey would enjoy that."

Rich followed her into the living room and sat on the arm of her couch and rubbed his chin. "A puppy? Damn, you sure you're ready to pile on another commitment in your life?"

Sarah's eyes narrowed. "What's that supposed to mean?"

"Last night? In your drunken ramblings, you made it a point to outline your goals and philosophies for me. Knowing all of that, I'd suggest you get a cat. A puppy might be too much of an emotional investment."

Chapter 15

Sarah skipped the pet store and headed to the animal shelter. She had enough black marks on her history—she needed every opportunity to start building good karma. The nagging wonder about what she'd revealed to Rich in her drunken confession kept her in an almost constant state of mortification. She wanted to ask, but she didn't want to know. What did she tell him about her feelings? Her history? Their history? Her cheeks blazed anew. She must not have told him everything…he was still there in the morning.

Sarah blindly walked past cage after cage of trapped animals, their whines and barks mere back drops to her internal dialogue.

"You should get this dog! He looks so sad," Stacey said, kneeling by the cage of a gray faced, ancient basset hound.

"I had planned on a puppy," Sarah said, looking at the slug of a dog with a raised eyebrow.

Stacey stuck a little hand through the cage and the old dog nuzzled into it.

"Aww, see Sarah? He loves me." Stacey slid another hand in and stroked one of the dog's long ears. "You love me, don't you, big fella?"

The dog whined, then stood, his black nose sniffing them from behind the cage.

Sarah looked around the room at the other, obviously more adoptable dogs. Then she looked down at the hound and his new fan. There was no question that this would have to be the dog. There was no way she could tell Stacey no.

"I suppose," she said, turning to a volunteer. "Sir, what do I need to do to get this dog?"

"This dog?" The man looked skeptical, but quickly smiled, like he was selling on commission. "Come with me, and I'll get you started."

~*~

"So, that's how we picked out the dog," Sarah said, unwrapping her foil wrapped hot dog.

"No, Rover picked us! As soon as we walked in the shelter, Rover barked, 'Over here! I need a home.'" Stacey held the leash in one hand and petted the top of the dog's head with the other.

"So, who got a new dog, you or Miss Sarah?" Rich asked.

"Duh, Miss Sarah. I'm just his interpreter and best friend."

"Hmm, seems he's wanting to take a walk," Rich said, leaning an ear to the dog.

"He said that?" Stacey asked.

"Most certainly did," Rich said.

Sarah's stomach tightened. Rich had evidently seen something while on the boat. Images of Kari in a situation she was too young to deal with made her stomach turn. A lifetime of scars, for being a stupid teen.

"Well, let's go, Rover," Stacey said, walking off slowly with the geriatric pooch.

"At least he won't take her for a drag."

"No, she may have to drag him back," Rich laughed.

"So, did you find them?"

Rich frowned. He leaned his body against a swing set pole and crossed his arms over his chest. The muscles in his forearms twitched. "Yeah, we did. They had a full boat load of teens, and it seemed to be on the up and up. Maybe you're right, Jess just can't relate to a young kid. Hell, she still acts like a kid herself."

"I suppose that's good to hear. I was just being paranoid. I should know better than anyone that my instincts are pretty off."

"Right or wrong, I appreciate you looking out for her."

"You've got good kids. I like them," Sarah said with a shrug.

Rich nodded. His body looked tense, and the frown he wore was topped with a furrowed brow. He took a deep breath. "I did get to have an interesting conversation with Doc."

She tossed the hot dog in the trash half-eaten. How could she chew and swallow when her mouth kept going dry? "And?" she asked.

"Seems Doc wants me to cut ties with you. Thinks I'm messing things up for your relationship."

"Relationship? It was a couple of dates."

"I know how you feel about him, Sarah. I know you want it to work. You told me yourself."

Sarah's hands went cold. "Really? Well, I was—"

"I told him what you told me. That he was a good man and that you would like to see it work out." He stuffed his hands in his pockets and rocked back on his heels. "I told him there was nothing between us."

"I like to think we're friends."

The muscle in Rich's jaw twitched. "Friends, huh?"

Sarah nodded. She felt lonelier than ever. Dried leaves blew across the ground, catching her attention as the sunlight and child's laughter in the park seemed miles and miles away.

"Doc is a good man. And he's got a lot more going for him than a single dad juggling mortgages and evil exes. You're making the smart choice."

She opened her mouth to tell him everything, but the words caught in her throat. No matter how hard she tried to spit out the truth, she couldn't. By staying silent, she had this...the opportunity to stand here in a park and spend time with him. Move the relationship closer than that, and she could lose everything.

Wasn't being a small part of his life better than nothing?

Chapter 16

For the next two weeks, Rich was polite, but hardly flirtatious with Sarah. He finished the offices and the windows, and barely offered her a goodbye beyond, "Well, I think we're done here." He packed up his tools and was gone. Sitting at her desk, drawing doodles on her ink blotter, she reminded herself that removing all romantic possibilities with Rich from her life was what she wanted.

"Hey sexy, I brought dinner."

Doc walked into her office with a bag of food. Sarah swallowed. She really needed to hire another secretary, because Rover was evidently a guard-dog-fail against intruders. She'd hired a secretary from the local community college, but had to fire her after she posted on social media—*Not going to believe who came into the office for a divorce!* When Sarah fired the woman, the blasé blabber threatened a lawsuit against her for violating her freedom of speech. If Sarah had a copy of the Constitution in her hands, she'd have slapped her with it.

Sarah pushed her chair away from her desk, ready to plead too much work to stop for food. "I—"

"Don't say you need to work. It's Friday night, and it's not like I'm asking you to go dancing. I just want ten minutes for dinner."

"Just ten minutes?"

"I'll take as many as you'll give me, but as your much-neglected boyfriend, I'm demanding ten."

Boyfriend? Her mind balked at the word. She was a little too old for such nonsense. *Boyfriend.* It took all her power not to roll her eyes and gag. Then the side of her that demanded she live a rational life told her, *This is why all of your relationships suck. You scoff at good guys who bring you dinner.* Taking a deep breath, Sarah offered him a smile. "I suppose I could call it a night. What time is it?"

"It's after eight."

"Eight? I didn't realize it was so late."

"You really should remember to lock up. I walked right in the front door."

Sarah rubbed the tight muscles in her neck. She'd remembered to turn the closed sign, but must have forgotten to lock the door. She led the way to the upstairs apartment, mindful not to offer Doc a peep show as he followed behind her.

"I don't know how you live so close to work. No wonder you're always there. You need a place that's distinctively separate. You're not very good at setting boundaries in your life."

Her first thought was to set an immediate boundary and tell him to mind his own damned business. She didn't need someone telling her what to do. *Be calm. Be normal,* she reminded herself with another deep breath in through the nose and out through the mouth. The door creaked open and she waved him in ahead of her. He took the invitation and walked straight to her kitchen and opened cupboards and drawers, getting out plates and utensils to set on the little dinette table.

It's good. He's a take charge kind of guy, she told herself, but still she could feel the blood pool on her cheeks from irritation.

Doc never noticed. He continued his work setting the table and popping open a bottle of wine. Sarah reached for the bottle and glass, but Doc smacked her hand playfully and said, "Sit. I will serve you. This is your treat."

"Marvelous," she said through slightly clenched teeth.

As she sat, her phone rang. She didn't recognize the number, but she quickly answered it anyhow.

"Sarah Andrews?"

"Yes, this is she."

"This is a little embarrassing, but do you know Stacey Cooper?"

"Little girl? Rich's daughter?" Sarah's heart stopped. *Please God, don't let anything be wrong.*

"Yes, that's her. My name is Rosa Walters, and we...my family...just moved to Dodd. My little girl and Stacey are friends, and Stacey was supposed to spend the night for Melonie's sleep over, but Stacey got homesick. I can't leave all these kids, and I can't get ahold of her dad, so she suggested I call you because she said your phone number is on the door of your house." Rosa laughed. "I assumed that meant you had a business, so I looked you up and took the chance. Thank God it was you."

The amount of relief in the woman's voice at finding a contact for Stacey made Sarah feel nervous all over again. "Is she all right?"

"She's been crying. For a while, I thought she was going to hyperventilate. I've tried to call her dad a hundred times, but he doesn't answer."

"That's not like him. Give me your address; I'll come and get her." Sarah wrote the address down and hung up.

Doc was shooting daggers at her with his eyes. He frowned and shook his head, getting up from his seat and throwing his napkin on the table. "Let me guess, Rich needs a rescue."

"Not Rich. Stacey."

"Because her father is a child and can't be found?"

Sarah was grabbing her purse and jacket as she talked. "It's not like Rich to ignore his kids. He may be a lot of things, but he is a wonderful dad."

"I can tell by the way you're heading out to take care of his spawn."

"Spawn?" Sarah paused buttoning her coat to look at his face to see if he was joking. He wasn't. There wasn't a trace of smile present. If Sarah was a betting gal, she'd bet he was pissed.

"Whatever," he said. "Go rescue the kid. It's not her fault her dad's an idiot. People shouldn't have kids if they don't want to take care of them."

"Holy crap, Doc. I thought you two were friends."

Doc shrugged. "Just because he's my friend doesn't mean I can't see him for who he is. Most women can't get past his charm to see it. I know all about him."

Her mouth dropped open, and she was about to argue, but she thought of a crying little girl in need of a rescue, and decided a full conversation on just what the hell he was insinuating would have to wait. "I don't have time for this."

"Of course you don't. I'll walk you out."

Doc walked her to her car and placed a chaste kiss on her forehead.

She mumbled something about calling him later and left. Arriving at the Walters' home, Sarah spotted Stacey watching for her from the front room window. Stacey waved as the car pulled into the driveway. All the anger and frustration Sarah had stewed in on the drive over disappeared. Oh, how she missed that little girl. Two steps from her car, Stacey ploughed into her, wrapping little arms around her neck and squeezing.

"Hey, sweetie. I missed you. Are you all right?"

The little girl's eyes were puffy and swollen, but she smiled. "I'm happy now. Can we go to your house and see Rover?"

"Of course." Sarah opened the car door and helped the child inside. Without thinking, she gave the little girl a kiss on her cheek. Stacey gave her a big, tiny-toothed grin.

As Sarah was driving down the road, Stacey said, "Thank you, Sarah. My belly started hurting, and I missed my daddy."

"You did? And you called him, and he didn't answer?"

"No. Then I heard Bonnie's mom tell Ashley's mom that my dad was out with Mandy and probably couldn't be bothered. And…and…." Fresh tears flowed down the child's cheeks. "I don't like her, Sarah. I don't! And I don't like my mom. And I don't like Kari's boyfriend. None of them like me. And I wanted to come see you, but Daddy says I'm not allowed to bug you." Her little face scrunched up and wails filled the car.

Sarah wanted to punch Rich in the face. Of course, she wanted to be bugged by the child. What was Rich's problem? Maybe Doc was right. Did he think he had to avoid her to hook up with the big-breasted bimbo? Like she cared who he was with. And how dare he ignore his kid? To think she had defended him. Pissed off her date for him. *That jerk.*

Her mind rant was interrupted by the sudden sound of gagging. She looked over at Stacey. The child was turning green and covering her mouth with her hand. Before Sarah could pull her car over, Stacey was heaving. All over herself. All over Sarah's car.

Stacey turned glassy eyes to Sarah. "I'm sorry. I'll clean it up."

"It's all right," Sarah turned the car around and headed away from her house and toward Rich's. "Does your dad keep a spare key at the house?"

"No."

"Oh." Sarah slowed the car and got ready to turn around again.

"But the garage is always open, and you can get in that way."

Hitting the gas, Sarah nodded. "That will work. Let's get you home for a bath and a change of clothes."

At the house, Sarah sat outside the open bathroom door and listened to the child bathe. Sarah wasn't sure if five-year-olds needed help or not, but unless it was requested, she wasn't offering.

"I'm done, Sarah."

"Okay," Sarah said. "Do you need something?"

Stacey laughed. "A towel, silly. And my pajamas."

Sarah stepped into the bathroom and handed the child a fluffy yellow towel. It smelled wonderful. Sarah doubted Rich used fabric softener. Evidently, Mandy was doing the laundry for him. *The conniving bitch.*

Dried off, Stacey led her to the bedroom she shared with Kari. The room was a mess. Sarah had to step carefully to keep from breaking a toy or her neck. Stacey dressed in a cartoony-princess nightgown. Sarah made her put on socks and a sweatshirt with it, for warmth.

Once she was dressed, Stacey looked up at Sarah, "So, should we go to your house now?"

"How about we watch a movie here and wait on your dad? That way he knows where you are."

Stacey nodded. "Tomorrow, can I come see Rover?"

"Sure."

Sarah picked her up and carried her to the living room. They snuggled together on the couch and watched something brain-numbing on a kid's network. In no time, Stacey's breathing slowed. The steady in and out of the child's breath was like hypnosis, and before she knew it, Sarah was fast asleep beside her.

A noise at the front door woke her. Voices and the jangle of keys. A woman's giggle. Rich's husky response.

Shit. Shit. Shit, Sarah thought as she scrambled to get herself extricated from the sleeping child and on her feet before the door opened.

She failed. The door swung open and Rich and Mandy fell into the room. Rich's hands were practically stuffed down Mandy's jeans, cupping her ass, which Sarah had to admit was quite an accomplishment considering the things were so damned tight they looked painted on.

"Ahh, that's so good, baby," Mandy said, shoving Rich against the wall and pulling his shirt over his head.

"I am so gonna — shut the hell up." Rich made eye contact with Sarah. "Sarah? What are you doing here?"

Mandy nuzzled her face into his throat, but he squirmed away from her grasp. The woman gave Sarah a look of disgust, with a full eye roll and everything.

"Stacey got sick at her sleepover."

"She did?" Rich plopped himself down on the couch and felt the little girl's head. "She doesn't feel hot."

"I think she was just homesick. But she cried so much, she threw up in my car."

"She did?" Rich's voice was full of worry. "My poor little princess." He smoothed the curls and kissed her forehead. "Why didn't she call me?"

"She did. Mrs. Walters said she called you about a hundred times."

Rich pulled his phone out of his pocket and looked. "I don't have any calls."

Mandy squirmed by the door. "So, like, I suppose I should go...if we're done here?"

Rich looked over his shoulder and nodded, and then as if he remembered he just had his tongue shoved down her throat, he said, "I'll walk you out."

Setting his phone on the table, he escorted Mandy back out the same door they'd just fallen through. "I'm sorry about this — " His words were cut off by the closing door.

"I'm sorry about this," Sarah mocked. "Seems responsibility

got in the way of my penis." Grabbing Rich's phone off the table, she unlocked it—Kari plus Stacey's birthdays. He was so predictable. One click on settings and Sarah saw the problem.

Rich walked back into the house. Sarah held the phone out to him. "I found your problem, stud. You're on plane mode."

"I didn't put it on plane mode." Rich turned his cellular service back on and his phone lit up with message after message. He shook his head. "What the hell? My poor baby girl."

"She couldn't remember anyone's phone numbers. Mrs. Walters didn't know who Aunt Tonya was. So, when Stacey told her my name was Sarah, and I had my name on my door, she googled the different businesses in town with the name Sarah."

"Holy shit. How did my phone get on plane mode? I never turn off my phone."

Sarah frowned. "Seriously? You can't figure this out?"

"Mandy?"

"Of course. I take it she's tired of interruptions?"

"Well, it has been impossible to close the deal—I swear, it's like my kids made it their job to be difficult."

"Real mature. Way to put your loins above responsibility."

"I didn't do it. And I swear to you, if she did this—"

"You'll what? Stop stuffing your hands down her pants? You really should wash them, you know. You've no idea where that ass has been."

Rich's cheeks flamed red. Sarah thought maybe she'd pushed it too far, but then he ran a hand through his hair and shook his head. "What the hell was I thinking? I know better than to get tangled up with…employees. I was just—"

"Hard up?" Sarah suggested.

"No." Rich's shoulders sagged. "I guess I was feeling lonely. I'm almost thirty-five, and what do I have?"

"Two great kids? A home? Holy hell, what more do you want?"

He shrugged and looked at her. His eyes were warm, and his lips looked inviting. Sarah wondered if he still tasted like peppermint. Her eyelids grew heavy, and a soft sigh escaped her as his lips moved closer. He was going to kiss her.

Sarah snapped her head back. Quickly she turned and gathered her coat and purse. She needed out of there before she did something she'd regret, like telling Rich her latest conundrum — how it felt like her heart was being ripped out of her chest via her throat to see him with another woman. She was a fool to think she could be his friend and calmly watch him move on and fall in love — not when she loved him. She mumbled a quick goodbye and bolted for the door.

Chapter 17

Rich stood in the kitchen with the blow dryer and yelled to Tonya, "You know, John can do this. It's not hard."

"I don't want John to know, or he'll yell at me for shutting it off."

Rich shook his head. "Why are you shutting it off?"

"Because the ice bucket fills up."

"Then dump it. Quit shutting it off. Dumping ice every now and then is probably cheaper than buying ice when it freezes up."

"But I like to buy ice. I like the little round cubes with the hole in it. That's perfect ice."

Rich shut off the dryer and tested the water feed. It worked. "So why am I fixing it?"

"Because John wants icemaker ice, and if he knows I shut it off, he'll yell at me."

"I'm going to have to agree with John on this one. None of what you just said made a bit of sense."

"Oh, bite me. Look around this place—I haven't demanded a mansion. Half my shit is broken, the other half is stained. Let me enjoy some small luxuries."

"Whatever. Maybe I should be grateful I'm single."

"Giving up on Sarah?"

Rich shoved the refrigerator back into its spot. "I was never pursuing Sarah."

"That's not what Kari told me. She told me you asked—"

"I was speaking hypothetically. Damn. How often do you two talk?"

"Hardly ever since Jess started monopolizing her. But a few weeks ago, she wanted my help. She wanted to play matchmaker for you and Sarah."

Rich leaned against the counter and shook his head. "There's no hope of that. Sarah's got Doc, and he's more her type."

Tonya pulled two colas out of the fridge and handed one to Rich. "But you have the girls, and Sarah is crazy about them."

"And she'll get to see them without me. I tried to keep Stacey from going over, and it was constant drama."

Tonya joined him, sitting across from him. "Doesn't matter. Sarah doesn't love Doc."

"She says that's why it's perfect."

"Sarah will always be Sarah."

"What does that mean?"

"Sarah has always wanted to be in love, to have a happy family. She never really had that with her parents, you know? She saw her mother at holidays and vacations. She never saw her dad. Her grandpa did what he could, but most of the Andrews focused on Sarah's potential, not on her need to be loved. Hell, they wouldn't even let her have a dog. Whatever was a hassle was forbidden."

"Good then—it's Sarah who's weird, not me," Rich laughed at his own joke, but it was a hollow sound, even to his own ears.

"Yeah, she's a little weird, but I love Sarah. She's loyal to a flaw. I mean, people say they have friends who will help hide bodies, but Sarah wouldn't just help, she'd buy the damn shovels. And she has the biggest heart."

"I can see all of that. I can. The problem is, she doesn't want me. I've been shoved to the friend zone."

"You're going to sit back and watch her date another guy?"

Rich hated it. He hated knowing she was out with another guy. But what could he do? "She was pretty clear. Doc is her future. He's more her type, anyhow."

"Pah. That's insane. I don't know what the hell is wrong with Sarah, but there is something wrong—and I'm not just talking about the obvious issues of being sexually repressed and uptight. The chick is over thirty, and has probably never had an orgasm."

His mind wandered back to that weekend. She'd been shy, but hardly repressed. Definitely not too uptight to have an orgasm.

Tonya slapped her hand on the table. "I knew it! I called her on it when I brought her to my house, and she denied it. I can't believe she never told me. I can't believe you never told me."

"Told you what?" He knew, but he had to buy time.

"You never told me you diddled her in college."

Rich's heartrate sped up. He didn't want anyone to know. It was a memory he treasured. A moment in time so perfect, if he tried to put it into words, he'd ruin it.

"You love her," Tonya said, her voice dropping low as if she was telling him a secret. "Oh my God. I was thinking you were just interested…I didn't know."

"I don't love her. I barely know her anymore."

"I can see it. You get this goofy look on your face when you think about her. And look." She pointed at him. "You're blushing!"

"I'm embarrassed. Who the hell wouldn't—? Damn it, I don't blush."

"You should talk to her. Tell her how you feel."

He shook his head and wiped sweat from the cola can. "That night I took her home from your house, she told me I was the worst thing that ever happened to her in her life."

"Ouch. What exactly happened between you two to justify

that?"

Rich licked dry lips. "I'm not really sure. You asked me to take her to prom, and I did. We had a great time. I thought she was smart and sweet, so when I got home for the summer, we went out a few times."

"You never said anything about dating her."

"She didn't want anyone to know. She said her mother would have a fit."

"Ugh. The woman is a controlling bitch."

"So, we snuck around. I never said anything to anyone, because I didn't want her to get caught. And then, one day, she was gone. I went to her house, and her grandpa said she'd left for college on the west coast. Sarah had my number. She knew my address. I never heard anything from her. What sucks…and I'm ashamed to admit…is that I was so depressed that fall, I didn't even go back to school. Then I met Jess, and the rest is history."

"Have you told Sarah any of that?"

"Holy shit, Tonya. She ripped my heart out sixteen years ago. And trust me, she's no sweeter on me now. You know what else she told me the night I took her home from your party?"

"I told you not to listen to her. She was drunk."

"Well, alcohol often speaks truth. She told me I was a constant reminder of what a lousy human being she was, and it was killing her."

"Damn. What did you say?"

"Nothing. What could I say? The next day, I talked to Doc, who pretty much told me Sarah could never move on, never be happy, if I didn't give her some space."

"Screw him."

"I want what's best for her, Tonya. I love her enough to want her to be happy. I've been thinking a lot about what happened between us. Maybe I pushed her too fast, too young. I don't know."

"Exactly what did happen? I mean, for someone who's family to one and best friend to the other, it seems I should be better informed. Were you guys, you know, intimate the whole summer?"

Rich shook his head. "Just the one weekend. It was my idea. I talked Sarah into telling her mom that her and Jess were going to take a tour of Indiana State for the weekend, but spending the weekend at the cabin with me."

"You guys used Jess as a cover instead of me?"

Rich cringed. How could he explain to his cousin that she was easily excitable, and had a tendency to blurt out whatever was on her mind?

"I suppose it's history now, but you should have told me. I know how to deal with Sarah better than anyone. Like, I'd have told you to make sure she knew she wasn't just any girl—I'm assuming she wasn't just a score, right? Cause I'd kill you—"

"Of course, she was special. But I've been thinking—she seemed happy at the time, but maybe she regretted it. Or maybe I was making more out of it than it was, and I was just entertaining her until she left for Stanford."

"No way. You two are perfect together."

"She wants to be friends, and I've decided I'm good with that. I mean, I tried avoiding her and that didn't work. I tried going out with Mandy—"

"You what?" Tonya stood so fast she knocked her chair over. Not bothering to pick it up, she yelled, "What in God's name were you thinking? Haven't you screwed your life up enough with gold-digging whores?"

"It was a mistake. It won't happen again."

Tonya set her chair to rights. "It better not. I'll bust that bitch in the face. I'm not playing with her anymore. Home-wrecking ho. How could you? You didn't…?"

"No." Rich rubbed the back of his neck as he remembered

falling through the front door with every intention of venting every frustration he had until Mandy couldn't walk straight. Then he'd seen Sarah and felt instantly dirty...like he'd been caught cheating. He still felt that way, no matter how many times he told himself he owed Sarah nothing and could screw anyone he wanted.

"Can you believe Mandy put my phone on airplane mode so my kids couldn't interrupt?"

"Duh. I hear she ditched her own kids on her mother. Left them in Florida and never looked back."

"I can't date a woman like that. Stacey got sick at her sleepover, and had to call Sarah to come rescue her."

"Mandy is a conniving little bitch. I don't know why men can't see it."

"She has a great rack."

"Seriously? That's all it takes? Men are so damned stupid."

"Normally, I'd never have even considered hooking up with her, but it's been a hell of a few weeks."

"This is insane. You should be with Sarah. You can't let her end up with Doc."

"She doesn't want me, Tonya."

"Oh no, she wants you. She just doesn't want to want you."

"Makes as much sense as your ice theory."

"Men. You're so thick. You just have to try harder."

"Not doing it. I'll take her anyway I can, so if she wants to be friends, then I'll be her friend."

"Well then, as her *friend*, you need to protect her from making a huge mistake. Saturday is Sarah's birthday. I know from Angie that Doc is hoping to take her on a romantic weekend get-a-way, so we need to put the kibosh on that. Is the back room of The Recline open?"

Rich took out his phone and looked at the calendar. "It's free from 10:00-midnight. Up until then, there's a baby shower."

"Baby shower? Really?"

Rich shrugged. "Hey, I don't ask. I just book it."

"Whatever. Put me down for Saturday, and I'll get on the planning. You're going to throw your *friend* a birthday party."

Chapter 18

"Knock, knock," Tonya said, knocking on Sarah's door as she walked in. Sarah swung her legs off the couch and sat up. The day had been hell, and Tonya was a welcome disruption. Sarah tried to pretend that last night's romp between Rich and Mandy had gone unnoticed, but that was a huge lie she couldn't sell to herself.

"So, I hear you busted Rich before he could drop his drawers for the bimbo?"

"I don't care what Rich does, or whom."

"Well, he certainly cares. He was over at my place this morning fixing my fridge, and oh dear God, was he humiliated."

"He should be. Shows a distinct lack of taste and judgment."

"That's what I told him." Tonya dropped herself on the couch beside Sarah. Poking Sarah on the leg, she asked, "When are you going to tell me about you and Rich and the magic weekend?"

"It was hardly magic."

"That's not the way he describes it."

Sarah's head whipped to look at Tonya. She had to know if the woman was joking. "What did he say?"

"It's not so much what he said, it was the look on his face when I asked him about the weekend. It was actually kind of creepy, because he's my cousin and all. But you can tell just by

119

looking at him…you mean a lot to him, Sarah. More than you could ever guess."

"I don't think—"

"Oh hell, stop thinking, would you?"

"Trust me, not thinking is what's gotten me here."

Tonya patted her leg. "Here isn't so bad. I'm damn glad you're here. I've missed you."

Sarah's nod was slow, almost hesitant.

Tonya didn't seem to notice her friend's lack of enthusiasm. She said, with all the cheer of a sales lady working on commission, "Okay, so next Saturday is your birthday. Spend it with me."

Sarah thought about it. Technically, she should spend it with Doc. He was hinting at doing something special, but she wasn't so certain she was ready for something special. Besides. she'd rather be with her friend, like old times. She nodded. "I'd like that."

"Good. I'll plan everything. You just be ready by 9:30."

"Morning or night?"

"Night. Good lord. Have you ever known me to be an early bird?"

Sarah shrugged. "People change."

"No," Tonya said, rising to leave. "I don't think they do."

Sarah's phone rang. It was Doc. She showed it to Tonya before answering.

"Hello, sexy lawyer lady. I wanted to know if you knew whether or not I can sue someone for trying to steal my heart?"

Sarah had to swallow the bile before forcing a grin and answering, "Sorry, sir, that sounds like a job for the police."

Doc laughed. "I was thinking. How about we rent a movie tonight? And grab a box of pizza?"

Hanging out with Doc was putting weight on her. For a doctor, his eating habits were deplorable. And he clocked so many hours at the hospital, he was always too tired to do anything much more invigorating than a movie.

But, it was comfortable.

And he was sweet. And patient. He'd totally forgiven her for ditching him last night after explaining what happened with Stacey and the cell phone.

"A movie sounds great. My place or yours?"

"If you wouldn't mind…."

"I'll be over around five."

"You know, Sarah, if you'd want to just stay…well, I mean, I have a big place…."

No. No. Do not say those words. Sarah's heart raced. "Hey look, I'm getting a call. See you tonight?"

She hung up before he could say goodbye, or determine who would grab the pizza. She wasn't calling him back. She'd rather just grab one.

Tonya gave her an arched brow and a scowl. "I think you're making a mistake. Please? Would you just call Rich? Just give him a shot."

"What would be the point? I've got…a…boyfriend." *Damn, why was that hard to say?*

"I suppose." Tonya stood. "I better get going. John and I are doing a date night. He wants a motorcycle, and he thinks he can use sex to get his way. He came in this morning with his pubes all shaved. He told me he did some manscaping for me."

"What made him think that would work?"

"I got a Brazilian wax, and he was so impressed, he got me a dishwasher."

"So, he thinks it's a sort of quid pro quo?"

"Exactly. But I could care less if he looked like freaking Sasquatch—hair doesn't bug me, and the lack of hair isn't going to make me shell out money for a mid-life crisis machine that will get my dumbass killed."

"You two are sweet. I'm jealous. You really have everything,

Tonya."

Tonya nodded. "You could have everything too. Just make the right decision."

~*~

Grabbing a pizza and a six-pack of beer, Sarah headed to Doc's house. He wasn't home yet, so she waited in her car. She was reading a book when he pecked on her window.

"I'm sorry, honey. I got held over. One of the, uh, nurses at work is having some trouble at home."

"Angie?" she asked as she got out of the car and grabbed the pizza and beer.

"Yeah, you know her?" Doc took the pizza off her hands.

"I went to high school here, remember? Hopefully, one day, I'll get to help her get divorced. Her husband sounds like a real ass."

"She won't divorce him. Threatens to every other day, never does it."

They made their way to the house. Doc suggested he shower while Sarah put the pizza on plates. He emerged in sweats and a tee. He truly was a handsome man. Shorter and more compact than Rich, but equally as handsome. Grabbing her around the waist, he pulled her close and kissed her. It was a nice kiss, gentle and warm. Not electrifying, but sweet.

When he pulled back, he said, "Angie and I once had a thing. Nothing serious, but still…."

"And you're telling me that, because?"

"Thought you'd want to hear it from me, not through the grapevine."

"Oh well, I think what happened before you met me is your business."

Doc laughed. "That your way of telling me you have no interest in divulging what the hell is between you and Rich?"

"That was shitty. And juvenile."

Sarah grabbed a beer and headed for the living room. Doc followed. She sat, arms crossed over her chest, feet propped on the coffee table. Doc sat beside her. She ignored him.

He pried her hand free and held it. "I wasn't trying to start a fight."

"Could have fooled me."

"Look, I believe in being honest, and I figured if you talk to anyone, then you'll hear about my having an affair with her."

Sarah's head snapped when she turned to look at him. "I thought it was just a kiss?"

Doc shrugged. "I suppose it was whatever Angie says it was."

"So more than a kiss?"

Doc shrugged. Sarah recognized the look of the broken-hearted. She'd seen it in the mirror for years. She asked quietly, "Do you love her?"

"Do you love Rich?"

Sarah's jaw clenched, and she tried to pull her hand away, but he held it tight.

"Seriously, Sarah, if I can't even mention the guy's name without you going through the roof, what the hell am I supposed to think?"

"You're not just mentioning his name. You're insinuating a relationship, completely different than just saying his name."

"I'm sorry. You're right." He growled and rubbed his face with his hands. "I just don't want to be in love with a woman who's in love with another man ever again."

"So, you do love her?" Sarah asked, patting his knee like you'd comfort a friend.

Doc shook his head. "Let's just eat our pizza and watch our movie."

"You can be honest with me; I can take it." Sarah cupped his chin and forced him to look at her. "I know what it's like to love

123

the wrong person."

"Rich?" He asked.

She nodded slowly, her palms suddenly sweaty. Sharing was dangerous, murky waters.

He took her hand in his. "Do you still...love him?"

Sighing, Sarah said, "I loved him when I was young and stupid, but not now. I suppose I do have an attitude toward him, because it sucked to be a kid with a broken heart and him not give a damn. Maybe it's my ego. He hurt me. He made me feel used, and I hate him for it."

Doc wrapped an arm around her shoulders and pulled her close, kissing her forehead. Then he looked down at her, his hands cradling her face. His eyes were bluer than she remembered. "That I understand all too well. Trust me, Sarah, I won't ever hurt you."

She wrapped her hands around his forearms and squeezed. "I do trust you. But I have to wonder, what happens if Angie ever gets divorced?"

"Honestly? She only uses me to get Donnie jealous. Has since we were in college. Donnie has always been her obsession. She comes running to me when they have a fight. I get her through it, and then she goes back to him. So, I'm done with all that, and I'm with you. I am with you, right, Sarah?"

A wave of dizziness hit her and she had to close her eyes. Images of Rich then and now filled her head, and her heart felt like it squeezed to a slow thud.

Before she could answer, he kissed her. It wasn't the usual, light-hearted lip brushes they often shared. This kiss was a game changer. Sarah instantly thought of pushing him away and running. But where would she run?

To Rich?

Never.

She knew Doc didn't love her, and she didn't love him, but

she trusted him. She knew he would keep his word. He would never hurt her. With a sigh, she leaned into him, kissing him back with as much feeling as she could muster. When his hands moved under her shirt, her breath caught in her throat and her elbow blocked him, but she said nothing. It was time to decide. To get in or get out.

Chapter 19

The pounding on the front door made them both jump. Doc was up in a flash, assuming a calm demeanor in seconds. Glancing back at Sarah, he paused at the door until she had her shirt pulled back down and properly adjusted.

Tonya stepped into the living room. "Hate to intrude, but can I borrow Sarah for a bit?"

Sarah slipped her shoes on as she looked at Doc wide-eyed, clueless.

"I suppose," Doc said with a shrug.

"Grab your jacket, Sarah," Tonya ordered.

"My jacket?" Sarah was about to complain, but then she thought of Rich. What if something had happened to him or one of the girls? Grabbing her jacket, she pulled it on. Brushing a kiss against Doc's cheek, she assured him, "I'll be back in a bit."

"Pick up where we left off?" he asked with a grin.

"If you're lucky," Sarah whispered.

"Oh, I'm lucky."

Doc was about to pull her in for a kiss, but Tonya yanked Sarah's arm toward the door. As she dragged her toward her car, she said, "This is all wrong, you know that, right?"

"What's all wrong?"

"You and Doc. It's just not right. I don't like it."

Sarah stopped dead in her tracks. "Excuse me? I don't think I asked for your opinion."

Tonya let go and circled the vehicle. "Well, I offered it anyhow. Get in. I need your help."

Sarah's pride told her to turn around and go back to her beer and her movie, but her feet headed toward Tonya's minivan. Climbing in, she buckled up. Tonya started the engine and rolled out of Doc's driveway.

Once they were on the main road, Sarah asked, "What's this all about?"

"Angie and Donnie…and Mandy…and Rich."

"What about them?" Damn if it didn't irritate the hell out of her that Rich's name made her heart do a little somersault.

"Donnie cleaned Angie's dad out. Stole all the money from the register and the safe. Her dad has cancer, you know."

"No, I didn't know. That sucks."

"I know. That's why Angie doesn't want to go to the police. She doesn't want her dad to worry. She just needs to get the money back before he opens the garage on Monday."

"And I'm supposed to help how? And what does this have to do with Rich?"

"I'll get to that. First, did you know your lover boy back there was making out with Angie at work? Tonight, in an ER closet… and yet Rich is the scumbag."

Sarah swallowed the lump in her throat. "Doc told me he was with her."

"Did he mention he had his tongue down her throat? Shit, Sarah. Those two play cat and mouse all the time. You think a relationship with Rich would be complicated—for a smart girl, you're pretty stupid."

"I'm going to let that slide because you're upset and Rich is your cousin, so you don't see it from my point of view."

"You do realize, when Angie said they kissed, that's code for affair, right? That Donnie asking for DNA might not have been uncalled for?"

"Holy shit, Tonya! I thought you two were friends?"

Tonya sighed and gripped the wheel. "She is my friend. I love her no matter what, but she's not perfect. And I'm pissed at her. She creates these messes and leaves them for everyone else to clean up."

"Like what? What the hell is going on?"

"Okay, here's the story in a nutshell. You may want to take notes...Mandy thought she and Rich were going to be a thing, so she dumped Donnie. Donnie then panicked and he dumped Angie. Angie ran to Doc, and while they were making out in the broom closet, Donnie goes to her parents' garage and robs the place blind. Then Donnie takes the money to Mandy to beg her not to leave him. Mandy takes the money and then tells Donnie to go to hell—she has Rich. Donnie then realizes he's committed a felony—I think stealing over $30,000 is a felony—so he calls Angie and tells her what a stupid thing he's done. Angie ditches Doc and runs to help Donnie. Ditched and lonely once again, Doc accepts the consolation prize—that's you—and Rich is now back on Mandy's radar."

"What about Rich?" Sarah tried not to sound too interested.

"Well, seems Donnie punched Mandy, thus putting her back on Rich's plate because he feels like he has to protect her."

Sarah gasped. "Donnie punched her?"

"Yes. Blacked her eye."

"Wow. Didn't see that coming."

"Evidently neither did she," Tonya snickered.

Sarah shook her head. "You're pretty sick, you know that?"

"Yeah, well, I hate that bitch. I won't lie about that."

"Did she call the police?"

"No, she ran to Rich. Asked him to let her stay with him, *because she was so afraid*...boo hoo."

"What did Rich say?" Sarah's stomach tightened. She knew that tramp would end up in his bed—probably tonight.

"He sent the girls to my house and took the tramp in. What do you think he did?"

Sarah shrugged. Her face was hot, and her voice lost.

"Now," Tonya said, rolling to a stop and turning onto a quiet back street of Dodd that led to neat ranch houses lined up in rows. "Donnie hurried back to Angie to proclaim his love and get her to help him. Mandy has Angie's dad's life savings. And the homewrecking twit is holed up at my dumbass cousin's house. Nothing is right in my world right now."

"So, what am I supposed to do about any of this?"

"First, we're getting Angie's money back."

Sarah's jaw dropped. She hoped Tonya was joking, but she wasn't. Her hands were tight to the wheel at a perfect 10 and 2 o'clock.

"We are taking Angie's money back?"

"Yep, Donnie said it is in a shoe box under Mandy's bed. Thirty thousand in cash."

"You're suggesting we what, break in?"

"No, we're sneaking in through an open skylight."

"That's called breaking in!"

"The slut took Angie's money. She needs it back."

"Why doesn't Donnie get it?"

"Last time he tried, he punched her in the face. Do I need to go back over this? She claims it was a gift, and she's not obligated to return it. So, it's up to us to get it."

"Oh well, I guess since we're adding theft to the B and E, we're hunky dory."

"Hey look, I'd do it myself, but I'm too fat to fit through the skylight. You, my dear, are the skinny one in the group."

"No. No way in hell. I'd get disbarred—after I get out of prison."

Angie pulled into a driveway. "This is Michelle's house. People will think we are here for girl's night out, so we have an airtight alibi. Mandy's house is only a block from here. We can cut through back yards, grab the money, and be out in time for margaritas at eleven...or you can go back to making out with Doc. Just remember he'd have screwed Angie in that hospital closet if Donnie hadn't called. But, it's your choice. It'd be the wrong choice, but still it's your choice." Tonya sighed as she grabbed her purse off the floorboards. "Look, I'm not an idiot. I know where all of this is going to lead...and frankly, it sucks. You're going to be with Doc; Mandy is *finally* going to get her claws into Rich; and Donnie and Angie will stay together. But it doesn't have to be that way. If you were to lock down Rich, Mandy would take Donnie off everyone's hands, and Angie and Doc could live happily ever after. If not, he'll marry you—the consolation prize."

"Would you stop calling me that?"

"If the shoe fits...."

Sarah shook her head. "There are obvious flaws to your logic. Angie could have left Donnie forever ago, and never does. And Rich...well, if you had seen him and Mandy together last night, you'd think they were perfect for each other."

"You won't be happy with Doc. Your heart's not in it."

Sarah grabbed the door handle. "Can we drop the discussion of my love life so I can go commit my first felony?"

Tonya laughed. "Sure thing, girlfriend."

They went into Michelle's. Michelle and Mary were ready for them. It was like a game of future-convict dress-up party. They had black clothes, stocking caps, and black face paint for Sarah.

"Aren't you coming with me?" Sarah asked Tonya.

Tonya added another dollop of blackening to Sarah's nose as she shook her head. "I told you, I can't fit."

"I'm supposed to go alone?"

"What good would me going do?"

Sarah's voice was shrill. "I don't know…moral support?"

"I'll be on the walkie-talkie. I'll tell you what to do, where to go."

Tonya took a rag and dusted all the fingerprints off the walkie-talkie before handing it to a now black gloved Sarah.

"Now, do you have any loose jewelry or anything you might drop that would identify you?"

Sarah pulled off her diamond ear rings and handed them to Jessie. "I have my cell phone, but I'm keeping it. I'll just tuck it in my pocket."

"I don't know about that…." Tonya frowned.

"No, I'm not going without it. I can't let my only lifeline be a pair of Ninja Turtle walkie-talkies. Where did you get these anyhow, the Dollar Tree?"

"I drove all the way to the Toys R Us in Middleton to get these. I even paid cash, so there's no link to me ever buying them."

"You're scaring me, Tonya." Sarah said as they pulled the knit hat over her hair, tucking in the stray blonde hairs.

"Let's just say, you don't screw with one of my friends, even the slutty ones, and get away with it," Tonya said.

Sarah caught a glimpse of herself in the hall mirror. She looked like a discount store cat burglar.

Chapter 20

Crossing through the yards took Sarah more than a few minutes. Tonya had not taken fences, dogs, and motion lights into consideration in her planning. Each time Sarah came face to face with a mutt, or stood like a wraith in a spotlight, she lost time.

"Have you made it to the house with the in-ground pool? Mandy's house is right next to it," Tonya's crackly voice asked.

"Not yet."

"What's taking you so long?"

"Umm, excuse me? There are dogs all over this neighborhood!"

Laughter, then silence. Sarah was sweating. Her face felt itchy from all the paint, but she kept moving forward. She was part of a sisterhood. Breaking into another sister's house? *No,* she thought, *home wrecking hussies have no sisters.*

She hit the house with the pool, and of course, it had a freaking privacy fence. Sarah had to go around the entire perimeter of the yard. As she rounded the left side of the fence, she was immediately in grass up to her knees. Evidently $30,000 wasn't enough to buy a lawn mower.

The house was lit up. Sarah called Angie. "Hey, you sure she's not home? The place is lit up."

"She just leaves them on. Don't worry. I just called Rich—

she's still there. He was making them dinner."

"Great," Sarah said as unwanted images made her want to barf.

"Jealous?"

"Bite me."

Sneaking through the yard, past the broken kid toys and faded lawn furniture, she stepped onto the back deck. A rotten board broke under her foot, and she had to do a quick side step to keep from falling through. Peeking through a hazy window, Sarah frowned. It wasn't like her to be judgmental, but the woman was a pig. Dirty dishes were piled high in the sink. Sarah pulled on the back door. It was locked. So were the windows.

"How do I get in?" She asked Angie.

"The roof."

"The roof?" Sarah looked up at the roof. It was at least ten feet above her head. "How the hell am I supposed to do that?"

"Grab a lawn chair."

Sarah put the walkie-talkie in her pocket. The tallest thing on the deck was the picnic table, but even from there, it was impossible. There was a tree by the house, a skinny little dogwood. Sarah checked it out. It looked sturdy enough, she supposed. Bracing a foot in the wedge of the trunk, she hoisted herself up and started to climb. She made it quickly to the top—all her Zumba classes paid off after all. There was a branch that hung right over the roof. All she had to do was shimmy right over and drop down on the roof. Easy as that.

Sort of. She didn't count on the cracking sounds making her heart race and her hands shake. She knew the damn thing was going to break, and she'd probably fall through the roof, break her back, and head off to prison in a wheelchair. Did they make handicapped accessible prisons? Was there much need?

Focus, Sarah!

Off the limb, she crawled across the roof toward the skylight.

A light shone up through it. Sarah peered down into the tramp's own den of iniquity. Her bed was unmade, and the sheets looked twisted and well worn. Sarah bet those sheets had seen a lot of action. An unwelcome image of Rich getting a notch on her headboard made her cringe. The skylight was closed, but it was easily pried open. How in the hell did Tonya know it would be so easy?

Once the little portal was open, Sarah swung her legs over the hole. She wasn't sure how she was supposed to get in from there. Just drop in, on the bed? Easing herself into the house, she clung for a few seconds by her fingertips before dropping. When she hit the bed, her knees buckled and she fell, rolling off onto the floor. The walkie-talkie crackled and squealed, then Tonya said, "Hurry. Rich is taking her home. He just called John, and asked if he could leave his girls at our house for the night."

"What the hell? If he's taking her home now, why...? Never mind."

"A little bangity-bangity, maybe?"

"He could've banged her at his house."

"Last time he tried that, you interrupted."

Sarah felt hot. Damn black stuff was practically choking her. She looked under the bed. "I don't see a shoe box."

"It's there. It has to be."

Sarah crawled around the bed, thankful for the gloved hands on the crusty carpet. She was about to give up, but then she saw it. Sliding it out from under the bed, she flipped the lid open. Holy crap. Stacks of cash.

"Donnie, you moronic troglodyte," she whispered.

Pulling the money out of the box, she stuffed it in the black bag Tonya had fashioned for her. Once it was filled, she shoved the bag into her jacket. She looked four — no, maybe five months pregnant.

She was about to head out of the house by the back door, but headlights flashed through the windows. She ran to the hall, but the front of the house was well lit, complete with lights blazing from the street and the yard.

She heard a car door close—muffled voices, a man and a woman. Sarah pulled the dresser under the skylight. Fear must have spiked her adrenaline, because she was able to move the dresser like a she-Hercules. As she climbed to the top, the front door opened and closed.

"I really appreciate you coming back with me, Rich. You don't know how much it means to me. I've just been a bundle of nerves all night. Can I get you a drink?"

"I better get home."

"Can you take just a minute? Let me check the house? Donnie waited in my bedroom for me this afternoon."

"Yeah, I can do that."

Sarah's heart leaped. *Oh dear God, I'm about to go to jail.*

With a speed Sarah didn't realize she was capable of, she climbed on top of the dresser and pulled herself through the hole, closing the skylight behind her. Crawling across the roof, she moved much quicker than before. She grabbed the closest limb and scurried across. Her quickened speed and lack of cautious weight distribution made the limb creak. Before she could utter a prayer or a curse, the limb snapped. It hit the roof and bounced, landing on the electric line. The line sagged, holding the weight of the broken limb and Sarah for a moment, before it too snapped. Sparks danced across the roof, and the loosened line whipped against the house like an irate snake.

Sarah only got to watch it for a moment before she fell. She tried not to scream, grasping the limb like a teddy bear and holding on tight until her body hit the earth. It felt like her back was broken, and she couldn't pull in a single breath.

Chapter 21

When the power line fell, the house went instantly dark. Rich came out the back door and looked around, then yelled to Mandy, "Looks like a tree limb knocked out your power. You need to call the power company before it sparks a fire."

Sarah got to her feet and took off. Her body felt like she'd just been beaten with a tree limb, but she still made good time moving across the yard. It wasn't until she came to the first fence she needed to climb that she was screwed. She couldn't lift her arm, much less hoist her weight over a fence with it. She circled the perimeter instead, only to find the next yard lit up like a used car lot. Rows of vehicles filled the once-empty space. A couple stepped up onto the back deck and opened the door, and the sounds of a party filtered out into the night air.

Sarah couldn't risk traipsing through the makeshift parking lot dressed like a two-bit burglar. She'd just have to take the road back to Michelle's. Moving quickly through the damp grass, Sarah rounded the edge of the house next door to Mandy's and was greeted with the sounds of sirens in the distance. Of course, Mandy had probably called them. The woman was nothing if not a pain in the ass. As the sound came closer, someone yelled fire from the neighbor's yard and within seconds, the party emptied out of the house, heading for Mandy's. The fire truck's air horn blew its abrasive honk, making Sarah jump as it rounded the corner headed toward her. Blue lights followed red, as police cars provided an emergency escort.

"Shit," Sarah said to the now-busy night.

She tried to wipe the black off her face with the sleeve of her sweatshirt, trying to look a little less culpable. Reaching into her sweatshirt pocket for the walkie-talkie, she found the pocket empty. It must be laying in Mandy's yard somewhere. All she had was her cell phone. The only local contact numbers were Doc and Rich. She took a deep breath and called Rich.

"Rich? I need help…."

"Sarah, where are you?"

Sarah looked around. A crowd had gathered in the street and yards surrounding Mandy's, all watching as sporadic flames danced shyly across her roof before the groan of wood made the structure collapse, sending sparks into the night that could have been called beautiful if they weren't unintentional arson.

Sarah swallowed hard. "I'm at Mandy's."

"You're where?" She assumed the question was rhetorical, because he didn't give her time to answer before adding, "I'll be there in a second. Can you meet me in the alley behind her garage?"

"Yeah." *Damn, why hadn't she thought of the alley?*

Siren sounds grew louder, then quieted as they came to a stop on Mandy's road. The red lights flashed, creating ominous patterns on the surrounding houses. Sarah groaned as she made her way to the garage. She hadn't meant to cause this much trouble.

In the alley, she wedged herself between two garbage cans and squatted in the shadows.

Rich was there in minutes. He stopped the truck and hopped out. He didn't say a word as he approached. With a shake of his head, he lifted her off her feet and carried her to his truck.

137

He set her in the bed and threw a tarp over her. "I'm going to have to hide you. Seems you chose the night of the Bruins-Devils football game to go on your crime spree. There are cops at every intersection on Main Street directing traffic, and now they're also looking for an arsonist thief."

"I didn't mean to burn her house down—"

"It's not burned down. You just scorched the roof. Now, stay put, cover your face, and stay quiet."

They drove less than a half-mile before getting stopped at a road block. A police officer ordered him to halt by stepping into the middle of the road. She shined her flashlight around the truck and then leaned against the window to talk. "Hey, Rich."

"Hey, Mags. Sobriety check? Or did someone steal the Bo Bruin again?"

"Bo is fine and still standing at the stadium. Devils only cause mayhem when they win. Fortunately, they hardly ever win." Maggie paused for a lifetime before informing Rich, "No, we've just been asked to be on the look-out for suspicious activity. Seems someone broke into Mandy's house and set it on fire as they left."

"My Mandy? From The Recline? I just left there, like ten minutes ago. Her power line came down with a tree limb. I told her to call the electric company. It probably sparked a fire."

"That makes sense, but Mandy's insisting it was arson." Officer Maggie White slid her flashlight back into her belt.

"Well, I'll be damned. Is she all right?"

"She's fine. Says she smelled the smoke and got out."

"Why does she think it was set it on fire?"

"Mandy says the house was trashed, and they stole several thousand dollars from her."

"Several thousand, huh? I didn't realize I was paying her that well," Rich said.

"Some women are more resourceful than others," Officer

Maggie said with a chuckle. "I told Chief Ed it's going to be hard to prove she had a bunch of cash, much less catch whoever stole it, but he said to just make an effort so we can log in the report. So, that's what we're doing. Seems a lot of fuss for nothing, but Mandy seems to have the ear, or the what-not, of Mayor Turnbridge."

"That old fart? I doubt he could handle fifteen minutes with Mandy," Rich laughed.

"You men are so pathetic," Maggie said. "Falling all over yourselves for a bit of tail every man in this town has tugged. There are probably a hundred pissed off wives who'd happily burn her house to the ground. How are we supposed to find the ONE?"

"I suppose she's not as popular with the ladies as she is the men, that's for sure."

"You wouldn't happen to know where your cousin and her gal pals are tonight, would you?"

Rich took a breath. "Why, it's lady's night, Maggie. You should join them." Rich nodded toward the clock on his car radio. "Hell, by now they're probably loaded up with margaritas and bitching about men."

"I could do my fair share of bitching about men. What do you think of Donnie? Did you see what he did to Mandy's face? Asshole. I'll tell ya', he was my first guess, if he wasn't still sitting in a cell for the assault. He blamed Angie. He said he gave Mandy some money, and figured Angie was out for revenge."

"Come on, Maggie, you know Angie better than that."

"What about Tonya?"

"Now, Tonya I'd suspect...if I didn't know she was at Michelle's all night."

"How about the new lady lawyer?"

"Why would Sarah have any interest in robbing Mandy?"

"True. Stupid hunch. I get these gut feelings, but they usually turn out to be way off. Wouldn't want to go accusing an attorney, right?"

"I guess not. Honestly, Sarah is such a cold fish, I couldn't imagine her even giving a damn about any of it."

"And you were with Mandy?"

"Yep. Couldn't have been me. Hell, how do we even know it's arson? I'm still betting on the power line."

"Ain't that the truth." Maggie leaned into the window and lowered her voice. "Between you and me, I hope someone got Angie the money back. I'd sure hate for her father to have another worry on his plate with the cancer and all."

"Maybe Mandy made up the money story and lit the place up herself. Hell, how will you know?"

"Well, let me know if you hear anything," she said, giving the top of his truck a knock as he drove off.

When he pulled up to the alley behind Sarah's, he lifted her out, tarp and all, and threw her over his shoulder. Every bump as he went up the steps caused her to bite her lip in pain. Letting himself in, he immediately shut all the window blinds, then went to her. She bit her lip against the tears.

"What in the hell did you do?"

"I...I fell out of the tree and hit something," Sarah said.

Rich went to the kitchen and got a warm towel doused in dish soap, and wiped the black paint off her face.

"Tree climbing in all black and face paint? Skinniest one had to go through the skylight, I assume?"

"So, they said." *So, he knows there's a skylight in the bedroom. Bastard.*

"Let me see," he said, pulling her black hoodie up, gently easing it over her shoulder as she cried out in pain. Rich shook his head and scowled at her, but his hands were gentle as he cradled her elbow and tugged gently on her upper arm. The pain in her shoulder eased to a dull ache, but the throbbing was gone.

"You dislocated it."

"It feels much better, thank you." Standing there in her bra and a much-too-thin undershirt, she felt naked. And she hurt like hell. Like her skin was on fire.

"Holy shit, Sarah. What did you do, roll in a cactus patch?"

"Stupid bimbo. Who has that many cactus in Indiana? Grow some damn marigolds, for crying out loud."

"I need to get tweezers." He held out his hand to her. "Come on, may as well get you comfortable. This could take all night."

"Oh, brother." Sarah followed behind him to her bedroom. Settling herself on the bed, he left the room. "My whole back burns," Sarah whined to the empty room.

Rich appeared with a shot of whiskey, cortisone cream, and a pair of tweezers. He handed her the whiskey. "This is for you."

She drank it in sips.

"Just swallow it. One shot, down the hatch."

Sarah tried to toss it back, and ended up sputtering and choking, but her whole body did feel instantly warm.

"Good girl," Rich said, taking the glass from her and setting it on her night stand. Then he settled himself on the bed behind her, making the bed creak with his weight. He cleared his throat before saying, "I need you to take your shirt off."

Pulling it off, she winced. Rich felt the shoulder and down her arm. It was at the elbow that Sarah let out a squeal. "Damn it, Sarah. You may have broken your arm."

"No, it's okay. Just a sprain."

"You need an X-ray."

"I'm fine. I swear. All but the cactus needles."

Carefully he pulled her undershirt shirt over her head. The bag of money was stuffed in her front waistband. Rich pulled it free and set it on the bed. "I'll drop this off to Angie later. Better not to have it in your possession…since you ladies seem to be in the suspects' cross hairs."

"I don't know why they'd assume it was us."

Rich chuckled. "Seriously? Angie's dad has his life savings emptied and supposedly given to his daughter's husband's girlfriend…and you ask how the law couldn't put the puzzle pieces together?"

Sarah sighed and nestled her chin into a pillow she pulled off her bed. Her words were muffled. "Well, they have no proof."

"Why did you do it?"

She shrugged, wincing as the movement shoved her shoulder into the tweezers. She took a suck of air.

"Hold still. This is hard enough without you wiggling all over."

"I'm not wiggling. I shrugged. You asked me why I did it, and the honest truth is…I don't know." The pillow cradled her cheek. Rich's hands were warm against her back as he tweezed away the spines. It was relaxing, like acupuncture. She let out a happy sigh, closing her eyes and sinking farther into the pillow. "It seemed wrong for Mandy to ruin Angie's marriage and take her money."

"You want to lay down?"

Looking back at Rich, she suddenly felt naked. "Why?"

"Calm down. You looked like you were about to go to sleep."

"No, I was just relaxing."

"Who knew rolling in a cactus patch could be so good?"

"Mmmm…who knew?" she said, closing her eyes. Warm breath tickled her skin as he moved closer to see the tiny hairs of the cacti spines.

"I think I got most of them." He ran a hand over her back. "How's that feel?"

Delicious. She shook the thought out of her head. *What is wrong with me?* Her mind was filled with images that made her cheeks turn pink and her conscience scream. *Doc. I am meant to be with Doc in a sensible, stable relationship.* Hugging her pillow tighter, her voice came out in a course whisper. "It's good. Feels good. Thanks."

Taking another couple of slow sweeps of her back with the cortisone cream, Rich gave her shoulders a squeeze. "You're damned lucky you weren't electrocuted. That was the stupidest damned thing to do."

Sarah shrugged.

Turning her to face him, he stared at her, his brows pulled in. "You could have died."

"Oh no, and before I named my heir," Sarah said with a laugh.

"Real funny. If something had happened to you...." He looked worried. Her lips parted, but no words came out. He looked nineteen again, sitting cross-legged on her sunny yellow comforter, tweezers still in hand.

Giving his leg a pat, she said, "I'm fine. And thanks. I really appreciate the help. Not just with the cactus, but picking me up, offering to hide the money." No wonder she'd never known his eye color. It seemed to be shifting with his mood, from hazel to green, to a golden brown.

"Well," he said, leaning toward her. "I'm glad you called me."

Slowly, ever so slowly, he came closer. She could feel the warmth from his body, breathe in his scent...bubblegum with a hint of smoke from the bar. A little closer and she could smell mint. A smile tugged at her lips as she wondered if he intended to have fresh breath. If he hoped to....

She didn't need to wonder a second longer.

He kissed her. Slow, patient lips turned her bones soft, so her body had no choice but to lean into his. Shoving the pillow to the floor, Rich pulled her onto his lap. Deepening the kiss, his hand moved up her naked spine, sending electric chills across her skin until it came to rest at the nape of her neck.

Pulling in his breath with her gasp, she held tight, wrapping her arms around his shoulders and her legs around his waist. "Arm's fine," she said against his lips.

"Good," he said as his lips trailed kisses from her throat to the tops of her breasts. Brushing a coarse cheek against tender skin, he looked up at her. The breath caught in her throat as images of what could have been and should have been flooded her mind. She was venturing into dangerous territory.

But for this moment, she didn't care.

Kissing the top of his head, she pressed him closer to her heart. In a single move he laid her back, towering above her on bent knees. His hands moved slowly up the curves of her thighs to her hips, pausing for a second at the waist of her jeans. As his thumbs brushed the silky skin above her belly button, her hips arched against him.

In an instant, she was cradled against him as he kissed her. Starting at her lips, he trailed hot kisses down her throat, to her collarbone, and between her breasts. She wanted to feel him. Running her hands under his shirt, she relished the feel of the silky skin and hard muscles of his chest. He felt solid, warm…his heart beat against her hand. Pushing his shirt over his head, she pressed herself against his naked skin. That brought out a growl as he slid her bra strap down her arm, kissing flesh as he exposed it.

Soon, the lacy material was on the floor and deft hands stroked her breast, while nibbling lips and a whiskered chin sent electric down her spine as he tasted the sensitive skin on her neck. Wrapping a leg around his hips, she thought she might lose it from the feel of his body gyrating against hers. The muscles in his back rippled as he moved, exploring her body. She couldn't think of anything she'd ever wanted more.

He leaned on an arm and looked down at her, gently stroking her cheek. "This what you want?"

No was the smart answer, but her body didn't care about smart. She nodded and pulled him back to her. His kiss was hard, almost painful, but his hands slid down her body, slipped into her still buttoned jeans, and squeezed her hip before popping open the button of her jeans. Nibbling on her ear, he whispered, "You have anything?"

"Have anything?" She closed her eyes and wished he'd shut up. "Like a disease?"

He laughed, bending forward and kissing the contour of her waist. "Protection?"

"No. Nothing." She sighed. Just once in her life, couldn't it play out movie perfect? "You?"

"I have one," he said, rolling onto his side. Pulling his wallet out of his pocket, he fished it out. It was a novelty condom with the *Star Wars* light saber, and the inscription, *Luke, I am not your father.* "I got this for Christmas about ten years ago, and never found a girl I thought was worth opening it for. You trust a ten-year-old-condom?"

Pulling herself up on her elbows, her stomach muscles tightening with the effort, she shook her head. "Seriously? Ten years? What were you going to use last night?" The thought of him just as lost and horny for Mandy made her jump up and grab a shirt from her night stand. "Oh my God, what was I thinking? This is insanity."

"What? No. I can run down the street. Come on, you have to admit, we are pretty damned perfect."

"Bullshit. You were just as intent on nailing Mandy last night. Oh my God, what's wrong with me?"

"Nothing is wrong with you. And I don't want her. I could have stayed with her tonight, but I didn't. I've felt like shit since I saw you last night. You're special to me, Sarah. I want you, not her."

"So says the guy with the hard-on. Forget it, Rich, I am more suited to a life with someone like—"

"Don't say it."

"Doc," she said, out of pure spite. For a moment there, she'd felt like they were meant to be together. But she was no different than Mandy. The only thing that made her special was that she was the one who was available.

"Damn it, Sarah." He stood, grabbing his shoes off the floor and digging keys from his pocket. He looked grim. "You know what your problem is? You have all the answers, and you have everything all figured out. Everything for you goes by some stupid, bullshit plan. I don't even know why I tried. You're so uptight and stuck in your own head, I'm sure you've turned into a lousy lay anyhow."

Sarah moved closer, going toe to toe with him. "What the hell does that mean, *lousy lay*?"

"It means you can't have fun in the sack if everything always has to go according to plans. Sometimes things are just better unplanned, with a little spontaneity. But not you, Sarah, no sir. For you, life has to be neatly laid out. No interference. No interruptions. God help anyone who steps between you and your perfect little plans."

Her brain was too full of all the ways spontaneity could ruin your life. Horrible memories that came flooding, causing her to feel like she was being punched in the gut. He had no clue, and she could never explain it to him, so she slapped him. Her hand screamed from the contact it made with his cheek. He looked at her and frowned, barely moved by her assault.

"I only want you to ask yourself one question." His jaw muscle twitched. "When you were in trouble tonight, why didn't you call Doc?"

Her face burned like she was the one slapped. She didn't have to explain herself to him. Truthfully? She had no answer. Her throat was growing thick and her eyes burned. Without another word, she stormed to her bathroom and slammed the door. It wasn't until she heard her apartment door slam and Rich's footfalls going down her steps that she slid to the floor and allowed the tears to flow.

Chapter 22

Work. That's what Sarah did best. She didn't even try to sleep after her and Rich's romantic disaster. She showered, changed into yoga pants and a loose button up, and headed to her office. Setting a pot of coffee to brew, she started working on the cases she had coming in the next few weeks. There was nothing substantial or exciting, but the client list was growing.

Her front doorbell chimed — someone was here. It was too late for clients. She rolled a kink out of her neck before rising to answer the door. As she made her way through the office, she noticed the sun was bright. Good lord, it was the next day. Her mind must have been very preoccupied.

Nearing the glass door, she recognized the face and walked a bit faster. *Kari.*

Sarah swung the door open. "Kari, hey, what brings you here on a Sunday?"

The girl looked over her shoulder and bit her lip.

"Come on in," Sarah said, escorting her through the office to the little kitchenette. "Can I get you anything? Hot cocoa? A pop?"

"No, I'm fine. I, uh, I just need some advice, and like I saw on TV that if you're a lawyer, you can't tell people what I tell you, right?"

Sarah cringed and twisted her hands together. "Technically, you're a minor. You tell me something that could cause harm to yourself or someone else, I'm obligated to tell. But Kari," she said as she pulled the girl down in the seat next to her. "Your dad loves you. There's nothing you can't tell him."

Kari shook her head and twisted a lock of hair. "Not this."

Sarah bit her lip. A plethora of possibilities danced through her head. Drugs. Sex. Pregnancy. Pedophilia. Sarah gasped. "Jess…um, your mom, her husband, he hasn't…."

"No, nothing like that…exactly."

Sarah's hands clenched, but she reminded herself to stay calm. It wouldn't help Kari if she thought Sarah was angry and misconstrue that anger as disappointment in the child sitting across from her. She asked cautiously, "What do you mean, *not exactly*?"

"I did something stupid. Really stupid." Kari chewed on her lip. "And my dad…he taught me to be smarter. He trusts me, and I…." Kari shook her head and said no more.

Sarah gave her hand a squeeze. "Listen to me, Kari. I know your dad well enough to know there is nothing, absolutely nothing, that you could do to make him not love you."

"I know," Kari said, breaking down into tears. Sarah allowed her to cry a moment as she got up and got her some paper towels. Taking her seat, Sarah said nothing as she handed them to the girl.

"Thanks," she said, wiping her tears and blowing her nose.

Once Kari seemed calm, Sarah asked her again, "What happened?"

Kari sniffed, rolling a piece of the paper towel nervously in her fingers. "First, you've got to promise me you won't tell my dad. Or anybody."

Sarah took a deep breath and promised, "I won't say anything."

"Never? No matter what? Especially not to my dad."

Sarah cringed inwardly. She knew this was a promise she shouldn't make, but she still said, "I swear. Whatever you tell me is between you and me. No one else. Though, I must be honest with you — you are hamstringing me. I'm sure this — whatever it is — could be handled better if your dad knew."

"No," Kari practically yelled the word at her. "You don't understand. My dad is the last person I want to know. My dad does everything for us. He's a smart guy. He could be doing something more interesting than running a bar and doing construction."

"I think your dad is happy with his life."

"He's happy because he thinks he has good kids. All the long hours. All the years he never had his own life. He did all that for my sister and me. How do you think he'd feel if he knew all that didn't mean crap? That even though he did everything right, his daughter is still a screw up?"

"Come on." Sarah's tone was sharp. "Listen to me, Kari. You're young. When you get to be my age, and you have a whole laundry list of crap you've done wrong, you realize there are very few foul-ups so bad that you can't recover."

Kari rolled her eyes. "Like you've screwed up."

"Sweetheart, I have messed up so many things in my life, I'm not sure I could count them all."

"Was dumping my dad one of them? One of your screw ups, I mean?"

Sarah rubbed her nose as she tried to manage an answer that was truthful, but not exactly honest. "I'd say it was a misunderstanding…because we didn't talk. Because I didn't trust him enough. Or maybe it was a matter of having too much pride to be honest with him."

Kari gave her a small grin. "Nice try, but I still don't want him to know."

"Damn. I thought for sure that would work." Sarah's hands shook, so she locked them together in her lap. *What if I had been honest with Rich sixteen years ago?* It was a dangerous question, because no matter what the answer, all she gained was regret and shame.

"Did you love him…back then?"

"Yes. I did."

"And now?"

Sarah took a deep breath. "Promise to never tell?"

"Seriously?" Kari laughed.

"Of course."

"I promise."

"The truth is yes, I loved him then, and I love him now."

"So, why? Why are you driving him crazy? He really likes you. He's planning you a surprise party tomorrow, you know."

Sarah's eyebrows popped up and her heart swelled. "Really?"

"Yup. It's his last-ditch effort. Is he wasting his time?"

Sarah sighed. "It's complicated."

"No, not really. My dad may be a lot of things, but complicated isn't one of them."

Sarah realized how two-faced she was being. Encouraging Kari to be honest and trusting Rich to forgive without judging, but then refusing to do the same herself. But there was a huge difference. Kari was his child. Unique and irreplaceable. Sarah was just one woman of many who would happily keep Rich company.

Barely above a whisper, Sarah said, "I suppose I'm in the same boat as you. There are things I've done…. If he knew, he'd never want me."

Kari studied her for a minute. "Like what kind of things?"

Shaking her head, Sarah stood and made a pot of coffee. "We're supposed to be talking about you."

"Please? I already promised not to tell."

"Oh hell," Sarah said with a grimace. She rubbed her face and let out a groan. The coffee maker started to gurgle and spit and slowly dump its dark magic into the pot. Sarah filled herself a cup half-way, then added some water from the tap.

"Come on, Sarah. Mine is probably way worse than yours."

"Fine. I'll tell you." Sarah gripped her mug in both hands. "I didn't come back to Dodd because I missed the area. I had a really good job in Indianapolis, making a lot of money, but I had to leave because I had an affair with my boss."

"Oh my God, that's nothing. People have affairs all the time."

"He was married."

"Yeah, that's bad. Did you know he was married?"

Sarah shook her head. "Not until his wife caught us."

"By caught you, do you mean she heard rumors, or…?"

"In the act. In his office. That's how I *met* his wife." Sarah's cheeks felt like they were on fire.

Kari gave her a sympathetic look. "Aunt Tonya says you caught Dad with Mandy. I'm sure he feels just as mortified. You guys could call it even."

The naiveté of the girl's simplistic determination caught Sarah by surprise. The two situations were hardly equal. Sarah frowned. "That's just one of many. I once had a boyfriend trick me into carrying cocaine into the country for him. If my mother didn't have a slew of powerful contacts, I'd probably have spent lots of time in prison."

"Now, that one is just funny. Dad would never hold that against you."

Sarah wished that was the end of her list. The worst of the unwelcome memories flashed through her head. Had she made better decisions—

"You okay, Sarah?" Kari asked.

Shaking off the memory, Sarah nodded. "Fine. I'm fine. Now, we've pretty-well covered everything you didn't come here to talk about. How about you tell me what happened with Phil?"

"Good redirect. Sharp. I like that."

"Dittos back to you. Now stop sidestepping and distracting and tell me what's going on."

"Okay, okay," Kari said.

The girl's shoulders relaxed. Sarah was glad to see confessing her own humiliations did seem to take some of the weight off the girl. Maybe Sarah could have been a good mom.

"My mom introduced me to this guy, Brandon, during one of my first visits. Totally cute. I mean, seriously perfect all the way down to his six-pack abs. Way out of my league, but he seemed to really like me."

"Was he your age?"

"Almost. He's seventeen."

"Did your dad ever meet him?"

"No. He has kind of long hair and a tattoo on his forearm of a cross and a rose. I figured my dad would take one look at him and have a coronary. Mom agreed. Dad would never understand Brandon. Mom told me he could be our secret. And at first, I thought it was great. Anytime I was at Mom's, I could see Brandon. She'd even let him spend the night."

Sarah groaned inwardly. The girl was probably pregnant.

"But after a while, I started to get bored with him. He was good looking and all, but he wasn't real bright. And he'd flip his hair, like this." Kari gave her head a small shake, flipping her brown hair over her shoulder. "And I felt really bad lying to my dad. And like, when I was out on a date with Brandon, every time he'd say something stupid or flip his hair, I'd imagine what kind of joke my dad would make…I guess I just got bored. So, I told him I wanted to break up."

"I'm impressed. Smart girl. A guy needs to be something more than pretty."

"Yeah, well, that's when things got weird. Mom and Phil

153

have been planning to move back to California. They asked me to go with them. Of course, I said no. I wasn't leaving my dad."

"How'd she take that?"

"Mom said she understood. She was saddened by it, but wanted me to be happy. But then Phil…." Kari took a deep breath, looking paler than ever. "Phil came to my room, and he threw this package on my bed. He told me I might want to reconsider breaking my mother's heart. If I didn't care about her, maybe he wouldn't care about my dad."

"What's that supposed to mean?" Sarah asked.

"In the package was a video of Brandon and me having sex in the pool house. Phil says unless I go with my mom to California, he will send the video to my dad."

"Is he an idiot? Your dad will kill him."

"No, Sarah. Dad can't know. I'd rather go with Mom than let my dad down."

"He won't—"

"You don't even want him to know you, an adult, screwed your boss. How do you think it feels for me? It's not even like it's a rumor I can deny—Phil has proof. High quality digital proof."

Sarah closed her eyes and thought it over. All it would take was one call to the police and Phil Demkey would be behind bars for even owning that video, much less blackmailing a minor with it. So easy to get justice if a person was willing to face the humiliation of their own bad choices.

"You realize he could be sent to jail for this?"

"Would my dad find out?"

Sarah nodded.

"Then no," Kari said. "Help me find a way out of this where my dad never knows."

"I'll…." Sarah thought she might vomit. She'd really tied herself up nice and tight in a pretty little noose.

"Please, Sarah." Kari grabbed Sarah by the hand and

squeezed. "I know you understand. I know you know what it feels like to feel humiliated. I could see it on your face when you talked about your boss. I know you can find a way to help me."

"I do understand, but—"

"Would you want someone you loved to have a video of you getting screwed by your boss?"

"No, but—"

"And who's to say if Phil thinks he has nothing to lose, it won't end up on the net?"

"It would still be smart to tell your dad and go to the police."

Kari was on her feet, her face red, her teeth clenched. "You promised me."

"And I'll keep my promise. I swear," Sarah assured. "I said that was the smart thing to do, not what I will do. Trust me, sweetheart, I rarely do the smart thing."

Chapter 23

Picking up the phone, she called Rich and told him to come down to her office, that she needed to talk to him. As she hung up, Doc called.

"Hey, pretty lady."

"Hey yourself," Sarah said.

"What's wrong?" He asked. She had to give Doc bonus points for perception.

"Nothing's wrong. I just...well, I thought maybe we should talk."

"Don't like the sounds of that. Something happen?"

Images of rolling on her bed with Rich flashed through her head, and she felt warm. "No, it's nothing like that. Tough morning, is all."

"Bad case?"

"The worst."

"How about dinner tonight? A nice dinner out, with wine and all that."

"That's not necessary. I didn't get to bed until late and got up early, I may crash before nine."

"You and Tonya didn't have anything to do with the fire at Mandy's, did you? Angie was telling me about the unfortunate blaze."

Sarah rubbed the back of her neck. "I'm not going to prison for arson, I swear."

Doc laughed. "Good. Tell you what, I'll bring wine and dinner to your place. You get tired, you can crash. Don't want you driving home tired…unless, of course you want to just sleep over at my place?"

She had to end this. But she owed him more than a phone call break-up. Her front door chimed again, so she cut him off. "If you could just stop by my house, that would be great. Sorry, but I've got to go. There's someone at the door."

With that, she hung up. What was she going to do? When was she going to begin that uncomplicated life she'd imagined? She was in deeper shit than ever before.

"You wanted to see me?"

Rich's voice made her drop her mug on the floor. "Damn, you scared me."

"Thought you'd be expecting me, sorry."

"It's all right. I was expecting you. I just have a lot on my mind."

He didn't look any better rested than she did. And if he knew what she knew about his daughter, he'd really look distraught. Or he'd be looking at her through bars, because he would surely kill the bastard. He shoved his hands into his pockets and waited for her to talk.

Clearing her throat, she said, "Kari came to see me this morning. And she made me promise not to tell anyone what she told me."

He went from stressed to panicked. "Is she pregnant?"

Sarah shook her head. "No, no. It isn't that. It's…well, she's uncomfortable with her new step dad—not in a sexual way, she's just not happy. She wanted me to make it so she doesn't have to visit them."

He smiled and ran a hand through his hair. "That's all? Jesus,

157

I was imagining some pretty bad shit."

Sarah nodded, feeling rather calm, even though she'd finally came to terms with the fact that she was certainly going to hell for all the choices in her life. "Now, I told her that I don't think the courts will agree to that, unless I can prove they are bad influences."

"Do you think letting her sneak around with the boyfriend, if he really does exist, would be enough?"

"I...I have an idea, but I can't share it without betraying Kari."

"What she told you? How bad —?"

"It's something a sixteen-year-old girl thinks is a crisis. Sort of like a child with their first cold. She'll find out, in time, that it's something you get over. She's building her immunity to the shitty side of life."

"Was she drinking?"

"Rich, please. I shouldn't even have told you this much."

He took her hand in his and gave it a squeeze. "I'll stop asking questions. I'm just glad she had you to come to. I know my little girl. She's smart. And she's a good girl. You promise me this is nothing that's going to hurt her in the long run, then I'll let it go."

Sarah gripped the counter. All of this excitement after being up all night was catching up with her, and she was feeling a bit dizzy.

"Are you all right?"

She shook her head. "I was up all night. I'm not sure I'm thinking clearly."

"Look, if Kari is unhappy visiting with them, maybe she's picking up on something, you know? Like getting a gut feeling. I don't know anything about Phil. He could be an ax murderer for all I know. Let's be honest, I've let a lot of odd things slide just because I'm afraid of rocking the boat and because I wanted my girls to be happy. But clearly she's not happy?"

"Not happy at all."

"Then whatever you need to do, do it. I trust you."

"You do?"

"Of course. You and I might be a disaster, but I trust you more than their own mother to do right by my kids."

Chapter 24

You and I might be a disaster….

Rich's words haunted Sarah, which was so beyond irrational it was bordering on stupid. Distance between them was what she wanted. It was what she needed to maintain her sanity — to maybe one day have a normal life.

But a disaster? That was harsh. Unless she considered the quagmire she'd just leapt into with Kari agreeing to stay silent about the sex tape. It didn't take a crystal ball to know this would bite her in the ass eventually. It was that thought that kept her from getting anything done. She wouldn't trust herself to sort her silverware. There was so much going on in her head, it hurt. She needed advice, so she called her mom.

"Two calls in one month. To what do I owe this pleasure?"

"I can't call my mother without it being a sign of the apocalypse?"

"Now, that's a little drastic. I was thinking more that your pilgrimage through Dodd hell is driving you insane."

"It may be."

Her mother sighed. "I can get you a job here in a heartbeat. London is alive with things to do, especially for a young girl like yourself."

Sarah laughed. "Girl? Mother, seriously. I'll be thirty-three on Saturday."

"My God. You're that old?"

"Yes, I am *that old*. And I guess it's starting to bother me that in those thirty-three years, all I've managed to accomplish is a few scandals. I could die tomorrow and—"

"Then change it. Get your act together. Leave that Podunk town. It's killing you. There is absolutely nothing to be gained from rehashing old failures. Mark them up to experience and move the hell on. Do you think I sit around and mull over all the things I've messed up?"

"No, but you're different. You've never loved anyone."

"Hah! How little you know."

"You loved someone? Was it my dad?"

"That loser? Hell no. He was made attractive by one too many glasses of wine. I had a professor in law school that simply made my heart do somersaults."

"What happened to him?"

"He was married and wasn't ever going to leave his wife."

"You had an affair?"

"Hey pot, careful how you judge the kettle. Yes, I had an affair. I was young and stupid and thought only love mattered. But here's a tip for you—love is nothing but a drug, and drugs should be avoided at all costs. They muddle the mind and make you do the stupidest things."

"I can see that. I do one stupid thing after another."

"You know, Sarah, when you know something is stupid, you should avoid doing it."

"That would be the wise thing to do, but…I made a promise."

"To whom?"

"Rich's daughter." Sarah filled her mother in on the details of her conversation with Kari, and the situation with Jess's blackmail.

"Hmm…," was all her mother said before a long pause. "Was

the PI any help?"

"I haven't heard back from her yet."

"I'll call and give her a nudge. Someone this sketchy has more to hide."

Sarah felt her first lift of hope. Maybe things weren't as bad as she thought.

"You also need to consider the concept of mutually assured destruction. You need to go on the offense. Stop letting Jess set the agenda. What she has on you is a personal hit. What you have on her equals personal destruction and jail time. Let her know — she hurts you; you will destroy her. You're not in as bad a position as you think, dear."

"I guess not." Sarah relaxed a little. For once, talking to her mother made her feel so much better.

There was a knock on her door. She suddenly remembered she had Doc to deal with. "I better go. There's someone at my door."

Doc stepped into her apartment. "You ignoring me?"

Sarah met him at the door. "Sorry, I was on the phone."

"I was just joking. I know you love me." He placed a quick kiss on her cheek and headed to her kitchen, making himself at home. "You have any parmesan?" He yelled. Sarah came to the door and was about to say no, but he was already digging through the fridge. He picked up a carton of Yoohoo and looked at her with a raised brow and a curled lip. "Seriously, Sarah, these are disgusting. I had you figured for a woman of taste."

She laughed. "Those are Stacey's."

"Oh," he said, dropping the cartoon and shutting the door.

"Oh, what?" She asked, crossing her arms over her chest.

"Oh, I didn't know he was still coming over."

"He doesn't *come over*. He's renovating my offices and I'm working on his custody case."

"So, working on his custody case means entertaining him

and his kid in your private residence?"

"His *kid* has a name." Sarah moved closer, prepping for a fight as she thought of just how huge Doc's balls had to be to be accusing her, when she knew damned good and well whom he was *comforting* after the money debacle. Ending this could be easier than she thought.

Doc shook his head and took a step toward her. "Look, I wasn't meaning to be a jerk." He tried to reach out for her, but she dodged him. "I'm sorry."

"Just leave."

"Excuse me?" He looked dumbfounded.

"I asked you to leave."

"Over calling Rich's kid a kid? What the hell, Sarah?"

"It's your presuming to tell me who I can and can't entertain, when I know you were with Angie. I spent half my life being bossed around by my mother. I don't need it from you."

"Shit, Sarah, I said I'm sorry. You're right. I was with Angie, but it wasn't like I was *with* Angie. She needed a friend."

"And I can't have friends who need a friend?"

He took a step toward her, rubbing the tops of her arms. "You're right. I'm wrong. Look...I'm jealous. Rich is the kind of guy who gets the girl in the end. And I see the way he looks at you."

"Hmmph," Sarah said, biting her lip to keep from asking him, *Exactly how does Rich look at me?*

"And of course, the way you act around him."

Sarah side-stepped him and headed for the refrigerator.

Doc's phone chimed. He looked at the screen and cursed. "I have to go. I'm on call and we have a three-car collision coming in. I'm sorry for acting like a jealous ass. I didn't mean it, and I hate to leave while you're mad—"

"Go. Get out of here. God forbid people die because you're dealing with relationship drama."

Doc flashed her a smile and gave her a kiss on her cheek. "If it's not too late, I'll be back."

Sarah shook her head. "I'm exhausted. Maybe tomorrow?"

"I want this to work, I swear. Can I take you somewhere tomorrow? Away from here, away from Rich and all his bullshit? Just you and me."

"Would you get out of here? There may be dying people waiting on you."

Once she was alone, she poured herself a glass of wine and a hot bath. She needed a quiet place to think…she had some plans to make.

Chapter 25

Rich laid out a lot of food for the cook to prep for Sarah's party, and dropped it off in the kitchen on his way to the back room. The amount of giggles and hoots he heard coming from that room had him nervous. He wanted this party to be nice for Sarah. He hoped the ladies weren't planning a roast.

One foot in the doorway, he shook his head. They'd used condoms for balloons. What he wouldn't have given to have had one of those the other night. He didn't know if he'd ever have another chance like that with Sarah. Her catching him with Mandy made him seem like a lowlife just looking for sex. He didn't know what the hell he had been thinking. Now, not only was Sarah repulsed by him, Mandy was all over him. He'd made her day manager just to get her off his shift.

"Check it out, Rich," Tonya said, grabbing his arm and dragging him over to a life-sized poster of a man in full, naked glory. Tonya handed him a huge paper penis. "It's pin the tail on donkey-man." All the ladies erupted with laughter.

Rich sighed. This wasn't exactly what he had in mind as a birthday party. He was shooting for classy. Okay, maybe nothing in this bar could be made classy, but it could have been a little less tacky.

"I can't help but wonder…were you the model for that?"

Mandy asked, rubbing her breasts against his arm as she talked.

He looked down at the penis in his hand and shook his head. "Hardly—I've been married. No man can walk away from a marriage with all his man-parts in place."

"I think you're way too modest," Mandy said, grabbing a handful of his junk.

Shoving her away, he shook his head. "Look, Mandy." He pulled her by the arm to a quiet corner of the room. "About the other night. That was a mistake."

She gave him a grin, her mascara-caked eyelashes lowering as she said, "It's got to happen to be a mistake. And you never know, you might change your mind."

"Not gonna happen. It never should have gone as far as it did."

Mandy put her hands on her hips and growled, "It's the skinny bitch, isn't it?"

Rich's initial thought was to deny it and claim they needed to maintain a working relationship, but he decided to go with the truth. Tonya was right…what did he have to lose, but pride? "Yeah, it's the skinny bitch."

Mandy gave him a hmmph and stormed off.

Shit. She'll probably rob the register and bust all my glasses. Damn it. How could I have been so stupid?

Tonya came over and patted him on the back. "Wise move. She'll get over it." Tonya looked over her shoulder at Angie. "Between you and me, Mandy was polishing Donnie's knob last night. John caught them parking in our driveway."

"He's too damn cheap to get a hotel?"

"I think Angie's parents caught wind of the gossip. Fred changed all the locks and passwords, and Donnie has no access to registers anymore. So no, he can't afford a hotel. And seems Mandy doesn't want to take guys back to her grandma's house."

"Does Angie know? About last night?"

"I'm not sure. I hate to ask. I didn't want to turn Sarah's party into drama central."

Mary unboxed the cake. Another penis. Rich rolled his eyes. "Yeah, it's best we keep this event classy."

Tonya laughed as Rich walked to his office.

He pulled Sarah's gift out of his pocket, wrapped in emerald with a silver bow…the same colors she'd worn to prom. Everything about the gift meant something. It was like a drowning man's life raft in one tiny package. He didn't want to give it to her in front of everyone else, so he hoped he could sneak her away for a minute or two.

The cook hit the bell and both waitresses went to the window and started carrying the trays of food back to the party. Rich slid the gift into a drawer and went to the bar and started filling pitchers with beer for the waitresses to carry back.

The husbands of the penis-obsessed decorators were the first to arrive. Tonya's husband came straight to Rich at the bar.

"Hey, Rich," John said.

"Whiskey shooter?" Rich asked.

"If you wouldn't mind, and if your cousin doesn't see."

Rich laughed. Tonya kept John on a short leash. Always had. John's dad had been a drinker who died of cirrhosis in his fifties. Tonya always joked that she had John beaten into submission, and she wasn't letting him die on her. Rich knew his cousin would die for the balding, soft-gutted guy.

"Did she let you get the motorcycle?" Rich asked.

"She agreed, but then she kept filling my lunch box with motorcycle crash pictures from the Internet. I decided I didn't want to worry her. I finally trained her to cook, I don't want to wear her heart out with worry and have to start over with a new one."

Rich laughed and handed him his shot of whiskey. "You're a wise man. And a lucky one."

John downed the drink and shoved the glass back at Rich. "You'll get your girl. Tonya says it'll happen. When my girl says something, you can bet it is what it is."

Rich scratched his ear. That almost made sense. The opening door caught his attention. The bells chimed and in walked Sarah, and right behind her, with a hand on her waist like he owned her, was Doc. The thought occurred to Rich that his party was probably going to get Doc lucky. *Damn it, why did I have to think of that?* There would be alcohol and laughter. Sarah would leave here relaxed and ready to unwind. Rich wiped the counter down with a vengeance, threw the dishtowel at the wall, and walked back to the party.

Sarah was instantly red-faced, but laughing about the decorations and the "donkey's tail." She gave all her friends hugs for putting the party together. Good old Tonya tossed him a lob ball when she said, "It was Rich's idea. He made the food and all. We just did the decorating."

Sarah turned her smile on him, and in two steps, she was in his arms. Her perfume was subtle and sweet. He wanted to breathe her in forever.

"Thank you," she said. "You didn't have to do this."

Not letting go, he said, "I wanted you to know, you're very special to me."

He heard the breath catch in her throat. Before pulling away, he kissed her. It wasn't as intimate as he'd share on a date, and far less chaste than what he'd give his grandmother. He knew Doc didn't have the gumption to call him out for it, but he did worry Sarah would slap the shit out of him for crossing the line. As he pulled away, he studied her face and was pleased to see she didn't even appear shocked. Instead, she smiled and gave his hand a squeeze.

He caught Doc's glare and couldn't help but offer him a smile and a wink in return. Doc shook his head and stormed off. He noticed his cousin was quick to nudge Angie, who took the bait and ran after Doc. Damn, his cousin was good. Even without a game plan, they had perfect execution.

They ate and drank. Then it was time for Sarah to open her gifts. From a penis hat to a vibrator, all of the gifts were jokes. Rich was immensely glad he'd left his gift in the office. He had to give Sarah credit, she took it all in stride. Someone struck up the juke box and everyone wandered away to dance, play pool, or shoot the breeze in smaller clusters.

Sarah was packing her sex toys in a gift bag when her phone buzzed. She picked it up from the table and read the message. Her face dropped and she put the phone down like it was poisonous, got up, and left. Rich was about to follow, but Doc was right on her heels. He wrapped his arms around her waist and took her out to the dance floor.

What the hell was he thinking? Did he really think one party would tip the balance and she'd fall right into his arms? He was going soft in the head in his old age. Standing at the edge of the dance floor, he felt more than awkward. Mandy caught his eye and gave him a little wave. He tried to smile, but it felt more like a grimace. He had to move. Mandy would feel his loneliness. She was like a super-predator that could smell the weak animals in the jungle. One last look at Sarah and Doc proved Sarah was happy, and that he seriously needed to move on. Turning on his heel, he headed to his office.

~*~

Dropping his body into his desk chair, he pulled her gift out of the drawer and fiddled with the bow. It was a stupid gift. He should probably pretend he never got it. This party was plenty from a friend.

A knock on his door startled him. His desk chair squeaked as he swiveled around, grabbed the handle, and pulled the door open. "Yeah?" he asked, then took a suck of breath. *Sarah.*

"Can I come in?" she asked.

"Of course," he said, standing and motioning her in, closing the door behind her.

"Did you really do all of this?" she asked.

"Are you blaming me for all of the penises?"

Sarah laughed. Her eyes sparkled. "The party, you jerk. The food, the beer...the plan?"

"It was Tonya's idea. She's just trying to make me look good."

"But you supplied all the food and the drinks?"

"That I did do," he said with a nod.

She took a step forward and kissed his cheek. "Thank you. It means more than you'll ever know, especially today."

His brow pinched together. He thought of the text she'd received, and wished they were on familiar enough terms that he could ask. As they stood now, he figured she'd consider it an intrusion. Although, she did say she wanted them to be friends... and a friend would ask, "What's different about today?"

Sarah looked guilty. "Why, it's my birthday. I, uh, turned another year closer to forty. Isn't that sort of a milestone for the first life crisis?"

She was really good at quick recoveries and redirection.

"Only if you think your life is going in the wrong direction."

Sarah bit her lip as his words sunk in. "Good point."

"Sarah...," he said. He wanted to tell her she'd be happier with him. That he loved her and could give her...what? A three-bedroom, two-bath ranch? A ready-made family? Doc offered three-thousand square feet on the lake with an indoor pool and an eagerness to start a new family.

"What?" she asked when he didn't answer.

"I almost forgot to give you your gift. Here." He grabbed the package on his desk and handed her the little box.

She smiled and tore into the paper. Inside the silver and emerald wrappings was a small velvet box. Sarah pulled it open.

Her happy squeal was music to his ears. Lying on a bed of white satin was a silver necklace with a frog pendant. "Oh my gosh, you remembered?"

"Of course. The day I took you pet shopping? I think the frog was my idea. He had more personality than the fish."

"That's exactly what you said." She gave the necklace a squeeze. "Thank you…for everything. You've made this night perfect. How could I ever thank you enough?"

"I could think of ways, but you'd probably not appreciate them."

Sarah laughed. "You had your chance. You weren't prepared."

A chuckle rumbled from his chest. "Would you be impressed to know I bought a box? Like a giant, warehouse-sized package… just so that never happens again."

Another knock on his door wiped the smile from her face. It was Doc. "You in there, Sarah?"

Sarah pulled the door open.

Rich expected her to make excuses, to be embarrassed to be caught with him. Instead, she was calm and — please God, let him be reading her right — detached. She showed no more emotion than if one of his waiters had knocked on the door.

"You ready to head home?" Doc asked.

Sarah shook her head. "Already?"

"I have to work in the morning. And I wanted to give you your gift."

"Oh well, I guess." Sarah looked at the necklace in her hand and said, "Thanks again, for everything."

His heart nearly skipped a beat when she leaned forward and brushed a kiss across his cheek. Then he felt like he'd have to scoop that same heart up off the floor and shove it, battered and bruised, back into his chest as she walked out his door with the obvious winner.

Chapter 26

Rich came into the bar early on Saturday because he couldn't take being at home another minute. Coming in through his outside office door, he flipped on the light and settled himself into his desk chair. He needed something to keep his mind off Sarah…and Sarah and Doc…and what private gift Doc had for her. Probably something much better than a frog. And her thank you to Doc was probably much more intimate than a kiss on the cheek.

Shit. I am in the friend zone.

He tossed his pen across his desk with the thought.

A knock on his door annoyed him. He was wallowing, didn't the universe understand that? He wheeled himself over and unlocked it.

It was Mandy. Rich sighed. If only life was as easy as Mandy.

"Hey," she said.

"Hey," he said back.

Mandy fiddled with the loose hair at the back of her bun. "I've got a situation…."

"And?" Rich wanted to tell her to get to the point or get the hell out, but he bit his tongue. It wasn't her fault he kept making an ass out of himself with Sarah.

"The thing is…I can't stand staying with my grandma a day

longer."

Rich rubbed his face. He never should have played tonsil hockey with her.

"Now, I know you've made it clear that there is no chance for you and me, right?"

"Right." He breathed a little easier.

She took a deep breath and sat in the chair by his desk. "So, Donnie asked me to move with him to Florida, and I'm considering it."

As much as Rich wanted her gone from his office and his life, he couldn't NOT mention the obvious. "Didn't he hit you? Blacken your eye?"

"Well yeah, but he was mad."

"That's not an excuse. I've been mad plenty...I still don't beat on girls."

Mandy laughed. "You've never wanted to hit Sarah? Not even a little bit? I wanted to punch her last night when she left with Doc. She should know you're crazy about her. It's wrong of her to lead you on."

Rich sat up a little straighter. Maybe he shouldn't have been honest with Mandy. Hearing his situation coming from her mouth felt far more desperate than when he just thought it in his head.

"She's never led me on, trust me. And the answer to the original question is no—even when she left with Doc, I didn't want to punch her."

"You probably wanted to punch Doc."

"No, not Doc either. No one should punch anyone—especially not someone they say they love."

Mandy shrugged. "Not all guys are good like you. The thing is, Donnie is crazy about me. So crazy, he lost it when he thought I was sleeping with you...and he needed the money back, and I told him to go to hell. I think between the money and the jealousy, he just lost it. He was worried he was going to go to jail."

"He should have thought of that before he stole it."

"He was feeling romantic."

"I see," Rich said, though he didn't see, not one bit. He loved Sarah. There were times when he thought the frustration of it would make him want to scream, but he didn't do stupid shit… beyond his almost hook-up with Mandy. "So, what do you need from me? Or is this your notice?"

"My notice?"

"Most people give notice when they quit a job."

"Oh yeah, well it is that. And I was also wondering if you'd give me a loan? My homeowner's insurance is going to cover the house since the fire *was* caused by the fallen electric line, but I won't get that check for another month. Do you think you could lend me a couple of thousand so we could drive to Florida and get us a place? I'll pay you back. I swear."

Rich's first thought was bullshit she'd ever pay it back. If her and Donnie owed him money, he'd never see them again. His second thought was never seeing them again wasn't such a bad thing. With Donnie out of town, Angie would tie up Doc. And of course, it was his cousin's fault that Mandy was homeless in the first place. Rich nodded. "I think I can manage that. You've been a good worker and a good friend. I want to see you happy." Rich pulled out his checkbook and wrote her a check.

She took it, staring at it like she was in shock. "Tonya told me you'd help, but I thought she was insane."

Rich almost grinned. He had to give his cousin credit, she knew how to bait traps.

Mandy folded the check and stuck it in her pocket. "You're a good guy, Rich, so I'm going to help you get the skinny bitch. I know for a fact that Doc spent the night with Angie last night."

Rich was dumfounded with her out-of-the-blue statement. It took him a full minute to point out, "Sarah and Doc left here together."

Mandy shrugged. "And he was back at home with Angie by midnight. Donnie and I took pictures—for the divorce, you know. To prove she hasn't been Ms. Perfect. You wanna see?" Mandy dug her phone out of her pocket.

Rich held up his hand. "No, that's all right. I'll take your word for it."

"If you want, I could tell Sarah," Mandy said. "Or give me her number and I'll text them to her."

As much as he wanted Doc to get busted, he couldn't condone Mandy doing it. He didn't want to be the one to hurt Sarah. The memory of her face falling as she'd read whatever was on her phone last night haunted him. He wanted to know what it was, what hurt her. But the reality was, he wasn't a close enough friend to ask. Sarah was an acquaintance. Her emotional well-being wasn't really his business.

No, it wouldn't be Rich who outed Doc's infidelity. He sighed, "Sarah is a smart woman. She'll figure it out, eventually."

Mandy patted the top of his head. "Hopefully sooner than later."

He nodded. "So, when are you and Donnie leaving?"

"As soon as my shift here is over. I got Marie to cover my shifts for the week. She's a doll."

"I appreciate that."

"I know things didn't work out between us, but you've helped me so much. I'll always owe you."

"Tell Donnie he better cool it and be good to you."

Mandy winked at him. "I will. Later, boss."

"Later," Rich said to the closing door.

Rich went back to his payroll, which after his donation to Mandy, was going to make this month tight. But if it would get Doc out of the way, he'd take out a damn loan. Work done, he headed home.

Chapter 27

Sarah was restless. Last night had been a mixed bag. The party was awesome. The love she felt for her friends almost made her cry. Then, there was Rich. On one hand, she wanted to call him and wave the white flag. Maybe something between them could work. On the other hand, if it didn't work out, it would break her heart. And how many more cracks could one heart take?

Then there was also the text from her mother letting her know she was questioned by an AP reporter about her daughter's affair with Evan Stollings. She denied it, of course. *Damn you, Evan.* She'd been totally duped by him. He was smart and charming. Everything about him was perfect.

That should have been her first clue.

That last day at Stollings and Reed, she'd gone to work happy, totally clueless that her whole world was about to fall apart. Sarah covered her face with her hands and let out a frustrated groan. What the hell had she been thinking?

Rich could never love a woman like her. If he knew about her and Evan, he'd never look at her like she was perfect. He'd hate her. At least with Doc, she knew he didn't love her. He didn't expect perfection. He wanted what she wanted…not to be alone.

Her phone rang, making her jump. It was her mother.

"Happy Birthday, counselor."

"Thank you," Sarah said.

"I hope you had a good one."

"I did…all things considered."

"The pictures were a downer, no doubt. I thought about waiting until after your birthday, but you never know when a reporter might show up. Best you be aware."

"You're right. I was just beginning to feel like it wasn't going to catch up with me. Maybe if he and I both say it never happened?"

"The woman said there are photos—you guys at a camp?"

"Oh."

"I take it you were at a cabin?"

"Yeah."

"You should have been more discreet."

"I didn't think he was married. I wasn't trying to hide."

"Did you tell Mrs. Stollings, like I told you?"

"I forwarded the message to her."

"What did she say?"

"She said she was on it."

Her mother assured her, "Elana Stollings has more to lose over this fiasco than you do. She'll fix it. Now, enough about your shady love life, I have news from my PI for you."

"Really?" Sarah sat. Excitement made her feel a little lighter. Maybe it would be something so damning that dealing with Jess would be a slam dunk.

"Calm down. It's not a case closer. It's more of an interesting tidbit."

Sarah grabbed the legal pad on her coffee table and flipped it open to a clean page. "I'm ready. What did you find out?"

"Seems the older girl, Kari? Her dad was rich. Talking old money, big connections rich."

"Jess said the guy was broke."

"Old money rarely flaunts it. They have nothing to prove.

Probably why Jess never caught on. According to the report, he was a do-gooder poet. Lived in a crappy apartment in the city like he was a pauper. He told his friends he and Jess fought when she tried to make him get a job. She was sick of being broke. That leads me to believe she never had a clue what this guy was worth. Or if she did, she must have decided she couldn't squeeze him. He did come from old money, and it's hard to steal old money. They're pretty good at protecting what's theirs."

"You think she's using Kari to get money out of him now?" That explained why she had no interest in Stacey.

"Not likely. Poor guy's dead. Died in a car crash six years ago."

"Oh. That's sad, but much less complicated for Rich. Do you think Jess is trying to get money from his family? Playing on their grief?"

"Excellent guess, my dear. I had the same thought, so I set you up a meeting with his mother. She only lives about forty-five minutes from you. I emailed you the details."

"Does she know about Kari?"

"I don't know. You'll have to go talk to her and find out."

"Thank you, Mother."

"Happy Birthday. I forgot to send a gift. I'll wire you money and you can buy yourself something nice."

"Don't worry. This was an excellent gift." She had a legitimate reason to talk to Rich.

Taking a deep breath, she snapped a leash on Rover and walked the couple of blocks to his house. She knocked on his door, crossing her fingers and hoping he was there. He opened the door, looking surprised to see her.

"Sarah. You want to come in?"

Sarah shook her head. "Can we talk? In private?"

"Of course," he said, stepping off his porch and walking with her down his quiet, tree-lined street.

There was an awkward silence. Sarah finally said, "Remember that PI I asked to check into Jess? I got some information today."

"Yeah? She find anything interesting?"

"Actually, she did. Did you know Kari's dad was rich?" There was a pause. Sarah threw in for clarification, "Her biological dad."

"Yeah, I knew what you meant. And no, I didn't. Jess said he was some sort of unemployed poet. I always figured she was making that up. I imagined a biker dude from a bar, knowing Jess."

"Well, seems she was partly right. He was a poet, but he wasn't broke. Seems he came from old money."

"She screwed up dumping him, didn't she?" Rich laughed.

"I'd say so."

"Do you think she's figured it out? That would explain the obsession with Kari. Shit, Sarah, I'm going to be screwed. How the hell am I going to fight off a guy with deep-as-hell pockets?"

"He's dead," Sarah said.

"Oh. Shit. That should make me feel better, but that sucks. Do you know how he died?"

"Car wreck."

Rich was quiet for a while. Then he asked, "What do you think this means for me?"

"I don't know. It's just…curious."

"What should I do? Should I tell her I know? Hunt these people down?"

Sarah sighed and wrapped Rover's leash tighter around her hand. "I'm going to meet with the mom—I guess Kari's grandma—just to feel her out. That's why I wanted to talk to you. What would you want this woman to know?"

"I feel like she should know she has a granddaughter. I mean, I don't know if this guy had any other kids, but imagine Kari is his only one. His mother has a right to know. I never really considered that Kari had family who would be good for her. I always imagined she was the result of a one-night stand — knowing Jess, you know."

"Yeah, me too. I suppose we shouldn't do anything too hastily. Maybe meet with her and see what kind of person she is."

Their conversation was interrupted by Kari yelling from the front door, "Dad, it's Ron at the convenience store. He says Mandy brought in a check for $2000.00 from you. He wants to know if she stole it, or did you want him to cash it for her?"

Sarah had to consciously force herself to breathe. She was eternally an idiot where men were concerned. She was ready to ditch Doc because Rich threw her a party and bought her a damned necklace? She swallowed hard. "I better get going. You know, if you ever want to finish what I interrupted between you and Mandy, you could bring Stacey over and give yourself a night to yourself."

Rich shrugged. "It's not like that. Her house was burned down, remember?"

"Poor baby," Sarah said. "I really better go. Doc is expecting me."

Rich gave her a look. She couldn't decide whether it was a look of disgust or frustration.

"There's nothing between Mandy and me. It was just a favor."

"Big favor. But hey, you don't owe me any explanations. I'll call you after I meet with the grandma."

"Sarah...."

She took a quick look at her watch and backed away. "I'm really running late. I'll be in touch."

With that, she turned and practically speed-walked away. If he wanted to play house with Mandy, fine with her. She walked all the way home in a huff. Poor Rover was panting by the time they hit the steps to the house. Worrying that the dog might have a coronary, she picked him up and carried him into the house, and gave him a can of dog food.

"I'm sorry, old boy. Rich is such a dick. It's not your fault." Rover didn't answer, or even look up. He was too busy shoving his bowl across the floor.

Feeling ignored — even by the dog — and desperate not to care about Rich a second longer, she dialed Doc's number and asked if he wanted to do something.

Doc sighed. "I would, babe, but I've got to be at a...uh... conference for tonight. Maybe tomorrow?"

"You enjoy that."

"You all right?"

"Of course," Sarah said, feeling guilty for making Doc worry before leaving for his conference. Especially when the thing that had her off kilter was the other man. "I'm fine. Maybe I'll do a little Christmas shopping."

"A little early, but that seems to be a Sarah trait."

"A Sarah trait?"

"Yeah, you're very organized and punctual. I've no doubt you have everything done by November first."

Sarah frowned. "Well, I suppose I like order."

"No shame in that. See you tomorrow?"

"Yeah, I suppose."

"Don't sound so excited," he said.

"Just another long day." Sarah rubbed the back of her neck, "You enjoy yourself."

"IBS treatments and symptomologies. So much to enjoy," Doc said, before telling her goodbye.

She poured herself a glass of wine, grabbed a book, and decided she'd take a hot bath — one with bubbles and a candle. The kind that's supposed to make people feel relaxed. Maybe it could work for her. Three pages in, she ditched the book and grabbed her iPhone. She set up a playlist devoid of love songs or sappy crap and popped in her ear buds. Rolling a towel, she placed it behind her head, adding a wash cloth to her eyes. Turning on the hot water with her toes, she let the warm water relax her.

Chapter 28

Sarah was only gone a few minutes before Rich regretted their conversation. Of course, it sounded awful that he gave Mandy money. He had to explain. He wasn't losing an inch to Doc in this battle, especially over a misunderstanding.

Opening the front door, he yelled to Kari that he'd be right back.

His daughter was quick to meet him with questions. "Were you and Sarah fighting again?"

"Sort of. I'm going to go explain to her."

"It was about the check, huh?" Kari asked.

"She'll understand, once I explain."

"I knew as soon as I said it; I screwed up," Kari said.

"It'll be fine." *Maybe.*

Stacey slid off the recliner where she was entrenched with coloring book and crayons. She tore a page from the book and brought it to her father. "Give her this, Daddy. Sign it for me, Kari...*to Sarah, I love you,*" Stacey said, handing her sister the page and a red crayon. "With a heart."

"Write it yourself."

"Daddy's in a hurry, and letters take me a lot of time." Stacey gave her foot a stubborn stomp on the floor.

Kari took the paper, signed it, and handed it to Rich, "Tell her we're making dinner—Stace and me. And tell her it's game night."

"Don't tell her that Kari cheats at Monopoly," Stacey said.

"I don't cheat at Monopoly," Kari said.

Rich stuffed the paper in his back pocket. He supposed he'd drive to Doc's first, since that's where she said she was headed. Maybe he could catch her before she got there.

He hurried to the car and backed out of the drive. On his way there, he started to lose his nerve. Was he just going to go up and knock on Doc's door and demand to talk to his girlfriend?

Yes, I am. It was awkward, but it had to be done. Sarah wasn't just any woman. It wasn't the sort of situation where he could lose, get over it, and move on. He'd lost her once, and he wasn't going to let it happen again. If she chose Doc, it wouldn't be for his lack of trying.

Rich was less than a half-mile from Doc's private drive when he recognized Doc's BMW. Rich's stomach tightened. Sarah couldn't be leaving with him. He had to talk to her. Looking through the front window, there was no doubt there was a woman riding along with Doc. As their cars passed and the sun's glare disappeared, he could see her. *Angie.*

Doc was with Angie. Rich breathed a sigh of relief.

He did a U-turn in the road and headed straight to Sarah's apartment.

~*~

"Sarah!" he yelled as he pounded on her door. There was no answer. Her car was still there, so she hadn't driven anywhere, and Rover was sniffling at the door, so she didn't walk anywhere. The key to her apartment was burning a hole in his pocket. Using it was an invasion of her privacy, but not using it…she could have fallen. Could be ill. He opened the door, popped his head inside, and yelled. Still no answer. Rover wagged his tail in greeting.

"You're a hell of a guard dog," Rich said as he closed the door behind him and stepped into the apartment. From his vantage point at the door, he could see the whole living space. She wasn't there. He went to her bedroom. Her door was open and the bed was empty. He called again. No answer. The bathroom door was open, and he could hear water running.

He yelled again. No answer. He waited several minutes, thinking she'd shut off the water when the bath was filled. Instead, it kept running and running. He thought of last night's text, and the look of grief that washed over her. Then he thought of Doc and Angie. Maybe Sarah saw them? Maybe she was upset. Irrational fears about things like suicide and head trauma made his heart rate speed up.

Giving the bathroom door a push, he found her lying in the tub. An empty wine bottle sat on the floor. "Sarah," he said, touching her arm.

Sarah screamed and simultaneously threw a punch at him as she tried to escape from the tub. A wave of water spilled over the side onto the floor from her efforts. Rich took a step back and raised his hands in the air. "I knocked. You didn't answer."

"What?"

He pointed to her ears.

She blushed, her cheeks turning as pink as her water-warmed breasts. She pulled out the earbuds. "What are you doing here?"

Suddenly feeling like an idiot, he stuttered as he explained, "You didn't answer the door."

Calming, she slid her body down below the bubble line. "How did you—?"

"I still have my key."

Sarah laughed as she turned off the water with her toes. Rich let out the anxious breath he hadn't even realized he was holding. She wasn't mad at him.

"I'm fine, but I appreciate the concern. One of my biggest fears is dying alone and not being found until I was bloated and fly specked."

"I can promise a daily check in, if you'd like."

Sarah smiled, but it didn't reach her eyes. As a matter of fact, her eyes were red-rimmed. She'd been crying. *Damn, Doc.* He wanted him out of her life, but dumping her on her birthday was a dick move.

"You all right?" he asked, squatting next to the tub.

"I'm fine," she said. "The water is a little cold. I think I ran the tank dry."

"You're lucky I put in an overflow. You'd have flooded the place falling asleep like that. Not smart to sleep in the tub. You could drown."

"I don't…usually. I didn't sleep well last night."

"Doc?"

Sarah blushed. "No, not Doc. He went right home after he dropped me off."

Good to know, Rich thought. But it still didn't rule out Doc breaking her heart. "Anything wrong?"

"Not really."

"Come on, Sarah. Talk to me. There's something wrong."

Rolling her head back against the tub, she closed her eyes and groaned. "I'm fine."

Eyes closed, head tipped back, he couldn't help but appreciate her chest. The soft swell of her breasts teased him. Her smooth ivory skin was all the more tempting because he knew how silky it felt to his touch. She was beautiful, and he wanted her.

A bit of silver caught his eye. Nestled between her breasts was the necklace he'd given her. His heart skipped a beat. That had to mean something.

Clearing his throat, he said, "Sarah, we need to talk."

Her eyes popped open and she looked suddenly nervous. "Is something wrong?"

He shook his head. "I, uh, wanted you to know I only gave

Mandy money to leave town. Not because I owe her anything, or because there is anything between us."

"I don't care what you do with your money," she said, touching the necklace on her chest.

"Still, I wanted you to know. I thought it might bug you if I had given her money for any other reason."

"It does make me feel better. Why, I don't know." Her laugh was nervous.

"Come on, Sarah, you know why."

"I do?"

"I'm too old to play games. It bugs you because you're lying to yourself to say there is nothing between us. I want you in my life. Not as a friend. Not as my attorney. I want you with me."

Her lips parted, inviting him. Wrapping a hand around the slender curve of her neck and through the damp tendrils of hair, he kissed her. Slowly, tenderly, hoping it said all the things he couldn't seem to find the words for.

She moved closer. Water dripped from her arms, making a splatter pattern on his jeans. The water from the tub sloshed over the side, splashing on the floor. Pulling back, she smiled at him. "I got you wet. Maybe I better get out, so we can talk properly."

His hand traced the curve of her shoulder. "I'm fine with things as they are."

Sarah laid her arms across the edge of the tub and let her chin rest on them. "Very tempting, but my water is getting cold. Would you mind handing me my towel?"

Handing her a fluffy white towel, he kissed her forehead and then stepped out of the room. He made himself comfortable on the couch and waited. She appeared a few seconds later wrapped in a blue terry cloth robe. She was a beautiful woman. The hair piled on top of her head with damp, curly wisps hanging loose around her face and neck was more perfect than the slick straight, never a hair out of place style she normally wore it in. She sat at the opposite side of the couch, her body turned toward him, a single foot tucked under her.

He was suddenly less confident than he had been when she was naked and in the bathtub. Rubbing the whiskers on his chin, he decided he'd just throw it out there. He had nothing to lose. It wasn't like she could dump him. "The girls are making dinner, watching movies, and maybe playing a few games. You should join us."

"That sounds like fun, but I couldn't…."

"Can't or won't?"

"I don't want to intrude on your family time."

Rich laughed, wiping at his mouth like he was trying to mold a straight face. "Seriously? Why won't you? What other plans did you have for today?"

"Well. I was supposed to see Doc when he got off work."

"That's your choice. It's the wrong choice, but yours to make."

Sarah bit her lip. "You're right. Doc is a nice guy, but it's a mistake."

"So, be done with him and give me a chance."

Sarah looked away from him, like the floral pattern on the couch was suddenly the most interesting thing on earth.

"Why can't you trust me?" he asked.

She shook her head. "I trust you, I swear. It's not you. It's me. It's always been me. I'm pretty much a relationship train wreck. I've made so many mistakes—from trusting Jess to be my liaison with you to the joke of a relationship with Doc. One mistake after another."

"Then stop making mistakes. Be with me."

Sarah shook her head. "It's not that easy. There are things I've done that can't be reconciled."

"What the hell is that supposed to mean? What could you possibly have done?"

Sarah got up and headed for the kitchen. Rich followed her.

Her hands shook as she tried to make a pot of coffee. Her efforts resulted in coffee grounds all over the counter.

Taking her by the hands, he pulled her into him. "Talk to me."

Laying her head against his chest, she nestled into him, but said nothing.

"Last night, at the party…you got a message. Is that what this is about?"

She nodded. "Partly."

Pulling back, his hands cradled her face, his thumb tracing the outline of her lips. "This can work, Sarah."

She bit her lip. "I don't know."

"Yes, you do."

Sarah closed her eyes a minute, then took a deep breath. She pulled her phone out of her purse setting on the table, tapped in her passcode, and then handed her phone to Rich. "I got this from an AP reporter about an hour ago." It was a picture of her and a handsome guy. The guy had his arm draped over Sarah's shoulder, his lips intimately close to her ear.

It only took Rich a moment to get over the initial stab of jealousy to recognize the guy in the picture. "You and Stollings? I kinda knew it. I could tell by the way you acted when I questioned you about him."

"He's a married man, Rich."

"You want me to shame you? Fine—Sarah, you shouldn't fall for married men."

"It's not a joke. It was a really bad thing to do."

"I agree. I'm shocked. I would never have guessed you'd be someone's mistress—but then I figure he lied. Probably told you that age-old line that he was unhappily married and getting a divorce."

"He never mentioned he was married. Being the moron that I can be, I didn't know who he was. I realize now that that sounds unbelievable. How did I not know who Evan Stollings was?"

Rich bobbed his head.

"The truth is…I went to school on the west coast, then I went to work in Oregon. I didn't maintain any ties with Indiana or its politics. But after a while, I started to miss home, so I put my resume up on a headhunter site and Stollings and Reed hired me. Evan was put in charge of training the new hire. I thought he was sweet and charming, and — well…you saw the picture."

Rich nodded slowly. "You still dating him?"

"Oh, hell no. As soon as I found out he was married, I broke it off. But evidently someone knows. And I worry…it could come out. I could be an embarrassment to you, your kids. That's why I'm not sure this…us…is a good idea."

"I don't give a shit. I'll never be embarrassed of you."

Sarah blinked back tears. Clearing her throat, she said, "I appreciate that, but I want you to give it real consideration. Evan is high profile. It could be the molehill people make into a mountain."

Rich scrolled past the picture to her mother's message. *I see the self-destruction continues.* "No happy birthday?" Rich asked.

Sarah's laugh was weak. "Mother is mother. She offered to wire me gift money this morning. Elana wished me a happy birthday when I forwarded the email."

"Elana? Elana Stollings?"

"Yeah."

"You sent her that, and she wished you happy birthday? Don't tell me it was one of those kinky threesomes."

Sarah's cheeks blazed. "No. Oh my God, no. Is that what you think of me?"

"No, but whose wife is okay with that? Becomes friends with her husband's mistress?" He regretted his words as soon as he said them.

Sarah looked like she might vomit, and her eyes were bright

with tears. "I wouldn't say we're friends, but she helped me make a choice in what direction my life was headed."

Rich laughed. "Away from her husband?"

Sarah's cheeks flamed.

"I'm sorry, Sarah. It was a joke. A bad one." He had to get a grip. He was acting like a jealous boyfriend. She was trying to be honest with him, and he wasn't making it easy on her. Taking her hand, he gave it a squeeze. "What advice did she give you?"

"She told me I was swimming with sharks, and I had to understand, I could not bleed when someone cut me. If I bled, the blood in the water would set off a frenzy and I'd never survive. If I wanted to swim these waters, I better toughen up. If I didn't want to toughen up...I should get out."

"How exactly do you toughen up?"

"I'm not sure...not exactly. I told her I wanted out. I just wanted a normal life, so she negotiated my severance package, and when Evan threatened to ruin me if I left, she took care of him."

"I bet he was shocked his wife knew."

She shook her head. "He didn't ever try to hide. That's one of the reasons I didn't realize he was married."

Rich pulled her closer to him, wrapping an arm around her shoulders and tucking her against his chest. "I don't see this as anything you should worry about or be ashamed of. Stollings is the only one who should be worried. He's the only one who should feel humiliated, and even if this hit front page, who cares?"

"I'd care. The girls would see it."

Rich smiled—a slow, lazy smile. "We'd cross that bridge if we ever came to it. Seems to me, Elana Stollings is a pro at cleaning up her husband's messes. And I imagine his closet is full of skeletons. At worst, you'll just be one of many. A small blip on the radar."

Sarah nodded. "That's pretty much what Mother said."

191

"Then don't worry about it."

"I won't…if you won't."

She closed her eyes. He kissed her ear, then ran his hands gently down her neck to give her bare shoulders a squeeze. "It will be all right. This isn't a big deal. You…me. That's all that matters right now, and I think it feels perfect. Tell me you feel it, too."

"I do," she said, then paused.

"Is there a but in there?"

Sarah's lip quivered.

He started to worry. "Come on, Sarah. Stacey sent you refrigerator art as a bribe." He handed her a folded-up paper from his pocket. It was a picture of a dog, brown and white like Rover. Above it was written in neat, feminine hand writing…*I miss you, Sarah*. She looked at the paper, then at Rich. He shrugged. "Kari wrote the words. She said to tell you she won't cheat at Monopoly if you come."

Sarah laughed. "Did she really?"

He nodded and grinned. "Come with me, ask her yourself."

Sarah nodded. "I think I will. Let me get dressed?"

"Of course," Rich said as he headed for the living room to wait.

Sarah stopped short at her bedroom door. Picking at the paint on the door frame, she asked, "Are you certain about this?"

"Get dressed, Sarah. I've never been more sure of anything."

Sarah returned in a hurry. She was wearing jeans, a V-neck tee, and a zip hoodie. Her hair was still in its sloppy bun on top of her head.

"Damn, but if you aren't beautiful. I honestly didn't think you could top the robe, but you managed."

Chapter 29

It was one of the best days Sarah had in years, maybe a lifetime. Dinner turned out to be cheeseburgers and onion rings. Kari added a special treat by making some break and bake cookies for the meal. After dinner, they played Monopoly. Kari kept her word and didn't cheat. She also let all of Stacey's bad counts to avoid her hotels on Boardwalk slide. The youngest of the group ended up winning with a whole lot of lucky rolls and good will.

Then they watched a movie about a princess. Rich made a fire in the fireplace. Sarah was so relaxed and happy, she didn't even over-think him holding her hand as they sat side-by-side on the brown wrap-around sofa. It wasn't until after the girls went off to bed that Sarah began to feel awkward. Grabbing her purse, she announced, "I guess I better be going."

Rich took her hand and pulled her down next to him. "Don't be in such a hurry." Leaning closer, he kissed her. Closing her eyes, she breathed in the scent of him. Bubble gum and wood smoke. His kiss felt familiar and thrilling, her body growing as hot as the crackling fire in the hearth. When his hands slipped under her shirt, she weaved her fingers through his hair and kissed him deeper.

She smiled. It felt good to be so close. To be here. "Being with you guys? There's nothing that makes me happier. I had the best time tonight."

"Good. We were hoping to finally lure you in with all the fun and excitement of this place."

"Sneaky," she laughed. "You saying the girls are in on the conspiracy?"

"Just Kari. She sees herself as the match-making queen, and suggested I invite you over and use your love for them to transfer to their old man."

Sarah's eyes burned. "They know I love them? Er, I mean, I care about them?"

"Yeah, seems they both think they could wrap you around their little fingers."

Sarah thought back on the evening and nodded. "They probably can."

"Well, we're a package deal, you know. Can't have my kids without keeping me."

Sarah laughed. "Is that so?"

"Completely," he said, rubbing a hand up her leg and pulling it across his lap.

Sarah fiddled with a button on his flannel shirt. "You really think this could work, you and me?"

He nuzzled her cheek with light kisses. "I've never been more certain of anything in my life."

The fire crackled in the quiet house. His hands roamed lower, squeezing her hips as they made their way to the small of her back. Whiskered cheeks were sharp against her hands as she held him, moving closer for a kiss. The intensity she felt stirring in him made her heart race. His breathing was ragged, and the pressure of his hands felt safe, comforting. When he tried to lower her back onto the couch, she wanted nothing more than to feel him pressed against her, but she thought of the kids. If they wandered out to use the bathroom, they'd be shocked.

She pushed against him. He looked more than a little

disappointed.

"What happens if the girls wake up?" she asked.

He rolled his head and groaned. "Shit. You're right."

"What do you normally do?"

"I don't normally bring women here."

She gave him a look.

Rich sighed. "Mandy was a fluke. Would you believe I was trying to get you out of my head? I was desperate."

Taking his hand, she nodded. "I think that's what I was trying to do with Doc. I thought I could force myself into something I could control."

"You can control me," he said with a grin.

"The hell I can." She laughed. "The first day I saw you, at the newspaper office, it felt like my heart was racing. I hated you for that."

"You hated my ad too, but I've been thinking…you realize I was looking for you."

"A fat chick with no goals?"

"Okay, so I'm not good with words, but the woman I was trying—and failing—to describe was the girl I remembered."

"A f—"

"Don't say it." He wrapped her up and held her close. "I love you, Sarah. I've always loved you. I'm not sure what happened; I've always wondered—"

"Does it matter? Can we just start right here, right now? I'm afraid—"

"There's nothing for you to be afraid of." He pulled her up, walking her across the room to the hall, where he stopped at his bedroom door and swung it open, "No pressure. It's just safer here."

The room was dark, so Sarah couldn't see much beyond the double bed centered in the room. "Promise me there aren't any Mandy cooties in here?"

When he lifted her off the floor, his hands under her thighs, she wrapped her legs around his waist. "No Mandy cooties, or any other cooties, for that matter."

"Good," she said, kissing him.

Laying her down on his bed, his hands moved across the warm, smooth skin of her belly, heading lower. The breath stopped in her throat.

"Too fast?" He asked, his hand slowing and creeping its way to her side to outline the curve of her hip with his fingers.

"No, it's just…been a while since it mattered."

She could feel his smile against her cheek. "Good."

It didn't take long for shirts to be stripped and tossed to the floor. His mouth, like a flame that leaves a trail of fire, stirred a yearning in her so deep, she could no longer keep track of what part of her body was being teased. It wasn't long before she was clinging to him, her body moving against him, seeking relief. He pulled himself away. Kneeling above her, he unbuttoned her pants, slipping them down over smooth hips. His hand slid between her legs, gently massaging the smooth skin of her inner thigh with the palm of his hand. His fingers trailed upward slowly, hesitantly. His touch was so tender and light it sent tendrils of electricity through her limbs to the very core of her body, causing her body to convulse, her legs to quiver.

Rich closed his eyes and took a sharp suck of air. "You're beautiful, Sarah."

Feeling a bit calmer, she smiled at him, stretching her arms above her head. "You got a condom this time, stud?"

He reached over and grabbed a box from his night stand. "Economy size. Only the best for you."

Sarah laughed. As he was tearing into the box of condoms with his teeth, Sarah thought of the bed. Every time he shifted his weight, the damn thing squeaked like it needed oiled. "Are you sure this is all right? The bed? It squeaks. A lot."

Rich sighed, his shoulders dropped. He looked more than disappointed sitting there on his knees, his excitement evident through his briefs, the box of condoms half chewed open. "They're heavy sleepers."

"I was thinking…maybe the floor?"

"Lady, I'll do it on the front lawn at this point."

Sarah laughed as they made a hasty bed of blankets on the floor. She made him do a double check on the door lock. No more worries left to contend with, it was that moment. Flesh on flesh, hearts hammering against each other. Sarah's throat felt dry. He kissed her, settling himself between her knees. He must have felt her hesitance, because he stopped. Brushing stray hairs from her cheek, he said, "Tonight has been perfect, Sarah. We don't have to do this. I'm in no hurry."

"No, it's what I want, I swear. It just never seems to end well for me."

Chapter 30

She could barely catch her breath. Her arms and legs were weak, like she lacked either the muscle or the bones to move them. He nipped at her breast. "That end all right for you?"

"Oh, dear lord. Can I bottle and sell you? Women would pay top dollar for that."

"You make it easy," he said, leaning on an arm, looking down at her.

"Was I very loud?" Mortification settled in. She was pretty sure she was more than a bit noisy.

"You were perfect," he said with a grin.

"I should go," she said, looking up at the clock on the night stand. It was after three. Goodness, how long had they been at it?

"It's too late. Just stay here."

"What will the girls think?"

"I'll sleep on the couch. They won't think anything."

"You don't need to give up your bed."

"I want you to stay. Think about it…they leave for school at eight. That gives us a whole hour in an empty house to see if the bed springs squeak."

Sarah laughed and kissed his shoulder. "I admit, you're smarter than you look."

"Thanks, I think." Helping her up off the floor, he pulled her in and held her tight. "The couch seems too far away. I could set the alarm, beat them out of bed?"

Sarah laughed. "I think we've pushed our luck far enough tonight, don't you?"

"Not really." He rubbed his nose against her cheek. "I can push it as far as you like."

"You better go," she said, handing him his clothes and shoving him toward the door.

"You've got too much self-control, you know that?" She bit her lip and was about to defend herself, but he kissed her. "I love that about you, you know?"

Leaning her head against his shoulder, she breathed a sigh of relief. "I'm glad you find my annoying traits lovable."

Rich kissed the top of her head, "I do. You know that, don't you…that I love you?"

Sarah gasped. "I, uh…."

"Shh...don't say anything. I'm just too old to play games. I've wanted you since you got back. You were meant for me, Sarah… sooner or later, you'll realize it."

With one more kiss, he was gone. She stood in the darkened room and wished she had the gumption to follow him and tell him…what? That she'd obsessed about him for the last fifteen years? Shaking her head, she crawled into bed and hugged the pillow with the familiar bubble gum scent.

~*~

Waking to the sounds of people was much more pleasant than an alarm. Sarah climbed out of bed and slipped her hoodie on over the T-shirt and sweat pants she found on his floor. For a guy, he wasn't too big of a pig, but he wasn't exactly Mr. Tidy. She wasn't sure if he meant for her to hide or come out and let the girls know she was still there, so she hung by the door and listened.

Kari caught on first. "Dad, Sarah's car is still here."

199

"Uh, yeah. It was late…and I uh…."

Sarah cringed. She didn't realize what a horrible liar he was.

"Way to score one, Dad! Give me a high five."

"I didn't score…I mean…. Dammit, shouldn't you be eating breakfast?"

Kari laughed. "I just meant, I know you like her, and you finally got her attention. So, is Doc history?"

"Sarah can live with us. I'll share my room," Stacey chimed in.

"Stacey, put Rover out. Sarah just stayed over because it was after midnight."

"I went to bed at ten, Dad. Sooo, gonna share the deets?" Kari giggled.

"There are no *deets* to share. Now get ready for school."

"Can I go wake up Sarah? Tell her goodbye before I go to school?" Stacey asked as the back door shut and the dog barked.

"I don't know, pumpkin," Rich said.

"I'm up," Sarah announced, coming into the kitchen. The girls greeted her with good mornings, Rich greeted her with a smile. He stepped toward her, but she dodged him. The girls finished dressing and grabbed for backpacks, gym clothes, and lunches. A horn blew outside. They gave their dad a kiss and ran to their Aunt Tonya's minivan.

Once the door was closed and locked, he turned to her. There was an awkward moment before he asked, "I take it you don't want anyone to know about us?"

"Just not the girls…for now. I think you should talk to them. Make sure they are okay with this."

"And by *this*, you mean…?"

"Us, as a couple. Kari was already suspicious. I wasn't about to make her think she was right."

"You really think she'd think we had sex? She's awfully young."

"Hate to break it to you, but your little girl is almost sixteen. I was seventeen when you lured me to your cabin."

Rich looked distressed, running a hand through his morning hair. "But she seems so much younger than we were."

"She's growing up. I'm sure she's heard about s-e-x." Rich's lack of awareness of his daughter's maturity only strengthened her resolve to keep the sex tape from him. Imagine how bad it would hurt the girl to see her father break down as his illusions of his baby girl were shattered.

"Well shit, that sucks. Why'd she have to go and grow up?"

Sarah shook her head and hugged him. *Poor guy.* He really was clueless. Patting his cheek, she assured him, "It's okay, you have at least five more years before you have to worry about Stacey."

"Ten? Why is she starting so young?"

Sarah laughed. Wrapping her hands behind his head, she pulled him to her for a kiss. "It will be all right, I promise."

"You'll stick around? Keep me distracted?"

"I suppose. You are pretty damned good at what you do."

Scooping her off the ground, he said, "Damned right. Now, you ready to test those bed springs?"

~*~

"You were right. That would have woken up the dead, much less my girls."

Sarah laughed as she snuggled against his chest, playing with the scattering of hairs. "See? I'm always thinking."

"That you are." He kissed the top of her head. "Come over tonight, after work?"

"I'd like that."

"Bring your toothbrush?"

"I don't know about that. Two overnights in a row? That's pretty suspicious. I'll come for dinner and leave by bedtime."

"What are you doing for lunch?"

Sliding up on an arm, she looked up at him and grinned. "I don't know — stop by and find out."

"Hell, work's over-rated. I say we stay here all day."

"Mmmm...can't. I have something really important I'm working on. I need to stay on top of it."

Tucking a muscled arm behind his head, he grinned. Reading his mind, she hit him with a pillow and rolled out of bed. "Mind if I use your shower?"

"Of course not. Can I join you?"

Sarah didn't answer, but backed into the bathroom with a shrug of her naked shoulders. She'd just finished adjusting the water when the curtain opened, and he joined her.

"Thought I'd wash your back." He grabbed a pink bottle of liquid soap and doused the sponge with it. The familiar bubble gum scent was heady.

"Bubble gum?" She asked.

"Stacey. She bought it for me one Christmas and was so proud. I had to make a big deal out of it. Now she buys it for me for every occasion."

Wrapping her arms around his waist, she kissed him. The hot water sprayed down on them, making his lips taste like rain. "I love it. Makes you damn near edible."

He growled and tucked her body closer to his. "We should go somewhere for a weekend. Just you and me. I want hours with your body, uninterrupted."

The feel of his wet, naked flesh made her decide work could probably wait for tomorrow, but then a door closed.

Footsteps moved down the hall. "Knock, knock. Richie, where are you?"

"Shit. It's my mother," he whispered against her lips.

"Your mom? Oh damn, oh damn," she said, looking around like there was a magic escape hatch in the shower.

"It's all right, I'll get rid of her."

~*~

Rich stepped out of the shower and wrapped a towel around his waist. "Mom?" He called, walking out into the hall.

"Hi dear, I brought your laundry. Here's the blouses I ironed for Kari. Hang them up or they'll wrinkle. And I have groceries in the car."

"Let me get dressed, and I'll get those."

"While you do that, I'll start cleaning."

"No, don't worry about that this week."

"It's my only free day. Your tight-wad father actually offered to take me to Niagara Falls. Can you believe that? Just out of the blue." Joni Cooper scratched the back of her neck and frowned. "You think he might be having an affair? Oh my, I hope he doesn't have cancer."

"I'm sure he's fine. And no, I don't think he's having an affair. He wants to do something nice for you."

"He tell you that?"

"Not in so many words, but yeah."

"What's that mean, *not in so many words*?"

"When Jess came back, he told me he'd never realized how one woman could ruin a man's whole life, and he guessed he got lucky to marry a woman with a good head on her shoulders and a big heart."

Joni sighed, "He did get awfully lucky."

"Yes, he did. Now, you ought to go on home and get ready to go. I can keep this place under control this week."

"I suppose," she said, not sounding completely convinced.

"Seriously, Dad's right. You've earned a vacation. You do everything for everybody." Joni walked down the hall toward the bedroom. Rich stepped in front of her, turning her toward the exit. "Go. Relax. Have fun. Buy me a key chain."

Joni came to a halt. "Well, my heavens, what's gotten into you? You're practically shoving me out the door."

203

"No, I'm not."

"What are you hiding? It's not the big-boobed bimbo, is it? She back over here? I thought I told you to not let her get comfortable here. She can find someone else to shack up with. I swear, I bet she set her own house on fire to get pity."

"Mandy's not here, I swear. I just wanted you to be able to relax and get packed up."

"My foot. Something's up." Joni side-stepped her son and moved quickly down the hall.

"Mom, what the hell are you doing?"

"I'm looking for Mandy. I don't want her here. I don't want her anywhere near my son."

"I swear. Mandy is not here."

"Tonya said the Andrews girl caught you practically mounting Mandy in your living room."

"What the hell, Mom?" Rich lowered his voice.

"More like 'what the hell, Richie.' When you hired her, you promised me you'd stay away from her."

"I have...for the most part. There was just that night, and Sarah reminded me what it was I really wanted."

"Ahh, sweetheart. Are you all right? Is that why you've been so depressed?"

"I'm not depressed. Seriously Mom, can we talk later?"

"What's your hurry? I'll make you some eggs and you can fill me in now."

"I like Sarah. End of story. Now, can I get dressed?"

"Of course, you can get dressed. So, what's your plan with Sarah? I've been meaning to stop by her office. I went to see Doc the other day, and he said she had to fire her secretary. I was thinking I could probably do that job. Maybe be your mole on the inside."

"I don't need a mole on the inside."

"We've got to get her away from Doc—"

"She's not with Doc," he said sharply.

"That's not what everyone tells me."

"Enough, Mom. You let me deal with this. Right now, I need to get dressed."

Rich turned and walked into his room, and his mom followed.

Rich turned, nearly pulling a muscle as he pulled on a pair of sweats. "Christ, Mom!"

"Lord's name, young man! Besides, I've seen it all before." She bent over and started grabbing dirty clothes off the floor. "I gave you a hamper, Richie, wouldn't kill you to use it." She started making the bed as she talked. "Now, about Sarah. I need to make sure you know what you're doing with her. Last time, she left you and you quit school. I don't want to see you hurt. I should definitely go feel her out…make sure her intentions toward my baby are good. That's why I need to be on the inside."

"Can we do this another time? Maybe after I dress?"

"So, dress. I'm not stopping you." She flopped down on the bed, setting the dirty clothes beside her. "Listen. The Sarah I remember is a sad sort of girl. Probably scarred by that mother of hers. Why, when she was little, I told her grandpa, 'Now damn it, Bill—and I said damn, I was serious—don't treat that girl like she's a prisoner, only letting her out for academic stuff.' I swear, Bill and her mother pushed that girl too hard. They were considering putting her in boarding school to make sure she stayed out of trouble. Maybe her dad was trouble. I don't know, I didn't know him that well. I only met him once. Talk about a loser. He hit on me at a barbeque. Did I ever tell you that?"

"Certainly not."

"Well, he did. I wasn't at all shocked when he disappeared. I heard through the grapevine that he left Claire and Sarah for some woman. I swear, some men only care about their man-parts." Joni bit her cheek. "You wouldn't do that, would you? Abandon your girls for some woman?"

205

"Never. You know better than that."

"Good, good. Some men do. After he left, that's when Claire got really weird. We were good friends in high school. She was a lot of fun. But after Sarah's dad left, she only cared about work. And Sarah's success." Joni Cooper sighed. "She's not like them, is she? All uptight and snooty?"

"She's fine, Mom."

"Well, if you are chasing her, don't try playing your games. I assume she's smart enough to see right through them."

"I don't play games."

"Better not," Joni said as she stood. Grabbing up the dirty clothes, she bent to grab another piece on the floor that was sticking out from under the bed. She pulled out a bra. Holding it up to Rich, her mouth formed a perfect O.

Rich shook his head and grabbed it from her. He put his finger to his lips. Joni blushed and nodded. Rich grabbed the clothes from her hands. It was Sarah's jeans and hoodie. Joni covered her mouth with one hand as her son quickly dragged her out the back door.

On the back deck, she asked. "You have a woman over?"

"Not a woman...Sarah."

"You're showering with her?"

"No, she hid in there when you came. She stayed until midnight playing games, so I told her to just stay over. And she's hiding because she doesn't want anyone to know about us until I talk to the girls...to see what they think."

"Well, that's wise. I said she was smart. So, did you guys...?"

"Mom, really?"

"When can I see her?"

The cold air whipped across his naked chest. Dancing from foot to foot on the cold deck, he was beginning to lose his patience. "Can we do this another time?"

Joni sighed. "I suppose. Go on inside, I'll leave the groceries on the deck."

As she turned to leave, Rich said, "Thanks, Mom. And I want you to know, if things go like I hope, you'll be seeing her a lot."

Chapter 31

Sarah hid in the bathroom until Rich popped his head in the door. "You waiting for round two, or just hiding?"

"Hiding."

"She's gone."

"I'm so embarrassed."

"I didn't out you, I swear. I told her you spent the night because we played games too late. She never guessed what a hot little beast you are on the floor and on the—"

"Stop." Sarah laughed as she planted her face in his chest. "You're not making me feel any better."

"Trust me, she thought nothing of it. My mother can be pretty clueless. She thought I suffered from the flu most of my senior year. I think Dad knew I was coming home trashed, but mom never caught on."

"Maybe I'm not the worst one in this relationship."

"Nobody ever said you were, Sarah. I wish you could see you the way I see you—you'd be impressed."

Unshed tears made her eyes burn. *I do not deserve this man....*

As if he could read her mind and knew her thoughts were headed down a dangerous path, he silenced them with a kiss. He pulled away slowly, brushing light kisses against her lips as he said, "We really should take the day off...together...."

"Mmm. I would, but remember I told you about the meeting with Kari's grandma? That's this afternoon."

"Really? That was fast." Rich took a step back. "This is all happening so fast. I mean a few weeks ago, it was the girls and me. Now, there's Jess and a mystery grandma, maybe even more—aunts, uncles...."

"I'm sorry. I know it's a lot of changes."

"Hopefully they're all for the better."

"Hopefully," Sarah said, though thoughts of Jess and her vile behavior made her feel like she'd just swallowed bitter poison.

"Should I go with you to meet the woman?" Rich walked to the cabinets and pulled out two mugs and filled them with coffee.

"Personally, I'd love a road trip with you. As your attorney, I can't recommend it. Indiana has grandparents' rights laws, and her child being deceased is grounds for visitation. Not going gives you plausible deniability. If the woman turns out to be a monster, you could continue to ignore her without the moral or legal obligation to inform her the child exists."

Rich nodded. "That makes sense. I suppose, if you think she's all right, you should tell her Kari exists. If it was one of my girls who died and I knew they had a child, I'd want to be in that kid's life. As a parent, I can't imagine losing a kid."

Sarah swallowed past the lump that formed in her throat. If only someone had told her a *choice* could make her feel like someone cut a piece of her soul out of her body. Shaking off the thought, Sarah asked, "Does Kari know that you're not her biological dad?"

"Of course. I'd never lie to my kids."

"Good. I didn't want to throw her into any more emotional upheaval if she had no clue you weren't her DNA donor."

Rich chuckled. "You have a way with words, lady. No, Kari has always known."

"And she's never been curious about who he might be?"

Rich shrugged. "If she has, she's never let on to me."

"That has to be a huge credit to you. I must have googled my dad at least once a month since the Internet became a thing. I was always curious what kind of guy he was — was I like him? Or was I simply my mother's child?" Sarah's laugh was immediately followed by a sigh.

"I think you're simply Sarah — simply perfect."

Sarah grabbed her purse and rose to leave. She planted a kiss on top of his head, allowing her lips to linger a moment. "It's good that I have you fooled."

Rich wrapped an arm around her waist and pulled her onto his lap. "Hurry back and I'll make dinner."

"Sounds like a perfect plan."

~*~

Sarah was surprised that she was surprised that Kari's grandma arrived at the meeting with a pair of lawyers from Stollings and Reed. It was the number one law firm in Indianapolis, and if the woman had the sort of money her mother had suggested, of course she'd be repped only by the best.

Collin Jennings, an older man with graying temples, recognized Sarah immediately. His assistant was a young man with blond hair, a baby face, and a beard. Sarah assumed he was fresh from law school and in training.

"Sarah Andrews." Collin's words were friendly, his handshake firm, yet warm. "We were sorry to see you go." Collin turned to Mrs. Milton, a sturdy woman in sensible shoes, a well-cut brown tweed suit, and the obligatory set of pearls. "You were right to ask us to come along, Maggie. I'm assuming Ms. Andrews would only take a case she thought she could win."

Sarah shook her head. "It's good to see you, Mr. Jennings. But rest assured, this isn't a situation about winning and losing. It's about making sure the right thing is done. My client has very recently been made aware that Paul Milton may be the biological father of his adopted daughter." If Mrs. Milton hired a Stollings associate for legal advice, Sarah assumed the woman wasn't playing games. Either she was easily defensive or already suspected something. Either way, Sarah decided it was best to be forthright. "My client has reason to believe his daughter is your granddaughter."

"Where exactly did your client come by this information?" Collin asked.

"My mother, Claire Andrews. She works for—"

"I'm aware who your mother is." Collin turned to Mrs. Milton. "Claire Andrews is highly respected and rarely mistaken, probably where her daughter gets it," Collin said, giving Sarah a nod. "So, your mother's informant thinks Paul may have a child?"

Sarah nodded.

"Mrs. Milton's son died in a car wreck six years ago. Her daughter also suffered an untimely death a few years ago. She is widowed, and those were her only children. If this is a hoax—"

"It's not a hoax. I cannot, of course, swear to the lineage of this young girl, but Mr. Jennings, if you would vouch for the character of Mrs. Milton, I'm certain my client would agree to whatever DNA tests you deem appropriate."

The older woman's chin quivered, and her eyes shone with unshed tears. "And what will that cost me?"

"My client isn't a rich man, so I think it only fair that the costs of the tests be divided fifty-fifty."

"No, my dear. What will it cost me to meet this child, if she is my granddaughter?"

It took Sarah a minute to understand. The woman thought she was shaking her down for money. Sarah shook her head. "No, ma'am. You misunderstand. My client loves his daughter. He wants what is best for her, and he believes knowing her family of origin is what is in her best interest." Sarah turned to Collin. "And let's be honest, the law is on your client's side if the tests prove positive. Mrs. Milton, you're within your legal rights to have visitation with your grandchild — especially with her natural father being deceased. My client and I feel for your situation. He is wanting to extend compassion, not a hand of greed."

The older woman lost her battle with the tears and reached into her purse for a handkerchief. Sarah laid her business card on the table and grabbed her briefcase. "I'm sorry for your loss, Mrs. Milton. Mr. Jennings, I'll leave you to discuss this with your client. If you have any questions, feel free to call. I put my private number on the back of the card."

Sarah hurried from the building, barely making it to her car before her own tears rolled down her cheeks. Sarah told herself that she was crying for Mrs. Milton and her loss. She couldn't be crying over her own loss — that didn't happen by accident, thus giving her no right to mourn.

Chapter 32

Sarah stopped by the hospital on her way home from the meeting with Mrs. Milton. She waited in a hallway while Doc was paged to the admission desk. Leaning against the wall, she tapped her fingers against the smooth concrete as she tried to decide exactly what to say to him. She'd never dumped anyone before, and it was uncomfortable—even if that person was already seeing someone else.

"Hey, babe," Doc said as he came down the hall.

"Hey," she answered as she ducked out of a hug.

Doc looked guilty. "Is this about the other night? I know I said I'd call, but something came up here at work."

Sarah shook her head. "No, it isn't that. I just…is there somewhere we can go?"

"Yeah, follow me." He led her back to a tiny, square office that barely had enough room for a desk and the filing cabinet next to it. "Head nurse's office. Sucks to be her, right?" He asked with a chuckle.

Once the door was closed, Doc leaned against the desk and reached out for her hand. Sarah tucked her hands in her pockets.

Doc gave her a quizzical look, "Did Tonya tell you I was with Angie last night?"

Curiosity got the best of her. "Were you?"

213

"Yes, but only as friends."

"The whole night?" Sarah asked with a raised eyebrow.

Doc sighed.

Sarah felt guilty for giving him hell when every muscle in her body was still sore. She reached out and rubbed his shoulder. "Look, Doc. I didn't come here to confront you about Angie. I don't know what you two have going on, but that's your business. I came here because I wanted you to hear it from me and not through the grapevine." Sarah felt her cheeks grow warm. Admitting this was hard, even when she knew she wasn't in the wrong. "It's Rich."

Doc snorted. "That's where you were last night? I came by your house and you weren't home. I figured you were out with Tonya."

Sarah shook her head.

Doc nodded. "I don't know why I thought I could beat him. I hope he's good to you."

"I hope he is too. I won't lie—you were the safer bet."

Doc laughed. "I don't know about that. It pains me to say it, but Rich loves you. It's plain as the twelve-hour shadow on his face. I knew it the day he brought you into the clinic."

"So, why?"

Doc shrugged. "I'm selfish. I'm pushing forty. How many beautiful, single women do you think come through Dodd?"

"A few?"

"Hardly. I've spent the better part of my life wasting my time with a married woman. Now, I've got what? You and me—that match made good sense."

"I thought the same thing. And if things were different...."

"I'm happy you're happy. I hope Rich knows what a lucky guy he is."

"I appreciate that." Sarah paused. "Can I give you some advice? As a friend?"

"Of course."

"If I had been emotionally invested in us, you'd have broken my heart. This relationship with Angie? It's insane. If you guys are going to be a couple, then be it. If not, ditch her and find someone else. There are more women out there. Hell, with your cash and good looks, you could be hitting on the twenty-somethings."

"Ah, gold diggers."

"Better than a married woman who will only keep breaking your heart again and again."

"I love her, Sarah. I don't want to, but I do. I want so badly to tell her to go to hell, but I can't. I know she's using me."

"Why do you put up with that?"

He shook his head. "Hell, if I know. I suppose you buy their bullshit stories because you want to. I mean, a guy like me has been left a lot. After a while, you don't have a real good measure of what's normal or not. Maybe I should see a shrink. Maybe it goes all the way back to mommy issues. She left me with my babysitter and was supposed to be back after she got her hair done. Evidently, she's still getting it cut."

"Oh Doc. You have to stand up to Angie. It's you or him. No more games. It's not fair to you; it's not fair to the next girl—if there is one."

He rubbed his morning chin growth. "If I hadn't been with her yesterday, I'd have been with you when you called. Then Rich wouldn't have gotten his foot in the door."

"Exactly." She grinned and gave him an elbow. "You want to lose another perfect woman like me because some chick has you on a short leash?"

"Shit. I'm regretting losing the one with me right now."

"Did you seriously think it would work? Two-timing me with Angie? I mean, nothing in this town goes unreported."

"I know. And no, I knew I was going to have to choose real soon. And whenever I thought about it, I chose you. You were

215

my plan for the future. It's just when Angie would call, I'd tell myself — this is it. I'm going to go tell her we're done."

"And never did?"

"Oh no, I told her. She'd just talk me out of it," he said with a hollow laugh.

"Don't you see how wrong that is?"

"She called me this morning to tell me Donnie left town with Mandy. Seems the burned down house and Rich's rejection made Mandy desperate."

"I should call Angie and see if she wants me to file divorce papers for her."

"I suggested that. She says she can't piss off her parents. They're hard core religious, and her dad is sick."

"Bull. All she needs to do is tell them what he's been doing."

"She says she'll think it over."

"Maybe you'll get lucky and Donnie will divorce her."

"Does that make me lucky?"

"Honestly? No. In my opinion, you've got to move on. If I had loved you, you'd have broken my heart. That's so wrong."

"You're right, Sarah. I need to leave here. Somewhere I never see her or hear about her."

"Change your number, stay off social media —"

"You know all about it, huh?" Doc laughed.

"Yep."

"Rich?"

She nodded. "I loved him with all my heart. I couldn't trust myself to be smart, so I cut all ties. Didn't come back until I thought I had grown out of it."

Doc hugged her and gave her a kiss on her forehead. "I do love you, Sarah. If it comes to that, yours might be the only number I keep. That all right?"

"That would be fine." She squeezed him back. "You deserve to be happy. Don't ever accept anything less, okay?"

216

He nodded against her shoulder.

Someone pulled the door open. Sarah jumped back. Doc cleared his throat.

"Sorry," a lady in blue scrubs said before slamming it shut.

"I better go," Sarah said, patting his cheek. "You'll stand up to her, right?"

"Yes, ma'am."

"Promise?"

"Promise," he said with a sad smile.

As Sarah was leaving the hospital, she was busy digging her car keys out of her purse and practically walked right into Angie.

"Sarah," Angie said. "I heard you were here."

"Yeah, I came to see Doc," Sarah said, happy to see the flash of jealousy that washed over Angie's face.

"Oh," was all Angie said.

"He asked me to go away with him this weekend. I told him I would, but only if the shit with you stops."

"Shit? With me?" Angie looked around the empty hallway.

"Yeah. I know you two were together yesterday, so I told him—no more playing friends with you. If we're going to make this work, I want him to cut the ties. Move out of this damned town if we have to."

"Leave town? He can't. What did he say?" Angie stood a little straighter.

"He said he loved you, but was done letting you break his heart, so he would do whatever I asked."

A red blush creeped across Angie's cheeks. "He said that?"

Sarah nodded, then let out an exaggerated sigh. "Look, I know he loves you, but I also know you have no intention of divorcing Donnie. It makes no sense to me why you would choose a lying cheat who steals from your sick father over a guy like Doc, but honestly, your stupidity is my gain."

"What the hell, Sarah? When did you get so mean?"

"I'm not being mean. I'm being honest."

Angie stepped closer, her voice low. "I do love him. I just worry about my family. They've always accused me of having an affair with Doc. And Mom and Dad firmly believe in the whole till death do you part thing, even if I'm miserable. If I choose Doc, they might disown me."

"You're a little too old to let your parents dictate your life. You're going to have to make a choice. Either send him up to bat, or I'll take that player out of the game. He's getting to the point in his life where a quick lay isn't enough. He wants a home and a family too. You think he wants to be your life-long booty call?"

"Good God, Sarah, I've never known you to be such a bitch."

"Shows how much you know me. Look, what you're doing is cruel. If you don't appreciate a guy like Doc, then I'll show him there are women who would."

"So, you would keep him, knowing he loves me?"

"One of the things I am guilty of is being rational. If that makes me a bitch, then so be it. I'm thirty-three. I want the same things Doc wants. We understand each other. I don't love him; he doesn't love me. But we'll make a good pair. And who knows — once we're out of this town and building a life together, love might come."

"Where will you guys go?"

"Ha," Sarah said, hitching her purse higher on her shoulder and stepping away. "Like I'd ever tell you. Like I told Doc, to make this work, we cut all ties. Move to another country if we have to. That's how we'll have our happily ever after."

With that, Sarah turned and walked away.

Chapter 33

Sarah reviewed the document one more time before sliding it into her briefcase. Smoothing the creases from her luckiest dress suit, she took a deep breath and said a little prayer, though she wasn't at all certain God helped a gal get away with blackmail.

Grabbing her briefcase, she was about to walk out her front door when she was greeted by an arm-swinging, red-faced Tonya.

"What the hell, Sarah?"

Sarah clenched her briefcase handle, and asked calmly, "What the hell what?"

"You're running away with Doc? After Rich came into the office whistling, which means you two obviously had sex."

Sarah laughed. "He whistles after sex? Is that sex with anyone, or — ?"

"Dammit, Sarah! It's not funny. He loves you. He's happy — finally."

"I love him, too."

"So, what's up with Doc? At first I thought Angie was lying, but then when you called and told Rich you'd have to skip lunch…I put two and two together."

"And got ten?"

"What's that mean?"

"It means you're way off. You busy? Want to make a business

219

call with me? I'll explain everything."

"You're not dumping Rich?"

"Not in a million years."

"Then why — ?"

"Angie deserved a bit of her own medicine. So, you want to come with me or not?"

Tonya took a deep breath and looked at her watch. "I suppose Rich can pick my kids up from school. I'm seriously dying to know how you're going to explain this."

"Well, come on. I'll drive."

Driving down the road toward Dodd Lake, Sarah gripped the wheel as she explained. "I did tell Angie all that, but only to piss her off. Doc is ball-less as a two-year-old girl, but he's a nice guy who's had the shittiest life. I just wanted to tweak her a bit and make her stop taking him for granted."

"And if she tells Rich?"

"She won't tell Rich. The girl's not stupid. Angie would not want Rich out of my life. He is her only hope of a single Doc. Honestly, I'm a little shocked she told you…no, I take that back. Telling you makes total sense. She wants you to verify if I'm serious. If you report back that I'm happily bedding Rich, she can continue to treat Doc like a spare tire."

"Wow. Rich must have done some impressive work. Look at you — all loosened up, talking balls and getting bedded."

Sarah laughed. "I do feel…good. God, I feel good. It's been so long since I've been happy, it's almost like being on a high."

Tonya laughed and let out a relaxed breath. "I know you wouldn't intentionally play Rich, but I was scared shitless that you decided to tuck tail and run for the comfortable choice. I told Angie that. I went off. I was like, 'I knew it! I knew she'd do this. She sees Doc as safe. I knew she'd end up with Doc.' I bet I have her crapping in her drawers."

"Good. She needs to quit playing these games. It's not fair to

Doc, or her, for that matter."

"You're such an evil genius, Sarah. Remind me to never piss you off."

Sarah bit the side of her cheek. "Speaking of evil…I'm going to let you in on something, and you have to promise me…and I mean promise…to never tell."

"What is it?"

"Promise first."

"I promise, what is it?"

"Jessie and her husband are blackmailing Kari," Sarah said, glancing at Tonya's reaction before returning her eyes to the straight country road ahead of her.

"My Kari? My niece, Kari?"

Sarah nodded.

"What with, the boyfriend?"

"You're going to lose it when I tell you, but you have to keep this promise. I swore to Kari I would never tell, but I just have to ask someone else who loves her if I'm doing the right thing."

"That freaking bitch — what has she done?"

"Kari came to me and told me Phil had a video of Kari and her boyfriend having sex."

"He what?" Tonya's voice echoed off the car windows.

"He has this video of Kari and her boyfriend having sex. And he told her that she needs to keep her mother happy, or he'll show the video to her dad."

"That son of a bitch. I'll gut him myself. Is that what we're doing today? Killing the bastard?"

Sarah's brows knitted together. "Of course not. We're civilized, for God's sake."

"I'm not feeling so civilized. I think my blood pressure is way up."

"Well, get ready to get hotter." Tonya took a deep breath and nodded. Sarah continued, "I think Phil planted the cameras in

221

the pool house to have a way to blackmail Kari. I mean, who puts cameras in a pool house where people change?"

"Or he's a pedophile and just wanted to see her change."

"I thought of that, but then I met Kari's grandma. Very rich. Very suspicious of being shaken down for that mountain of money. I think Jess and Phil know Kari is a golden egg, and they don't want visits with her; they want custody. That's why they're blackmailing Kari—forcing her to move across the country with them."

Tonya grabbed at her chest and shook her head. "You're kidding me?"

"Wish I was. If my hunch is right, they probably hired the boy to date her. I've asked a private investigator to find this boy and talk to him. I would bet you every dime in my account that *relationship* didn't happen by accident."

"I never trusted Jess, but that's seriously maniacal."

"I think Jess is capable of anything if it gains her something."

"Oh my God, do you think they are selling it as kiddy porn? I saw that on TV—"

"I think it's a shade less diabolical than that. I honestly think it's about the money."

"Shit, Kari's dad's family—what are they, freaking Kennedys?"

"I have no clue about their net worth, but the grandma hired a lawyer from the firm I used to work for. None of those lawyers come cheap. The woman has some very deep pockets. My guess is Jess needs Kari to get money out of the dead dad's family."

"Oh my God, that poor baby." Tonya's face was red and her hands shook. "So, what are you going to do?"

"I could go to the police. Both of them would rot in prison for years."

"Sounds good."

"But then Rich finds out, and I've broken my promise to Kari that I would keep him from ever knowing the truth."

"Would there be a trial?"

"Of course," Sarah said.

"That would be humiliating—damn video would probably make its way to the Internet."

"Most likely."

"So, what's the other option?"

"I'm going to blackmail them. I'm going to let Jess and Phil know that all this information will go straight to a friend of mine at the FBI if she doesn't sign complete custody over to Rich. That she'll not make Kari visit anymore and won't have contact with her, unless initiated by Kari once she reaches adulthood."

Tonya nodded. "I hate that Jess doesn't get punished. I want her to feel pain. A slow, painful torture. She doesn't care about her kids. Not seeing them won't matter at all to her."

"It's the best I can come up with—the only way that keeps my promise to Kari. But then I think about Rich finding out and he'll kill me. Am I screwing up royally here?"

"Remember that time my dad caught me and John going at it in the bathroom?"

Sarah giggled. "Good times, right?"

"Not at all! And at least I married him. But to this day, when I think about it, I want to crawl into a hole. Poor Kari. If it gets spread across the net like all those other sex tapes…oh my God, that poor girl."

"I know, and that thought makes me feel like I'm doing the right thing. But then, I think…I could lose him forever."

"But then, if you tell him and Kari hates you, the relationship isn't going to last. He's not going to keep a woman his daughter can't stand."

Sarah nodded. "And a promise is a promise. I have to keep it."

Chapter 34

Tonya and Sarah turned left off the country road onto Wooster Drive. Tonya whistled. "Jess sure did move up in the world. Living it up in Wooster?"

"By the address, I'd say it's lakefront too. You know Jess always swore she'd have nothing in life but the best."

"I wonder why she ever married Rich?" Tonya asked with laugh.

"She did it to hurt me. She knew I loved him. Evidently I was a fool to think she was a friend."

"I would have told you that—had you trusted me."

Sarah sighed. "I know, I know. I regret not going to you every day of my life."

"Well, I suppose if you're eternally remorseful, I can forgive you."

"Eternally remorseful…you could put that on my headstone."

"Ha! I'm sticking with you, chick. I won't let you make any more horrible decisions."

"You say that as we set off to blackmail the mother of your niece?"

"Oh well, sometimes you do evil for good. It's justifiable."

"We'll probably end up in hell."

"Nah…I know a good attorney."

Sarah shook her head at Tonya, but the smile on her face felt good. Sarah was home.

Circling a cul-de-sac lined with large, perfect yards, they slowed, looking for house number 209. All the houses had stone-surround mailboxes displaying the house numbers, so they found the house easily. It was a mammoth, with large arched windows and tall entry doors.

"It looks like a church, don't ya think?" Tonya asked.

Sarah tipped her head and looked. It did look like a church, from the washed-out brick to the steepled roof. All it needed was a bell tower and a cross on top.

"It does. Leave it to Jess to buy the biggest one on the street."

"Sad thing is, Jess had it all. Great husband. Wonderful kids. If that wasn't enough, I doubt there is enough money in the world to make her happy."

"Well, obviously this isn't enough. She's angling to get more." Sarah parked and grabbed her briefcase. "You want to wait here or go with me?"

"Oh, hell, I'm going. I wouldn't miss this for the world," Tonya said, climbing out of the car.

Sarah rang the doorbell, fully expecting a maid to answer the door. Instead, it was Jess, dressed in yoga pants and a bra top. The girls were right. Her "girls" were several sizes larger than they were in high school, and her waist was several inches smaller. Sarah supposed she missed the obvious being too focused on the blackmail threats.

"Sarah," Jess said, wiping at sweat on her neck with a towel. "Still meddling? I thought you were smarter than that. And Tonya, I see you never took my advice about those yoga classes. But still, good to see you."

Tonya shot Sarah a look. Sarah shook her head.

"Come on in," Jess said, stepping back and ushering them in. "I was just doing my work out. You just missed Javiar. I'd recommend him to you Tonya, but he's very expensive. Sarah, you could probably afford him…if you were saving the money you made with Stollings and Reed before you got fired."

Sarah took a deep breath and closed her eyes a moment to remind herself to stay calm.

Jess wiped sweat from her neck as she led them to a kitchen any restaurant would love to have. Jess pulled fruit and vegetables out of the fridge and started prepping herself a smoothie, chopping up chunks of fruits and veggies and dropping them into a blender.

Sarah pulled the file from her briefcase and laid the papers out on the counter.

Jess ignored her, flipping the blender on, filling the room with the buzz of spinning blades. Sarah reached out and yanked the cord from the wall.

Jess gave her a look. "Excuse me?" she asked.

"I'm not here for a visit, Jess. I'm here to protect your daughter."

"My daughter?"

"Yes, Kari." Sarah pulled out the custody papers from the file and slid them in front of Jess. "Just so you know, as we speak, I have a PI interviewing the boyfriend you and Phil hired to get compromising pictures of your daughter."

Jess grabbed a towel off the counter and wiped her hands. "We didn't hire him to compromise anyone. I just wanted Kari to enjoy herself here. And Brandon is Phil's nephew, so if he gives his family money, that's his business. My husband is a very generous man."

"So, I hear," Sarah said. "Kari says Phil is very generous with his threats too. Did you know he was blackmailing her with a video of her having sex with Brandon?"

"Blackmail? That's absurd."

"You calling your daughter a liar? She says Phil told her he'd

226

show the tape to her dad unless she made you happy."

"What the hell do you think he means by that, Jess?" Tonya asked.

"I don't know what you guys are talking about," Jess said. "Phil loves Kari. We both do. As a matter of fact, Phil is being transferred to the West Coast, and he wants Kari to go with us."

"So, you guys are blackmailing the kid to make her move with you?" Tonya asked. "Or does Phil get a little tingle in his willie for little girls?"

"Seriously, Tonya?!" Jess said. "You're disgusting."

"Look," Sarah said calmly. "Kari came to me…she said Phil made her feel uneasy — her words, not mine. Then she said that Phil had a sex tape of her and was blackmailing her with it. Now, if you say you know nothing about that, I believe you. But I also believe Kari. The kid isn't a liar. And you, as her mother, should protect her."

"Of course, I would do anything to protect her. I mean, I know you guys think I'm the bad guy in all of this, but I only left her in the first place because I knew I needed to get clean, and I haven't even forced Stacey to spend time with me because I know my little girl doesn't even know me."

Jess blotted at her eyes with the towel.

Sarah frowned. "Look, let's pretend there is no sex tape, and Kari is just a scared young girl not wanting to move out of the only home she's ever known. How about if you sign custody of the girl over to Rich, this all goes away?"

Jess chewed on her thumbnail.

Sarah shoved the papers closer to her. "All you need to do is sign these, I'll take them to family court tomorrow, and it's all done."

Jessie looked the papers over. "Why would I give my daughter to Rich?"

"You're not. You're just giving him custody. You know he

wouldn't come between you and your daughter. This just ensures that we never have to go to court. Never have to tell a judge that your husband blackmailed a child with a sex tape...which is so many levels of illegal. I mean, even owning that sort of thing makes him a sex offender — you know that, right?" Sarah looked up at the high ceilings adorned with skylights and ornate hanging lights. "I'm guessing Phil has a pretty high-profile position. You think being listed as a sex offender will hurt him much?"

"Kari told you this?" Jess asked.

"Yes, Tonya and me." Sarah looked to Tanya, who nodded.

"Well, I hardly believe Phil did anything like this, but if Kari is so distressed that she's willing to say such bizarre things, I think giving Rich custody is probably in her best interest."

Sarah handed her a pen. "Wise choice."

Jessie signed, her hands shaking. "So, is that it?"

Sarah scooped the papers off the counter and stuffed them into the file folder. "I'll take these to the courthouse tomorrow. The judge will meet with Kari and ask her a few questions, to be sure this is what she wants. Then he will make the order official."

"Do I need to be there?"

"No, Tonya is a notary public. She can verify this is your signature."

"But if I wanted to be there, what time is it?"

Sarah sighed. "I'll call you with that information once it's set up."

"I mean, I'd like an opportunity to explain to Kari that I am doing this for her. Not because she lied, but because I want her to be happy."

"Thank you, Jess. You're doing the right thing. I may have misjudged you," Sarah said with a smile. Then she and Tonya bolted, not wanting to give Jess the opportunity to change her mind.

Chapter 35

Sarah raced home, changed into jeans and a sweater, and headed to Rich's for dinner. She got there just in time to catch him and the girls carrying boxes of pizza into the house.

"Sarah!" Stacey cried, and came barreling down the sidewalk for a hug. Kari offered her a much more subdued, "Hey," but her smile spoke volumes. Rich, on the other hand, frowned.

"Girls, take these inside and get your homework done," Rich said, handing Kari the pizzas and Stacey a grocery bag. Then he cracked his neck and leaned against the door of her car. "Angie called me."

"Seriously?" Sarah was truly shocked. She thought for sure Angie would keep her mouth shut.

"Not going to say, *about what*? Or any of that?"

"No, I know what she said. And I did say it. I was just trying to help Doc."

"Helping Doc by making out with him in the nurse's office?"

"I what? Oh my God, she said that? That lying little tramp." Sarah's mouth hung open in disbelief.

Rich was quiet.

Finally, she said, "No, I never made out with him. I talked to him. I told you I was going to talk to him, remember?"

"Yeah, I remember. I just don't remember lip on lip action

being part of the necessary conversation."

"There was no lip on lip action. She's just mad because I told her if she didn't start doing right by Doc, I'd take him off the market."

The muscle in his jaw twitched. "You would, would you?"

Sarah's heart beat a little quicker. "Of course not."

"Then why say it?"

"I told you. I wanted to help Doc."

"So, he's still a priority? Helping him is more important than not making me look like an ass?"

"I never thought she'd repeat any of it. I thought she'd get smart, tell the guy she loved him, and they'd live happily ever after."

"You really thought it'd be that easy?"

Sarah shrugged. "I honestly did. I mean, if she had any sense and she feared me taking Doc from her, the last thing she'd do is cause trouble between you and me."

Rich shook his head. "I guess I don't follow, because I'm not really a game player."

"I'm not...look, I screwed up. I'm sorry. I should have thought it through, but I didn't."

He continued to stare at her like she was a school kid caught cheating on an exam.

Her nerves were starting to scream. She was suddenly Claire Andrews' dipshit daughter, who couldn't be trusted to pick out her own clothes, much less make choices that would affect the rest of her life. Her eyes burned, but her spine stiffened. "So, do we get over this, or are we done?"

His eyes narrowed a bit. "It'd be that easy for you to walk away?"

Sarah shrugged. "No, it would hurt like hell."

"Were you with him at lunch today?"

Sarah shook her head and tried to clear the constriction from her throat. "No, I dropped by on my way back from Indianapolis. I cancelled our lunch because I was meeting with Jess. You can even verify that with Tonya. I took her with me."

"Why would you and Tonya meet with Jess? Did Mrs. Milton say something?"

"No. But she did seem like a nice lady. No, I wanted to talk to Jess on behalf of Kari. Seems Kari feels as awkward visiting there as Stacey does. So, I went to talk with Jess and she informed me that her husband was being transferred to the west coast—which might explain the sudden fear of visits on Kari's part. I explained to Jess that Kari had told me she didn't want to visit anymore, and that maybe the girl was just nervous about having to go so far from the only home she knew."

"She wants to take my kid to the west coast?"

"Not anymore. After we discussed it, she agreed it was in Kari's best interest to give you full custody of Kari."

"She what?" Rich was up off the car and fully alert.

Sarah reached into her bag for the file folder and handed it to Rich. "Here's the papers. They're signed. I called and scheduled a meeting with the judge for tomorrow, and Jess says she will meet us at the courthouse and make it official. Kari will need to be there because the judge will want to speak with her, make sure this is what she wants."

Rich flipped through the pages, his eyes wide. Then he smiled at her; a full, glorious smile. "This is where you were today?"

Sarah nodded. "For Kari. As her attorney."

"Well, son of a bitch, if this isn't just the best news all day."

Sarah chewed on her lip. Her gut told her she should tell him the whole truth, but she wouldn't. She couldn't. He'd never know that she and Tonya had taken the papers to Jess with their thinly veiled blackmail option. They could both go to jail for their work today—that was a thought that stuck in the forefront of her mind.

Then to come here and get interrogated about Doc? And to be

231

called a game player? Well, that was a pretty clear indication that she wasn't so damned good at predicting outcomes. Her stomach tightened. This little escapade could ruin her for good. She suddenly wanted to be at home, in a hot tub, with at least a gallon of wine. "Those are copies. I've already filed the originals with the court. Meet me tomorrow in family court at two. Hopefully this will be the end of it."

Sarah turned to leave.

Rich grabbed her by the hand. "Where are you going?"

"Home. I'm tired. I just wanted you to have those papers and tell you about the court time." Pulling her hand away, she walked to the driver's side.

He was right behind her. "Don't go. The girls were so excited." Pulling the keys out of her pocket, she shook her head. He grabbed the keys from her hand and pulled her in for a hug. "I'm sorry. I had all sorts of shit going on in my head. I imagined you going to see Doc and the two of you making out at the hospital. And then taking it back to his place. It wasn't a pleasant day for me."

She nodded, laying her cheek against his chest. "I didn't think it through with Doc. I bumped into Angie and the ugly just got hold of me."

He laughed. "The ugly?"

"Yeah, that side of me that makes me want to strangle people and make them do the right thing. It's not that hard to do the right thing."

"Did you have to strangle Jess?" He asked with a laugh. "Or did you have to bribe her?"

"Neither. I just presented the situation from Kari's point of view."

He smoothed the hair down that fell across her shoulders. "Whatever you did, I thank you."

Sarah nodded, not at all certain he'd approve of the whole

truth.

"You're good for them, Sarah. I'm glad Kari had you to go to." Tipping her chin until she had to look up at him, he said, "You have a big heart, and I know you'd do anything to help the people you care about. I'm sorry about Doc. It's just...well, from my point of view, he's been the opposition. For weeks, he had what I wanted. Understand?"

She nodded.

Rich kissed her, sweet and deep.

"I never meant to hurt you, or embarrass you. I swear, I really didn't think she'd mention it to anyone, least of all you."

"It's done. We're past it. I think we should go in and tell Kari the good news. And then we'll celebrate."

He kissed her again and she held him tight. They'd survived yet another Sarah-created fiasco. Would a third be a charm or a strike out from the game?

Chapter 36

Sarah dressed in her best grey suit. Her hands shook as she buttoned and zipped. She tried to drink a cup of coffee, but her stomach wouldn't allow it. Even a bite of toast made her want to vomit. Sitting on her couch, she took a deep breath. Rich had been furious over Doc. If he knew what else she was into, he'd hate her for sure.

That little ruse had blown up in her face, but the end result was good. Angie was finally filing for divorce.

Sarah checked her watch—it was almost noon. She gathered her papers and headed out. She decided to walk to the courthouse. It was not too far down the street and the day was sunny, like fall was offering them one last weak day of warmth before the bitter cold swept in.

Angie was waiting on her. Sarah felt like slapping her, tattle-tale telling traitor. She regretted telling her she'd waive her legal fees—she should have charged her double. Sarah led her to a small room lawyers often used for consultation and went through all the paperwork with her, explaining the time frames. She'd had a phone consult with Donnie's attorney in Florida—seems him and Mandy were settled in and hoping to buy a gym. For now, they were both working for Disney World. Donnie wasn't contesting Angie's right to custody of their son as long as she agreed to waive child support. Donnie never was convinced Tyler was his kid, anyhow.

Sarah didn't worry over it—she was just happy this was going to be clean and simple.

"I told my parents Donnie filed for divorce," Angie said.

"That's your prerogative," Sarah said, her voice clipped.

Angie sighed and hugged the purse in her lap. "I'm sorry, Sarah. I know you loved him."

"Love him. Present tense."

"Well, I hope you realize—me doing this—it means I plan for us to be together. I hope that won't ruin our friendship."

Oh hell, Sarah thought, *she's talking about Doc.* Sarah frowned. "I'll get over it. Don't worry about it." She made a few X's on the paperwork and then handed it to Angie. "There you go. Sign where indicated, and in about sixty days, you should be a free woman."

Angie signed. A tear rolled down her cheek. Sarah grabbed the papers and practically yanked them away from Angie as she signed them. Angie sniffled a bit more and Sarah couldn't hold her temper any longer. "You should be celebrating, Angie. Donnie is a jerk. He's a lying, cheating, woman-beating ass. I cannot for the life of me understand why you stayed with him so long."

"It's just that a part of my life is over. My family is broken apart. I suppose it's not something you can understand. You've never had a real family. You'll never have to explain to your child why his dad isn't coming home."

"It might be harder to explain why his dad thinks he belongs to your boyfriend," Sarah said. Collecting the papers, she looked at Angie. "I think Doc is a fool to take you back. I think he could find a hundred women if only he'd look. I think you're mean and cruel to use him like you do."

Angie stood. "Screw you, Sarah. You're always so high and

mighty. How are you any better? I know you're screwing Rich and baiting Doc. How are you any better than me?"

"Don't you dare compare what I've done to what you've done. I'm not married to anyone. If I was, I'd either honor that vow or get out. I wouldn't play games with someone's affections and ruin their life."

"Maybe you ought to ask Rich about that. You broke his heart fifteen years ago. Put your career ahead of everything, including him. And now, I suppose you'll go running back to him just because you're out of options. That's not exactly noble."

A heaviness washed over Sarah pulling her shoulders down. "You're right, Ang. I shouldn't be throwing stones, that's for sure."

~*~

Sarah was in the small family law room waiting when Rich and Kari arrived. Rich looked happy; Kari looked as nervous as Sarah felt. Sarah sent Rich for sodas, giving her a minute alone with Kari.

As soon as the door was closed behind him, Kari leaned in and asked, "He doesn't know, right?"

"Right."

"It won't be brought up?"

"No. I talked to your mom yesterday, and she agreed your dad should have custody."

"That easily?" Kari bit her lip.

Sarah took a deep breath. *Yes, it was too good to believe.* "Yes, that easily."

Rich returned with the drinks. Sarah was so shaky she could barely open the tab, much less drink it. Her hands felt icy and thick.

Jess and Phil arrived, accompanied by men in suits, Sarah assumed they were lawyers. Her stomach dropped.

Jess looked gorgeous in a pink sweater and white wool pants.

Sarah felt like a mouse in her gray. Jess came over and said hi to Rich, rubbing his shoulder and leaning across his lap to hug her daughter. Phil stood in front of the table staring hard at Sarah. Once Jess was done making small talk, Phil reached a hand out to Sarah. "Sarah Andrews, it's a pleasure. Evan Stollings and I are good friends. He's told me so many *interesting* stories about you."

Jess gave Sarah a cat-like smile. "If only we had the time — the stories about Sarah that I could share. Right, Sarah?"

Sarah's smile was shaky, her hands trembled. Kari reached across the seat and took her hand and gave it a squeeze. Sarah looked at the girl. Her big, brown eyes were wide, like she was offering silent support.

Jess seemed to catch the exchange. Once her gaze landed on Sarah and Kari's clasped hands, her phony-friendly demeanor was dropped. Jess sneered and leaned across the table until her face was inches from Sarah's. "You scheming, lying little bitch. You won't get away with this. I know what you're doing. You're trying to take my daughter from me — screwing Rich and playing mommy. But they're my kids. Mine. You understand? It's not my fault you killed yours. You will regret this Sarah; that I swear to you."

"Shut up, Jess," Rich's words were harsh.

Jess turned to him. "You — you sanctimonious prick. Acting like you're some saint because you raised some other man's brat. She's my daughter. Not yours."

The bailiff, an older man with a thin build and graying hair, approached the table. "Is there a problem here?"

Jess flashed him a smile. "Just having a chit chat before the hearing starts."

"Please take a seat," he ordered.

"Of course," Jess said with a smile.

Once everyone was seated, the bailiff ordered, "All rise for the Honorable Judge William Morgan."

Sarah was grateful the sound of chairs scraping on hardwood floors drowned out the hammering of her heart.

Judge Morgan was a chubby, elderly man with a chin waddle and thin, grey hair. Following close behind him was Mrs. Milton, who sat in a chair in the corner, ankles crossed.

The judge called them to order and asked Sarah for the custody agreement. Before Sarah could rise from her seat, Jess's attorney was up, addressing the court. "Your Honor. Those papers were signed under duress. Seems Mr. Cooper's attorney has gone so far as to blackmail my client with thinly veiled and incredibly bogus accusations of child sex abuse. I'm sure Miss Andrews understands the severity of her accusations…and I suspect she is also aware that failure to properly report such information, if it were true, could lead not only to her being disbarred, but to jail time also." The attorney stepped forward and placed a brief on the judge's desk.

Judge Morgan adjusted his glasses and looked it over. He cleared his throat. "Miss Andrews, did you meet with Mrs. Demkey last night and threaten her into signing the papers?"

Sarah stood on trembling legs. She looked down at Kari. The girl's eyes were huge. "Your Honor, I simply met with Mrs. Demkey to appeal to her on behalf of her daughter. The child wants to remain with her father, and has expressed feeling uncomfortable with Mr. Demkey. I never said he made any sexual advances or overtures toward the child, and none were implied. I simply said the girl felt uncomfortable in his presence."

Judge Morgan nodded. "Is that true, young lady?"

Kari leaned forward and said, "Yes, sir. That's true. I want to stay with my dad, and I don't like Phil." With that, Kari started to cry.

Sarah wrapped an arm around her and held her tight.

"Well, Counselor…Mr.," Judge Morgan looked over the

paper. "Pulaski. Seems at best, I am inclined to give Mr. Cooper custody until the court can better look into these accusations."

"Your Honor, you can't be serious! Miss Andrews blackmailed my client as Mr. Cooper's counsel. And if I might inform the court, it doesn't take much research to look into Miss Andrew's legal history and see that she is hardly opposed to crossing the line of good ethics and appropriate behavior. As a matter of fact," he stared at Sarah. "I barely had to scratch the surface to find out the relationship between Miss Andrews and sex scandals is a common theme. I wonder what we'd find out if we were actually investigating. Is that what it will come to, Miss Andrews? Dirty little tit for tat?"

Judge Morgan's voice boomed in the room. "Are you seriously threatening opposing counsel right in front of me? Son, are you stupid, or just incredibly arrogant?" Judge Morgan wiped the sweat from his brow. "Or maybe you think, with your fancy suit and your expensive shoes, that you've stepped into some Podunk town where the judge is an idiot? Well now, I can assure you, I am no idiot, and my order stands. Full custody granted to Mr. Cooper, with a referral to social services for investigation."

Jess stood and yelled, her finger shaking at the judge, "Aren't you even going to ask her if she threatened me with a sex tape?"

Judge Morgan sighed. "Miss Andrews, did you blackmail Mrs. Demkey with a sex tape?"

"Your Honor, if such a sex tape exists, I've never seen it."

"Counselor," Judge Morgan repeated, rubbing the bridge of his nose. "Did you blackmail Mrs. Demkey? You lawyers and your dancing around the questions."

Sarah took a deep breath. "No sir, I did not."

"Thank you. My order stands. Mr. Cooper, you may take your daughter home. Social services will be notified."

Before striking the gavel, Judge Morgan ordered Sarah to meet with him in his chambers. Then the bailiff ordered all to rise, and the judge left the bench.

Sarah gathered up her papers and stuffed them in her case.

Rich grabbed her arm. "What's going on, Sarah?"

"I need to go talk to the judge."

"Sarah," Rich's words were sharp. "What the hell was he talking about, sex scandals and tapes?"

"I don't know," Sarah said. "Jess is crazy."

~*~

Rich watched Sarah pack up her papers. Her face was white as a sheet of paper, and her hands shook. Then he looked at his daughter, who kept her eyes on Sarah. Before Sarah left the room, she gave Kari's arm a squeeze.

Once she was gone, Rich turned to his daughter. "What the hell just happened? Did any of this make sense to you?"

The child burst into tears.

Jess approached their table. "I'll tell you what happened. Sarah forgot who the hell she's dealing with. That little piss baby was never a match for me. And my husband is a powerful man, and I can promise you, Sarah will regret she ever tried to play games with us. That bitch will rot in jail, for sure. Did she tell you why she left Indianapolis? You might want to ask her…see what kind of woman you have spending time with my kids. And while you're at it, ask her what she did with your baby."

"Leave her alone!" Kari sprang to her feet. "Did you know? Did you, *Mother*?"

Jess took a step back.

"Answer me," Kari screamed. "Did you know what your *husband* was doing to me? You send Sarah to jail, and I swear I will go straight to the police. What have I got to lose? Sarah was trying to stop people from knowing what he did. Now it doesn't matter, does it? Everyone knows."

Kari threw her unopened can of cola at her mother and ran from the room. Rich caught up with her in the hallway. He grabbed his daughter by the arm and pulled her into his chest, kissing the top of her head. "It's okay, sweetie. It's okay."

"I'm sorry, Daddy. I'm so sorry. It's my fault. I got Sarah in trouble. I made her promise not to tell."

"Not to tell what?"

Kari's tears flowed faster. "I can't," she mumbled.

He held her until she calmed down, then asked again, "What did Sarah do?"

"She's lying for me."

"Lying for you...about what? Did Phil...touch you?"

"No, but he...."

"He what? Baby, you've got to talk to me."

"Phil told me if I didn't move with him and Mom, he'd...."

"What did he do to you?" Rich's words came out much louder than he intended. He could feel Kari flinch. "I'm not mad at you, sweetie. I need to know what happened."

Kari wiped at her tears and nodded. "Mom and Phil introduced me to this boy."

"The one Stacey said you were sneaking around with?"

Kari nodded. "You'd have hated him. He had long hair and tattoos, but I thought he was cute and Mom said what you didn't know wouldn't hurt—that you weren't exactly my real dad anyhow."

The muscle in Rich's jaw twitched, but he cautioned himself to remain calm. "You're right. I wouldn't have liked that kind of guy. How old was he?"

"Seventeen."

"So, you dated this guy, and then...."

"I...oh, Daddy...I can't talk to you about this. It's why I went to Sarah."

Rich thought back to Sarah telling him Kari had come to her and made a confession. Assured him it was nothing that would scar her for life. That it was nothing any worse than any other

241

sixteen-year-old would do. He walked Kari out of the courthouse and led her to a bench in a sunny area of the courtyard. He sat, giving the empty space next to him a pat. Once she was settled in, he asked quietly, "I'm going to guess you and this guy were, uh…intimate?"

Kari nodded, her cheeks instantly bright red.

"Did he force you?"

Kari shook her head.

"Where do your mom and Phil come into this?"

"Phil had cameras in the pool house, and that's where…."

Rich took a deep breath. He wanted to beat the hell out of Phil. The sick son of a bitch probably set his kid up. What kind of bastard puts cameras inside a pool house? At best, the pervert was trying to sneak peaks at people changing for a swim. If Jess knew about this and allowed it to happen, she should never get to see her children again. Rich tried to remain calm, but it took suppressing every natural instinct in his body. With every muscle tense, he spoke calmly through gritted teeth. "And Sarah chose to hide all of this from me?" Surely what Phil did was child abuse, if not sexual assault and voyeurism.

"Sarah didn't hide anything."

"She didn't tell me."

"It wasn't her information to share. It was my business, so it should have been my choice."

Rich shook his head. "It doesn't work that way. You're my daughter, and I had a right to know. You'll understand when you have kids."

Kari rolled her eyes as she picked at her lower lip in thought. "I won't ever understand how you can blame her."

"It won't just be me. She'll have to deal with the law too."

"Oh God." Kari clutched her stomach and rocked back and forth. "It's all my fault. Sarah begged me to tell you. I told her I'd never talk to her again if she told you. I told her she knew how it felt to be humiliated — would she really do that to me? She just tried to fix things for me. I'm so sorry, Dad. I know you probably hate me."

"Don't be ridiculous. You're my baby girl."

"But I knew better; if only I'd followed the rules. If you'd have met Brandon, you'd never have approved."

"Listen, I've done plenty of bad things. Breaking rules is part of the teen experience."

Kari swiped at her tears and took a breath. "It's part of helping friends too. That's why Sarah shouldn't be in trouble. I need to talk to her. I need to tell her I'm sorry. I need to tell the judge not to send her to jail."

"I'll talk to Sarah." Rich wasn't sure what he'd say. He was still in a bit of shock that she'd done it. She was a smart woman. How could she be so stupid? Rich frowned. "Right now, I'm calling your Aunt Tonya to come and pick you up."

"No." Kari pulled away from her dad. "I need to see Sarah. I have to talk to her."

"I don't want you talking to Sarah right now. I need to get some things worked out with her first."

"You're blaming her?"

"She should have told me what was going on."

"I begged her not to tell."

"You're my daughter. It wasn't her right to decide."

"But she's my friend."

"Adults aren't supposed to be your friend, Kari. They're supposed to be smart. Damn foolish woman and her game playing. I should have known — whether it's breaking into houses or lying to help boyfriends, she operates on her own standards. And I'm not sure that's good for you."

"Not good for me? She did what I asked her to do. She barely knows me, yet she loves me more than my own mother ever has. And I'm sorry, Dad, but you don't get it. Men can't get it. A video of a guy screwing a girl hits the net and that guy is king. If mine goes viral, I'm a whore. Sarah understands that. Like she said—she knows what it's like to hate looking at yourself in the mirror."

"I'll talk to her," Rich promised.

"If you hold this against her, I swear, I will never, ever talk to you again. I'll…I'll go live in foster care or something."

Chapter 37

Sarah could not understand what Phil and Jess had thought they would gain by bringing up the tape. Sarah never saw that coming. But then again, Sarah was beginning to realize that she wasn't at all accurate at predicting human behavior.

"Are you going to answer the question, Counselor?"

"Of course," Sarah said. "The truth is—I did blackmail Jess. Kari came to me and said the stepdad told her he had a video of her having sex with her boyfriend in the pool house. According to Kari, Phil told her the video would go to her father and possibly hit the net if she didn't move with them to the west coast."

"And you knew this, and instead of reporting it to the proper authorities, you instead blackmailed the mom?"

Sarah nodded.

"I'm assuming in hindsight that you realize that was a mistake?"

"Oh, I knew it was a mistake from the moment I agreed to keep my mouth shut. I could try to BS you, Your Honor. I could try to pretend that as an attorney, it was privileged information. But we all know minors can't make contracts. I could also pretend I didn't know I had a duty to report, but that just makes me look like an idiot. The truth is, I made a promise to someone I care about regarding a kind of situation I am far too familiar with.

245

And I knew from the moment I made that promise that it could land me in jail or get me disbarred."

"And yet, you still did it?"

"Yep. I could also lie and say I am full of remorse, but the only thing I regret is that it didn't work. Now, everyone knows what Kari wanted to keep a secret."

"Do you have proof this video exists?"

Sarah shook her head. "No, but Kari said Phil said —"

"That's hardly proof. What if he was lying, or she was lying?"

"She wouldn't lie."

"I'm trying to give you wiggle room, Ms. Andrews."

Sarah wiped sweaty palms on her skirt. "Instead of wiggle room, could promise me you'll have his computers seized and his house gone over with a fine-toothed comb? What kind of sick pervert puts cameras in a pool house? And I seriously don't think the man is sane. This wasn't a smart move to out me like he did. That was vengeance. He was more interested in getting me in trouble than keeping himself out of trouble. If he has a video, what's to stop him from downloading it to the net? I'll happily go to jail if you can stop that."

Judge Morgan rubbed the fat waddle under his neck. "Go home, Ms. Andrews."

"Am I going to jail? Should I stay in the area?" Sarah asked as she stood.

"Go. And please, don't sound so eager to get locked up. I'm not saving you from facing that girl's father."

~*~

There were so many thoughts clogging Sarah's mind, it was beginning to hurt. Judge Morgan was right, she preferred jail to facing Rich. She didn't want to face him. Didn't want to see the anger and disappointment in in his eyes. It was bad enough that she'd done her best to ruin her own life, now she was bringing chaos to his. And to Kari's. Her lies and games — she was ruining

246

everything. Sarah was a game player, a liar, and worse.

Sarah let her body drop onto the couch. "Maybe I just shouldn't face him. He is obviously fed up with me. And with good reason. Hell, I can't even think of a defense for myself." Sarah rubbed her eyes. Jess's words haunted her — *you killed yours.* Rich would ask about that. "I can't. I just can't." Sarah honestly thought she might vomit. She covered her mouth with her hand and took a few deep breaths. "I was wrong. Kari isn't my child… even if I wished it were so."

Rover waddled over and sat in front of her. Big brown eyes bore into her, floppy ears tilted as if waiting for her to explain to him why she was talking to an empty room.

"Stop it, Rover. Don't look at me like that."

Rover whined.

She scratched his over-sized ears. "Truthfully? I don't know what I'm doing. The judge didn't tell me to stick around, and Mother has been begging me to come to Europe." Rover licked her hand. "Of course, I'll miss you, but I have to save some tiny bit of sanity." Rover rested his head on her knee and let out a long sigh. "I just can't stay here, buddy. And I can't take you from Stacey either. So, this may be where we say goodbye."

Sarah wrapped the dog up in a hug, kissing the top of his furry head. "He hates me, pooch. I heard him…okay, so maybe not hate, but close. And how could he not? I'm nothing but one big bad decision."

She gave the dog one more squeeze, then stood. Taking a deep breath, she got a box and gathered his toys, food, and treats and set the box by the door. She texted Kari and asked her to watch Rover. Dog settled, she turned her attention to packing her own bag. She only needed one carry-on where she was going. Her mother wouldn't approve of most of her clothes anyhow, and would insist she get new ones.

Changing quickly from a suit to jeans and a sweater, she

stuffed the rest of her necessaries, like her passport, contact solution, and RC bear, in her oversized purse. Hugging the leather bag to her chest, she took a deep breath. In a few short months, this place had become home — her home. Memories of painting with a little girl with wild red hair, and how Rich would get so lost in his carpentry he never realized she was watching him swept over her. *Missing him. Missing what should have been.*

A wave of warmth left her eyes hot and her throat tight. *I have to go.* There was no sense thinking of such things. She had a rule against wallowing. Years ago, she'd accepted the fact that life sucked, and had gotten over wishing for it to be better. In this world, children got cancer, moms beat their babies, and the bad guys won more often than the good guys. That was reality. Survival depended on learning how to adjust and move forward.

With only a short pause at the door, she left her apartment without looking back.

~*~

Rich took the steps two at a time. Kari was in a panic that Sarah was going to do something stupid. The more he knew what Sarah was capable of, he realized impulsive and irrational was what she did best. He pounded on her door and yelled her name. She never answered. He unlocked the door and went through the apartment straight to the bathroom, expecting to find her in a hot bath. His heart sank when she wasn't there.

He went back to the living area, where he noticed the box of dog stuff with a note with his name on it.

Rich,

I'm sorry. I didn't mean to cause the trouble that I did, but you're right — too many lies, too many games. I'm not good for you or your kids. Tell Kari I'm not going to jail, and she owes me no apologies. I'd do it all again. She's my friend, one of the best ever. And tell Stacey Rover needs a home. I promise, I'll send money for his care. I feel some guilt saddling you with a dog, but I couldn't take him from her.

248

Tell them I have an opportunity to take a really good job, so that's why I am leaving. They'll be hearing from me. I promise.

Take care,

Sarah

"No!" Rich crumpled the letter.

"Rich?" Tonya popped her head in the door. "I got your message to pick up Kari at the courthouse, but I went there and you all were gone. Then I ran into Angie and she told me there were fireworks this morning, and that Sarah was being arrested?"

"Arrested? Her letter says she got a new job."

"I don't know. And you know Angie. She can be an idiot, but I can't imagine her making up Sarah being arrested without something giving her the idea. How in the world would Sarah be in jail?"

"Sarah blackmailed Jess."

"I know. I was there."

"You what? What the hell is wrong with you women?"

"What's wrong with us? What's wrong with you? She was trying to save Kari some humiliation. From where I'm sitting, that shouldn't be a strike against her—she should get an at-a-girl."

Rich sat on the couch and ran a hand through his hair. "Why am I shocked you're taking her side? You were in on the break in at Mandy's."

"I wasn't *in* on that, cuz, I organized it. Sarah wasn't a fan of the idea, but she did it. You know why? Because I asked her. That's who Sarah is."

"But she should have told me about Kari."

"But she should have told me...." Tonya mocked. "As opposed to getting you full custody and protecting your kid?"

"It backfired on her."

"Didn't for you, did it? Who gets to keep their daughter?"

"I do."

249

"Who got hurt in the attempt? You? Hardly. Just your pissy-manly pride that drives you to be in control of everything. Kari—maybe, but that's her bitch mother's fault. I'd have castrated Phil for doing what he did. If anything, Sarah moderated Kari's humiliation by assuring her that she is never alone in her humiliation, both in spirit and in reality—Sarah could be sitting in a jail cell as we speak. That's sisterhood."

Tonya gave him a look that seemed to dare him to argue with her. Like she would just love the opportunity to punch him in the face. He decided against taking the bait.

"I don't know where Sarah went. She left a note that says she got a new job."

"Probably making license plates."

"Would you stop saying she's in jail? They won't put her in jail." Rich stood. "I need to find her. Talk to her."

"Tell her you love her. Tell her thank you for putting your kids before herself."

"Really? You think I should thank her for lying to me?"

"Of course. I only say what I mean, jerk."

Chapter 38

Rich checked the courthouse first. The judge was gone for the day, but the clerk in his office assured him Sarah was not in jail and there was no order for her arrest. Rich breathed a sigh of relief. As his initial anger wore off, it was replaced with worry — where was she? He'd left at least a hundred voicemails and texts. No response.

Sitting in his car outside the courthouse, he didn't even know where to begin looking for her. Or did he? He took a deep breath and as much as it killed his soul to do it, he called Doc. "Have you heard from Sarah?"

"Not for several days. At least not since she dumped me. I can't say the best man won, but I'm glad she's happy. She's one of the good ones."

"Yeah, she is." Rich hung up the phone and threw it into the seat next to him. How could he have been so stupid to blame her?

His phone rang and he grabbed it like a drowning man reaches for the lifeboat. He didn't recognize the number, but maybe Sarah had lost her phone. That's why she was ignoring him.

"Sarah?"

"No, Mr. Copper, it's Martha Milton. I was actually trying to reach Ms. Andrews myself, but she's not answering."

"I...maybe she lost her phone."

"Perhaps. When you see her, could you give her a message from me?"

"Of course," he said as his brain tortured him with the thought—*you may never see her again.*

"Good. I have a friend who knows some people at the bureau, and he assured me there will be a warrant served on Demkey and his residence by dinner time. He won't get away with this, and we won't even require Ms. Andrews going to jail to make it happen." Mrs. Hinton chuckled. "I like the girl's spunk—I'm guilty, put me in jail, but be sure to go over that house with a fine-toothed-comb. If the girl says the tape exists, it exits. That's what she told Robert. He had to order her out of his office before he lost all decorum and hugged her. She looked so distraught. I wanted to hug her too. I might still." Another chuckle. "I appreciate her discretion and her loyalty."

"She is a special lady."

"If I may be so forward, and if you agree, I'd like to invite you all for dinner. I would love to meet you all."

"I'll talk to my daughter this evening. I'm sure once she knows she has more family; she'll be eager to meet you."

"Will it be shocking to her? I could pretend to be a family friend...."

"No, ma'am. You can be her grandmother. I've never lied to my daughter. She knows I'm not her biological dad."

There was a quiet pause, then a small sniffle. "Thank you, Mr. Cooper. You have no idea what this means to me. And please, if you don't mind...the little one—"

"Stacey?"

"Yes, Stacey. I think it only right that she be told she has a new mystery grandma too. If that's all right with you."

"I think that is very generous of you. She does hate to be left out of anything."

"I was the youngest of three girls. I understand completely. When you tell them, be sure to mention that I have a stable full of horses…and a pony for the little one."

Rich smiled. "You have horses and a pony? Oh, they will lose their minds over that."

"Oh, I will have that stabled filled and more! I've been a lonely old gal, Mr. Cooper. Your family's visit will be like all of my best Christmases rolled into one. I'll be in contact about the details. Please tell Ms. Andrews I expect her to come too."

"I'll let her know." *If I can find her.*

Chapter 39

Months passed with no word from Sarah. Rich tried every way to find her. He even called the secretary she'd fired to see whose cases she was working on. If one of those cases wasn't closed, maybe Sarah was still in contact with these people. It seemed like a really good lead, but it was a dead end. Yes, there was one case still open. Fredericka Barnes's trust fund. Rich called the woman and found his hopes dashed again—Sarah had transferred the case to another lawyer. Rich immediately called the replacement lawyer, who explained to him that he'd never met Sarah. She'd called him and said she was leaving the country on personal business, and needed someone to wrap up her cases.

So, Rich waited. In October, he got a letter regarding a meeting with Judge Morgan. He went to the meeting eagerly, hoping maybe, just maybe, Sarah had set it up.

But she hadn't. It was just a simple hearing granting him full, permanent custody of Kari and Stacey. After the hearing, Judge Morgan gave Rich his heartfelt appreciation for his inclusion of Mrs. Milton into his family.

"Martha is a dear friend. I am in your debt, son."

Rich was quick to take advantage of the good graces and asked about Sarah.

Judge Morgan shook his head. "I'm sorry, but I don't know

where she is. She turned herself into the bar and was given a slap on the wrist. I believe she lost her license to practice for a year. I wasn't going to turn her in, but I guess she didn't want the fear of being reported to the bar hanging over her head forever. One of the only things I know for sure — keep an eye on the front page. You can thank Sarah for what's coming." With that, Judge Morgan gave him a wink and exited the courtroom.

A week later, the story broke. On the front page, there was a shot of Phil trying to shield his face from photos. Rich read the story over his morning coffee with a grin. Phil Demkey, the former owner and operator of several private rehab facilities, was arrested for embezzling, child porn, and distribution of controlled substances. Phil was looking at many, many years in prison. The FBI was put on the case after an anonymous tip.

Rich set his paper down. Sarah.

Where are you, Sarah? He missed her. All his anger was gone, replaced by worry and longing. He missed that look she gave him — arms crossed over her chest, lips twisted in a bit of a smirk — right before she sparred with him. There was no other woman like Sarah. He had to get her back. But that was turning out to be an impossible task. He assumed she was with her mother, but that didn't help him find her. Claire Andrews wasn't on any search lists, and Sarah's phone was turned off. He suspected Kari had her number, but she wouldn't share it or even speak to him about Sarah.

In desperation, he finally complained to Stacey that he missed Sarah so much he didn't feel like eating any pizza. The little girl gave him a pat on the arm and said, "Tell Kari when you miss her and Sarah will call you. That's what I do."

When Rich asked Kari, she told him she didn't know what Stacey was talking about. Rich supposed he had been right all along — Sarah had a strong influence on his daughter. He told himself maybe he should he happy she wasn't their stepmom.

She definitely lived in a world of gray.

But he loved her. Like he'd never loved any woman in his life.

Gifts for the girls showed up with return addresses that turned out to be law offices. Money showed up in his account from a bank in Geneva. When he called the bank for information, all they could tell him was the payments were wired from a bank in London. He had a crazy thought of climbing onto a plane and heading for England. But London wasn't a town like Dodd, where he could stop a fella on the street and get information on any resident who lived or visited there.

October turned to November, and soon, it was time to hang the Christmas lights. He didn't feel at all festive and was fed up with the waiting game, so he went to his daughter. He found her in her room listening to music.

"Stacey says if I miss Sarah, you can get her to call me."

"Dad, I told you —"

"Just listen...I miss her. I love her, Kari. I need you to tell me how I can get her back."

"I can't make her do anything, but —"

"The hell you can't. Bring her back, Kari. She'll listen to you."

Then he went outside and started hanging Christmas lights. Being festive was the last thing he wanted to do, but he knew it meant a lot to Stacey. He'd gladly fake happy for his little girl.

Days passed with no word from Sarah. Fear and worry were replaced with anger. How dare she leave without a single explanation? It was just like last time. When Sarah decided to be done, she was gone. Last time, he'd quit school and turned his life upside down with grief, but not this time. Every night after work, he hung more lights. If he couldn't be happy, at least he could be excessive. By the time he was done, his house would rival the Griswold's in tacky glow. His Christmas spirit would not be dampened by a woman. He'd fill every square inch of his yard with festive fun to prove it. Tonight's addition was a blow-up Santa that popped in and out of a chimney. Stacey had seen it at the local discount store and fell in love with it. Rich bought it with the Rover funds — Sarah sent way more than was needed for dog food. At first he was going to bank it and return every penny to her, but then he thought the hell with her. If she wanted to ditch them, Rover included, then she could pay for it.

"Little lights aren't twinkling, Clark."

Rich recognized the voice instantly. *Mandy.*

"Why are you back?"

"Well, hello to you too." She stuffed her hands in her coat pockets and made her way from the road to his yard.

"I'm just surprised. Thought you and Donnie were still soaking up the sun."

"Meh." Her head tilted to the side as she shrugged. "I can't take his constant jealousy. And my grandma had a stroke and needed someone to take care of her. So here I am…back in Dodd."

"Sorry to hear about your grandma. I can't say I'm surprised about Donnie."

"I didn't figure you would be. I hear the skinny lawyer skipped town."

"Seems like."

"She hasn't been in touch at all?"

Rich plugged in the Santa and watched him move up and down. He didn't want to talk about Sarah. Tonya called him almost daily with new and improved theories…defending her friend to the end. "So, how did Angie take the news that Donnie is single again?"

Mandy shivered. "Offer a gal a cup of coffee and I'll fill you in."

Rich hesitated for a moment. His first thought was Sarah wouldn't like it one bit. His second thought was screw Sarah. "Sure. I've got an hour or so before my girls will be home from the mall."

"Still hiding relationships from your kids?"

"I thought we were talking about coffee, not a commitment."

Mandy laughed. "I'm just sayin'. Would it kill your girls to see you having coffee with a friend?"

"It's just less complicated that way. I let them fall for Sarah… look where it got them. They're broken-hearted. They can hardly enjoy Christmas."

"Are we talking about them or you?"

Rich scowled at her. "Did you want a damn cup of coffee or not?"

Mandy laughed and locked her arm around his. "Yes, I want that coffee."

He escorted her to the kitchen and poured them each a mug full. "Cream or sugar?"

"Straight black. I'm uncomplicated like that." Mandy winked at him. Rich handed her the mug and she took it with a smile, wrapping both hands around it and blowing into the cup.

Rich sat and took a swallow before asking, "So, how did Donnie take you leaving him?"

She set her mug on the table. "Truth be told…he dumped me. I was just too embarrassed to admit it."

"No shame in getting dumped—I hope." He laughed and took another drink.

"She's an idiot."

"Same could be said for Donnie."

"I agree. I put up with his crap for years. I'm done now. Angie can have him."

"But Angie's with Doc, right?"

"Not anymore."

"I thought they were planning a wedding…going to get baby Tyler DNA tested and live happily ever after."

"They did have him tested. Turns out the little fella is

Donnie's." Mandy took a long, slow sip. "That's how I lost him. Now that he knows Tyler is his baby, he wants to raise him, so we came home from Florida. One week with my crazy grandma and my kids and Donnie was ready to beg Angie to take him back."

"Did she?"

Mandy nodded. "Just like always."

"Ouch. Poor Doc."

"Yeah, he took it hard. You know he's leaving? He quit at the hospital and his house is for sale. I ran into him when I took my grandma in for an X-ray. He said he was taking Sarah's advice — when you needed to get over someone, you cut ties totally and completely. No contact, not even on social media."

"She is the expert at cutting ties."

"She's a fool, Rich. You really should find a woman who would treat you like a king."

Rich laughed.

"I'm serious. Sometimes the perfect one for you is right under your nose, or right across the table from you."

Chapter 40

Sarah lifted her arm to knock on Rich's door, but paused in mid-air when she looked though the window. Kari swore he missed her. Was dying without her. But it looked to her like Rich had moved on. With Mandy.

Sarah turned and was half way down the sidewalk when Rover barked. And barked. The fool dog was flipping out, scratching at the picture window that looked out over the street. Sarah barely made it to her car before the front door swung open and Rich stepped out.

"Sarah?"

Sarah shook her head and leaped into her car, and practically peeled out of his drive way.

~*~

As she sped away, Sarah tried to breathe past the crushing pain in her chest. She thought she had this figured out, but dropping in on Rich and Mandy wasn't part of any of the scenarios she'd rehearsed while away. The few months Sarah had spent with her mother reminded her that family was what Sarah really wanted. Her mother's life was work. Her friends were nothing more than associates. Her lovers were men she kept at arm's length. Sure, she had an office and a salary that was to die for...which was exactly the price she was paying. The time that Sarah had stayed with her, she'd seen her for a few hours each week. The rest of the time, her mother was either traveling or in meetings. The woman was in her mid-fifties, with high blood pressure and an ulcer-ridden stomach. Sarah didn't want to be her. But it still took her a month and begging from a child to work up the courage to buy a return ticket home.

Her mother wasn't thrilled to see her daughter go. In Claire's mind, Sarah had walked away from at least three very impressive jobs to run after a man. With a sigh, Claire admitted, "You do what you want. I won't say a word. I've come to realize I never wanted a daughter."

"Really," Sarah said with a shake of her head. "Thanks for that revelation, Mother."

"It's the truth. I didn't want a child with an independent personality. I wanted a mini-me. I'm as bad as one of those men who live vicariously through a son. Only I also wanted to make the improvements through you that I wish I could make in my own life."

"But I'm not you."

"That's what I'm saying. And it's taken me over thirty years of being a sort-of parent to realize how wrong I was. Thank God I let you stay with Grandpa Bill. You were such a quiet, moldable child. If you'd have lived with me, I'd have made your life miserable. I did enough damaging parenting from a distance."

"You weren't a totally bad mom."

"I scared the hell out of you. If there is one thing I most regret, it's bullying you most of your life. If there was one gift I could give you, it would be to teach you to stand up for yourself. To accept that you're human and that you screw up. But that you're still the best girl in the world."

Tears stung Sarah's eyes, but she smiled. "Spoken like a typical mother."

"You're not just going home for that guy, are you?"

"I'm not going home for him. I'm going home for me."

~*~

As she continued driving away from the worst-case scenario, she wondered if she'd made the right choice coming home. She had been so certain of the decision while in London, but now that her heart felt like it was trying to escape her chest, it didn't feel like such a good choice. She couldn't even drum up a good cleansing anger at Rich—it was her fault he was with Mandy, not his. She drove toward home, but panicked and took a left when she should have taken a right. Her path was random; she just kept making turns until the skies were dark, her shoulders ached, and her eyelids felt heavy. She stopped at a convenience store and picked up a few bottles of wine, and then checked into a hotel.

She filled a plastic cup with wine and settled herself on the hotel bed. Flipping on the TV, she scanned through the channels, but found nothing of interest, so she left it on the news. Swallowing her drink in a gulp, she poured another glass. Her goal for this evening was to get so wasted her brain would go numb, and she'd pass out.

As she poured a second glass, a pounding on her door made her dump the cheap chianti on the floral bedspread. Rubbing the wetness in with her hands, she ignored the knocking. No one could know where she was.

"Open the door, Sarah. Right now."

The voice made her heart speed to a stop. It probably wore itself out. She climbed off the bed and went to the door, looking through the peep hole. *Rich.* Her worst fear and ultimate wish in the flesh. Her mouth went dry; her body froze.

"If you don't open up, I'm calling the police and telling them you're suicidal, and they'll break it down."

Sarah pulled the door open, and he stepped in.

"How did you—?"

"You'd make a horrible spy. I've been tailing you since you left Dodd."

Suddenly awkward, she made her way back to the bed and sat cross-legged.

"Where have you been?" Rich asked.

"London. Uh, visiting my mom."

"I'm sorry to hear that. I assume she's dying?"

"No. Why would you—?"

"I'm assuming you would only leave me…leave us…because someone was dying."

"No. I just…needed time to think and work things out."

"And you couldn't call and let me know you just needed a vacation?"

"I thought—weren't you paying attention in the hearing?"

"I was. I had a few questions…questions I never got to ask because you ran away."

"I didn't run away."

Rich sat on the bed beside her. "The hell you didn't. You're always running away from me."

"No, I wasn't. I just needed space to think."

"And let me guess, Dodd is too small to think in?"

Well, when he said it, it sounded sort of stupid. "No, I just…."

Grabbing her by the shoulders, he turned her until she had to look at him. "Kari told me what happened. You put yourself at risk lying for her."

"I don't know—"

"She told me about the sex tape. She told me about the boyfriend."

Tears rolled down Sarah's cheeks. She wiped them away. "You didn't yell at her, did you?"

"No. I was floored, but I think I took it pretty well. I wanted to bust Phil's skull in and kill Jess, but I was calm. I feared if I flipped out, Kari would think I was mad at her, or ashamed of her, and I'd never be ashamed of her. She's my little girl."

"You're the best dad. You really are. She's a lucky girl."

"The only thing I would still like to know is why didn't you guys trust me? Tell me what was going on?"

Sarah bit her lip. "No, that's not it. It's just…she was so humiliated. And I know how it sucks to have your indiscretions made public. When she told me, I felt her pain. I couldn't make the situation go away, but I could try to minimize the damage. In her mind, you knowing was the worst-case scenario. She's daddy's girl, and she didn't want to lose that. And of course, I made that stupid promise, so I was kind of painted into a corner. So, I blackmailed Jess. I told her Phil was blackmailing Kari, and if it went to court that way, he would sound like a creepy pedophile. It seemed like the logical solution at the time."

"You lost your license. You could have gone to jail."

Sarah shrugged. "I don't need a license to work. I've been working for my mother finding loopholes in contracts. It's actually pretty lucrative. And I wasn't worried about jail. I hear federal prisons are pretty nice, and I could have used the exercise. I bet they have a lot of free time. Maybe I could have written a book—"

"Would you be quiet? You're rambling."

Sarah pressed cool hands to warm cheeks. "I'm nervous."

"No being nervous. You're going to trust me."

She nodded.

His hand slid into her hair, brushing it between his fingers. "What exactly happened in Indianapolis?"

"I already told you," she said, swallowing hard.

"You had an affair. That's it?"

Sarah bit her lip. "Pretty much." *His wife walked in on us and he never bothered to stop. I had to smash him in the face with a stapler to get him to quit.* Sarah decided he didn't need the gory details.

The room was quiet.

Sarah pulled a pillow off the bed and cradled it in her lap. "I'm sorry I didn't tell you about Kari. Hate me if you want, but I made a promise to her."

"When did I ever say I hated you?"

Sarah shrugged. "I heard you talking to Kari outside the courthouse. I know you were disappointed in me."

"I was upset. There was a lot of stuff I didn't know about — me, the dad who thought his babies told him everything. I'll be honest, I'm not a fan of the lying, but I appreciate the fact that my kid trusts you. That you'd go to jail to help her."

Sarah rolled her eyes. "Federal prison. It's not like I'd have been crushing rocks on a chain gang." Sarah tucked the pillow under her chin. "I really am sorry for the mess I made."

He pulled her close, tucked her head under his chin, and held her. "It's all right, Sarah. I've come to understand why you did what you did."

She nodded again, absentmindedly fiddling with the buttons on his shirt. He looked handsome in his baby blue flannel and well-worn jeans.

"You remember the older lady in the courtroom that day?" Rich moved his head back, looking down at her as he talked.

"Yeah," she managed. "That was Mrs. Milton, Kari's grandma."

"I forgot, you met with her. She's also a fan of yours."

Sarah sniffed and looked up at him. "Really? I was surprised to see her there. I meant to ask Judge Morgan if that was legal to allow her to sit in."

Rich laughed, his eyes crinkling in the corners. "Coming from the lady who used blackmail to protect her interests?"

"True."

"Mrs. Milton backed me in my case against Jess. My crazy attorney impressed her. The idea that someone would go to jail to protect her granddaughter's image is in her words, 'commendable.' Seems she is appreciative of your…how did she put it? 'Discretion and loyalty'."

"Seriously? I didn't sink you?"

"Not at all."

"So, what did Judge Morgan decide?"

"I got full custody of both girls."

"That's great. What about Jess? Did she flip out?"

"A little. With Phil in prison and no way of bleeding Mrs. Milton, I assume she had to go somewhere and get a job."

"Poor baby."

"And given her involvement in blackmailing Kari, she isn't allowed to have contact until they turn eighteen and initiate the contact themselves."

"Ouch."

"She testified against Phil about how he set the whole thing up, paid the boy to hit on Kari, the taping…all of it. She kept herself out of jail, but failed to realize her testimony was evidence in family court."

"I knew it! I knew they set her up. Goodness, I missed a lot."

"Yes, you did. And I've been very lonely without you."

"Is that why Mandy's around? For comfort?"

"Would it matter to you if she was?"

Sarah's cheeks grew warm and her jaw clenched. "I suppose you had the right to do whatever you wanted."

He studied her through narrowed eyes. "Is that jealousy? For a guy you don't care enough to make contact with for months? You know what kind of torture that was?"

"I didn't leave to punish you. I love you."

"Crazy way of showing it."

Sarah stood, pacing the small space between the TV and the bed. "I left because I didn't want to know you hated me. I promised no more games, and I still did what I did. I was certain it was over."

"Shouldn't I have had a say in whether or not it was over?"

"That's why I'm here now. I realize we only get one chance at life. You are my chance, and I thought—I needed to be brave enough to take that chance. Little did I know I was going to come back to you and Mandy having a little tete-a-tete."

"It was a cup of coffee in the kitchen. That was it. Today was the first day I saw her since she left town. I'm not having an affair with Mandy. Not now. Not ever."

Sarah breathed a sigh of relief. Unexpected tears burned her eyes, but she blinked them away. There was hope. She just needed to ask, but she didn't know what words to use…could she tell him everything? If he knew everything, could he forgive her? Could he still love her?

As if he could read the questions in her mind, he asked, "That only leaves one thing…."

Sarah took a gulp of air. "What?"

He stood and tipped her head back until she was looking at him. "What was Jess talking about?"

"It's been so many weeks, and she said a whole lot of stuff…."

"I think you know what I'm talking about."

"I don't want to do this. It's nothing, and has nothing to do with anything."

"Sarah, come on. I need you to talk to me."

"No, please. It doesn't matter." Her chest started to hurt again, like someone was squeezing her ribs into her lungs.

"When you left that summer, were you pregnant?"

"I said it doesn't matter. Why do you want to dig up things that no one can do a damn thing about?"

"I take that as a yes?" Sarah turned to walk away, but he grabbed her arm. "No more running. Talk to me."

"No," Sarah whispered.

He pulled her closer until she sat next to him on the bed. "Were you pregnant?"

Sarah shrugged and bit her lip so hard she tasted blood.

"Sarah...."

"Yes! Yes, I was. Is that what you want to hear? Yes, I was pregnant. But it's gone. It no longer matters." She took a shaky breath. "My mother made me. Or at least it felt like it. I was such a wimp. Afraid of everything."

"You're rambling again, Sarah. Tell me, what happened."

"My mother found out that I snuck away with you that weekend. So did my dad, and suddenly the guy who I only saw a few times in my life was making waves and threatening to challenge her custody of me. He said my grandpa wasn't keen enough to keep up with me, so my mom made me come live with her. She didn't want my father to know I was pregnant. It would have strengthened his custody argument, and I still had six months until my eighteenth birthday."

He kissed her temple. "I'm sorry, Sarah."

She held onto his arms, gripping them tight.

"It was mine?"

A wave of queasy warmth washed over her. She nodded.

"Why didn't you tell me?"

"Jess told me that you said you didn't want to be bothered. You were only nineteen. That you didn't even have a job, much less a way to take care of a baby. You could help pay for the—procedure, but that was all you could offer. She told me that while I was gone, you two had grown close. That she never meant it to happen, but sometimes friendships just evolve. She told me you two were dating. I hated you, but still I wanted the baby. I was trying to hide it. I thought if I could just make it to Stanford, I could get away with it. But I couldn't. Jess told my mom about everything. She was such a good friend." Sarah shook her head. "Always looking out for my best interest."

"Jess never told me."

"I know that, now. Jess told me she never gave you the

message when she first came to town. She threatened to tell you about it if I didn't back off the custody case. Told me you'd hate me for it."

"I could never hate you. And I'm glad she didn't scare you out of helping me."

Sarah shook her head. "Your kids needed you. Their mother is a monster."

"They're lucky to have you."

Sarah bit her lip. "I think Jess was right — I was trying to steal her kids. It's like I know what I lost. I feel it every day. I see kids that should be about that age, and I wonder, what would ours have been like? And then suddenly there are these kids in my life and they need me. I couldn't not love them. Being around them stopped the nightmares. I'll never forget — "

Sarah stopped. She couldn't put it into words. The images and feelings of that day. Crying and begging for her mother not to make her do it, her mother grabbing her by the arm and screaming at her, "It's your fault, Sarah. You did this. You have nothing, are nothing, without me giving it to you. You can't even feed yourself. How are you going to take care of a baby? A baby no one wants. Your life will be over before it starts. You're not old enough or wise enough to make this decision. And if your father finds out, you'll be living with him. I swear, you fight me on this, I won't even buy you a goddamned plane ticket home. Then what will you do?"

Sarah gripped the fabric of Rich's shirt. Memories flooded through her mind, images and snippets she'd tried to force into dark corners long ago. "I told the nurse at the clinic that I didn't want to do it, but she just patted my arm and said it was for the best and would be over soon. When it was done, my mother stuck forty thousand dollars in my bank account and handed me a plane ticket to California. Every year, more money appeared in my account. I refused to visit her. Refused to let her visit me. I didn't see her until I graduated from law school. She told me she was so proud of me. I wasn't sure who I hated more — my mother or myself."

Chapter 41

The light was gone from the room. Sarah had cried for hours, saying nothing. Rich held her, rocking her like she was a child. Finally spent, she stood. "I need a shower. You probably need a clean shirt," she tried to joke.

"I'm fine," was all he said.

"I'll be back. I really just need to clean up." She covered her face with her hands. "Oh lord, I feel like hell. I need a drink."

She reached for the bottle of wine, but he stopped her. "Take the shower. You bring any clothes to change into?"

Sarah sighed. "My suitcases are in the trunk."

"You go shower. I'll go get you something to change into and some dinner. Then we'll talk."

"Okay," she said, biting her lip to stop it from quivering. More tears were coming, so she turned and made her way blindly to the bathroom.

She heard him leave. She showered fast, then wrapped herself in a towel and waited with a chilled heart for him to return. Her stomach was twisted in knots.

Rich knocked on the door and she ran to let him in. He had a sweatshirt and sweatpants that he laid on the bed.

She took the clothes to the bathroom and dressed slowly, pretty certain he hated her. Hated her for being a coward. And a liar. And a failure. She pulled the Hoosiers sweatshirt over her head, then pulled on the matching pants. They were a few sizes too big, but she'd stolen them from Rich to wear home after their first night together. They were a reminder that if she'd made better choices, she'd be happy right now.

She went back into the room. Rich was sitting in a chair, staring blindly at the television. Stepping in front of him, she touched the top of his head, brushing her hands through his hair. "You okay?" she asked.

"I'm all right. I just...honestly, I keep asking myself, how do you do this?"

"I'm a coward. I was so used to my mother telling me what to do, that I just didn't have the courage to stand up to her."

"Not that, Sarah. Damn it, you were just a kid. I mean the knowing, the what ifs...the idea that had your mother not pushed you, we'd have our own sixteen-year-old."

Sarah sat on the edge of the bed facing him. "I think about that every day." Sarah clutched at her belly. "The hardest part—the part that makes me hate myself, that haunts my sleep—was that I hid the pregnancy from my mom for so long, I could feel little flutters. I thought if I was too far along, it would be illegal. But it didn't matter. I was entrusted with that life, and I failed it. If I'd only made it one more month, I'd have been back in the States and in college."

"Oh, Sarah." He leaned into her and nestled his cheek against her neck. "No wonder you hated me."

"I came to hate anything I couldn't control, most of all myself."

"You realize this changes everything?"

Her eyes burned. "I figured."

"I had planned on taking it slow...maybe dating for a year or so, then talking you into marrying me."

She took a deep breath and got ready for it.

"But not now."

"I understand. I really don't blame you."

Lifting the hem of her sweatshirt, he traced circles on her belly with his thumbs. "I can't live for years wondering what if, thinking about just how unfair all of this is."

Sarah squeezed his shoulders. What could she say? Sorry just didn't fix some things.

"I want it now. Not later, not in a year or two."

"What?" *Was he forgiving her?* "What are you saying?"

He looked up at her, then kissed the tender skin next to her belly button. "I want to start now. I want my baby."

"Your baby?"

"Our baby."

"You're not breaking up with me?"

"Why would I do that? I told you, I love you. My kids love you. The last few weeks haven't just been hard on me. The girls miss you. Stacey colors you a picture a day for when you get back. Okay, so Stacey has been fine. That kid has never doubted that you'd be back."

"I've been calling them. I wasn't sure if that was okay, but I didn't want them to think I left them."

"Just left their dad." Rich hung his head and grinned.

"No, I had to sort myself out. I've had a lot of demons I've been trying to run from. It was time to face them."

"They're all faced. Time to come home."

Sarah wiped at her tears. She couldn't speak; she was overwhelmed. It sounded perfect. Rich was saying everything she wanted to hear, but she was afraid that at any moment her world would come to a crashing halt and she'd lose it all.

"On second thought—I can't trust you. If I let you go home, you'll do something stupid."

"I—"

"I'm not waiting. I can call Mom or Tonya—one of them

273

will keep the girls. You're an attorney — where's the fastest place we can go to get married? Off the top of my head, I'm thinking Vegas."

"You want to marry me?"

"Of course. Should I ask? Get down on a knee and all that?"

Sarah shook her head. Her tears dried. "I don't think I can have a baby. I would love to, but what if…after what I've done…I can't?"

"Stop punishing yourself, Sarah."

"I'm not. I just —"

"You're just going to tell me you'll marry me. As soon as possible. And you're just going to try to make a baby, and if it takes an entire lifetime to make it happen, then you promise to keep at it."

"And if it never happens?"

"Then I always have you. And you always have two girls who need you to love them, because their own mother sure as hell doesn't."

Sarah's chin started to quiver and the tears fell fresh down her cheek.

Rich scooped her up and held her. "What is it, Sarah? What's wrong?"

"That's everything."

"What's everything?" He dried her eyes with his thumb.

"You know *everything*."

"That's a good thing, right?"

Sarah nodded. "It's just that I've always thought I'd be alone. That even if I had someone, I'd be alone."

"I love you, Sarah Mae soon-to-be Cooper. And I forgot my economy-sized box of condoms in my hurry to chase you down, and if you have an issue with that — well then, we're not on the same page."

Sarah smiled, biting her lip against any further tears. "Not a problem. I'm pretty sure we're on the same page."

"Good. Then kiss me."

The End

About the Author

Elizabeth divides her time between her beach cottage and her scrupulously clean house in the hills of West Virginia.

Ooops. That's fantasy Elizabeth. The real Elizabeth spends her days schlepping after her four boys (five if you count their father) and the assortment of pets they swore they'd take care of.

She does live in West Virginia; the house is clean when the mother-in-law visits; and she does have serious dreams of living at the beach.

Elizabeth is a Marshall University graduate with a degree in counseling. This has proven very beneficial when dealing with the make-believe friends she hangs out with all day (she calls this 'writing').

Follow her blog at: http://www.eseckman.blogspot.com

www.ingramcontent.com/pod-product-compliance
Lightning Source LLC
Chambersburg PA
CBHW050718180626
46814CB00002B/503